The Titus Diary

The
Titus
DIARY

GENE EDWARDS

Tyndale House Publishers, Inc.
Wheaton, Illinois

Library of Congress Cataloging-in-Publication Data

Edwards, Gene, date
  The Titus diary / Gene Edwards.
    p. cm. — (First century diaries)
  ISBN 0-8423-7162-1
  1. Paul, the Apostle, Saint—Journeys—Greece Fiction. 2. Silas (Biblical figure)—Journeys—Greece Fiction. 3. Timothy, Saint—Journeys—Greece Fiction. 4. Bible. N.T.—History of Biblical events Fiction. 5. Church history—Primitive and early church, ca. 30-600 Fiction. I. Title. II. Series: Edwards, Gene, date. First century diaries.
PS3555.D924T58 1999
813'.54—dc21   99-24807

Printed in the United States of America

05 04 03 02 01 00 99
8   7   6   5   4   3   2   1

In Memoriam
*To the one man in modern history who has lived a life as
full of dangers, failures, joys, and triumphs as did the men
whom you will meet in* The Titus Diary.

*To
Prem Pradham
Apostle to Nepal
1924–1998*

PROLOGUE

I have just received word that Silas is dead. Silas was arrested and imprisoned on the isle of Rhodes and shortly thereafter was sentenced to death.

While in prison Silas wrote asking me to continue the story that he had begun. (I am Titus, of the city of Antioch, friend and coworker of Paul of Tarsus.) Silas has left us a record of the first journey of Paul to the world of the Gentiles. That adventure took Paul and Barnabas to a land called Galatia. Since then Paul and Barnabas have fallen asleep in Christ, both meeting their death under the blade of a Roman sword. We are grateful, then, that Silas recorded their adventure in Galatia.

Though Silas was not on that first journey, still, in the years following he became a close coworker with Paul and was, therefore, very familiar with the entire *Galatian story*. (Silas became Paul's traveling companion on Paul's second journey—which took them to the land of the Greeks.)

I felt it far better that Timothy tell the story, rather than it be told by me. After all, as Silas was not with Paul on that first journey, I was not with Paul, Silas and Timothy on Paul's second journey. Timothy was present with Paul through the entire four years that Paul was in Greece. Hence, I wrote to Timothy asking *him* to record Paul's journey to Greece.

In his reply, Timothy made a wise observation: "Had either Paul or Barnabas recorded the first journey—that is, the Galatian story—neither could have told the story as well as did *Silas*.

Paul and Barnabas were too central to the story. In the same way, you, Titus, can tell the story of Paul in Greece far better than Silas or I could. We are both too much in the story. We would both leave out things that were of a personal nature. You, Titus, are the best person to preserve the record of that great adventure in Greece. You know the story as well as anyone. In fact, brother Titus, I would leave out a great deal of the journey because it is too embarrassing to tell. You, on the other hand, care not if you embarrass me!"

I, Titus, had to agree with Timothy's words; therefore, I consented to tell the story of Paul's four years in Greece.

When I agreed to Timothy's words, Timothy unexpectedly lost a battle. I, Titus, agreed to chronicle the story of Paul in Greece, but only with the understanding that Timothy would tell the story of Paul's *third* journey, the *Ephesian* story.

I, Titus, was present in Antioch some seven years ago when Peter came there to visit the Antioch church. I was present when a Pharisee named Blastinius Drachrachma came from Jerusalem and caused much confusion in the church in Antioch, for Blastinius demanded that we Gentiles be circumcised. Yes, I witnessed Paul rebuking Peter in Antioch before more than a thousand people. I then went to Jerusalem (with Paul and Barnabas) to resolve the conflict between the church in Antioch and the church in Jerusalem, as well as the issues of Blastinius's demands that all Christians obey the 620 laws of Moses. In Jerusalem I met the Twelve. Silas has already told you that story.

I, Titus, was a witness to the writing of the letter which the Twelve drew up saying they approved of Paul's gospel to the Gentiles.

I was present when Paul and Silas departed Antioch, on Paul's second journey, a journey which took him up into Galatia and then to Greece.

I, Titus, am at the very heart and center of Paul's *third* journey. I played no small role in Paul's travel in Asia Minor and his three years in Ephesus.

I shall, therefore, end my part of this story at the point where Paul and Timothy visit Jerusalem. Why at this particular place? Because, to me, Paul's second journey *ended* there. From Jerusalem Paul and Timothy came to my hometown, Antioch. Upon his arrival there, Paul asked Timothy and me to go with him to Ephesus. A few days later, the three of us set out for Ephesus. So began Paul's third journey!

Timothy has agreed to continue the saga from that point. Let us hope that Timothy keeps his word and tells us of Paul's third journey.

I shall tell the story of Paul's journey into Greece, beginning at the point where Blastinius Drachrachma, a man set on Paul's destruction, reentered Paul's life. This man, who hounded the steps of Paul wherever Paul went, began his second great effort to destroy Paul's ministry just as he set out on his second journey.

Blastinius Drachrachma was a man who professed to be a follower of Jesus Christ, but he was a far, far stronger advocate of Jewish laws than of Christ. It was not beneath Blastinius to enroll unbelievers to aid him in destroying Paul. It was toward this end—the destruction of Paul—that Blastinius called a secret meeting in Jerusalem. His purpose? To induce a secret society called Daggermen to assassinate Paul!

It is there we shall begin our story.

CHAPTER 1

I *will* destroy Paul! I have invited all of you to this room to tell you why Paul must be stopped."

The voice was that of Blastinius Drachrachma, the most zealous Pharisee in Jerusalem.

"Last Sabbath I entered the holy temple, and there, standing before the altar, I made the most sacred of vows: Paul of Tarsus will be stopped. I will do all that is granted me by God to prevent this man from preaching the Messiah to those who are *not* Hebrews."

Those listening nodded in approval.

"I will prevent Paul from corrupting the sacred teachings handed down to us by God through Moses.

"I have recently learned that Paul has left Antioch and is on yet another journey—a second journey into the Gentile world, destroying the sacred law. At present his destination is unknown. But I will follow him. I will soon leave Jerusalem and find this enemy of Moses . . . this friend of the unclean. . . ."

"And Peter?" asked one of the men sitting in the darkened room.

Blastinius's black eyes narrowed.

"I have been told by many not to engage in conflict with

Peter, that he is too loved, too powerful, too highly regarded. Yet Peter confessed that he proclaimed the Messiah to Gentiles, nor did he require those heathens to be circumcised. No man, not even Peter, must be allowed to do such blasphemous things. This Paul has blinded Peter. Either Peter must be shown his error, or . . . he must be exposed as an enemy of the law.

"I have called you here to give voice to what all of you feel. That Peter, that Paul, that Rome are destroying the traditions of God."

A long discussion followed. Common ground was at last found by both those in the room who professed to be believers and those who were unbelievers.

"We must stop the uncircumcised from following the Messiah."

With that ground established, Blastinius dared make his surprise move.

"There is someone here whom we should now hear from, but before he speaks, all torches in the room must be extinguished."

"The rumor is true then. He is here?" asked someone as the room fell into darkness.

"Yes, a *sicarius* is present."

"What!" exclaimed another. "One of the Daggermen, *here?*"

"There is no need to be afraid, I have invited him here," reassured Blastinius.

At that moment, someone stepped into the room.

"I have been listening." The voice unmistakably carried the accent of one who had grown up in the rural land of Judea. "You have asked a question I desire to answer." The voice was cold, almost cruel.

"There are rumors that we who are called Daggermen have

marked Peter for death. This is *not* true. Tell him so. We wish no misunderstanding. Peter is not on our list."

There was a long silence.

"Each month we gather in secret—this is our way. We each call out the names of all who are undermining the traditions of Israel. Each time only a few names are selected for . . . for their just reward. We then pray for those who are about to die!"

A long pause ensued.

"Peter has never even been discussed. But tell him that his name may soon be discussed!

"As to Paul, we know little of this man. He does not reside in Judea. If he did . . ." There was another pause. "If Paul did live in Judea, his name would be *discussed.*

"Until now we have never sent anyone outside of Israel to kill God's enemies. But the thought has been . . . *discussed.*"

Another voice interrupted. "Then I suggest that you discuss Peter, and add Paul's name to those whom . . . you will pray for!"

Nervous laughter followed.

"We," the cold voice deliberately paused to emphasize the word *we*, "We advise you to heed Blastinius Drachrachma's words: Pursue this man Paul wherever he travels. Stop his mischief—by any means.

"Now a final word. We, the sicarii, will see to it that Rome will be stopped. All Jews who derive their wealth from Rome will be eliminated. The traditions of our people will prevail. Israel will no longer suffer shame."

A door opened, then slammed shut. Torches were relit, but the room was quickly empty.

A few days later there was another such gathering. It was decided there that Blastinius and a few men of his choosing should depart Jerusalem with the sole purpose of following Paul on his new journey.

But where was Paul? His first journey was into the Gentile land of Galatia. Rumor had it that Paul had begun his second journey by returning to Galatia. From there?

The answer to that question was to be discovered by Blastinius. At that very moment, Paul and Silas were in Galatia . . . and were making last-minute preparations to continue northward. Accompanying them would be Timothy, the young man from Lystra in Galatia.

No wonder John Mark gave up carrying your luggage and went back home," said Timothy as he lifted one of the bags of food lying at his feet.

Under the watchful eye of his mother, Eunice, Timothy began pulling food out of the bags.

"Let's see . . . this will spoil in one or two days . . . and this will spoil in about three days . . . and this will surely spoil before we get around to eating it . . . and none of us like this. And we Jews are not supposed to eat any of this."

Silas's eyebrows rose. "We Jews? *Yesterday* you were a Gentile!" Timothy continued rummaging through the bags until he had reduced them to a manageable size.

Silas stared at the pile of discarded food. "We will starve! Where is John Mark?"

"I will strike a bargain with you," responded Timothy quickly. "I will carry *all* of the other bags if you will carry *one* that has food in it."

Silas pulled at one of the bags of food, then studied the others. "An excellent bargain—for *you.*"

"What shall I do with all this discarded food?" wondered Eunice aloud.

"Tell one of the other young brothers I will give him all this food if he will carry one of these bags the first ten miles out of town."

Paul had looked on the scene with bemused interest. "This Timothy of ours is definitely not a John Mark," he observed. "This one will surely end up bargaining his way out of carrying *anything.*"

"Perhaps," responded Timothy, "but it is better that we go hungry than for you to send me back to Lystra with a broken back."

Paul threw up his hands in mock defeat.

"Timothy is not easily intimidated," observed Silas. "We should have expected as much, having heard of the way he confronted Blastinius when he made the mistake of trying to circumcise Gentiles in Lystra and Derbe."

"It is time," said Paul. "It will be light in a few hours. Remember, I am still a wanted man here in Galatia. I prefer not to be stoned *twice.* The second time would probably be boring."

Eunice slipped to her son's side, embraced him warmly, and bade him good-bye. The three men stepped out into the streets of Lystra. A few moments later they were on the Aegean Road, headed north and west.

Just after passing through the city gate, Paul paused before the Temple of Zeus. He paused soberly at the very place he had been stoned and left for dead. "The stoning was worth it," he said quietly. "The assembly of our Lord that now gathers in this city grew out of this dirt and blood."

By daybreak the men were safely out of the jurisdiction of Lystra. "Beyond this point I am not a banished man," remarked Paul.

At this very same moment, back in Antioch, Syria, a letter had come from Jerusalem, addressed to Paul. The letter had been received at the house of Simon Niger, with whom Paul always stayed when he was in Antioch. In Paul's absence, Simon passed the letter on to Luke. The writer was Justus Barsabbas. The letter began, "Justus Barsabbas, To Paul." It was brief, but its contents were unbelievable.

Having read the letter, Luke immediately called all the brothers in the Antioch *ecclesia* together. When they heard the contents of the letter, all agreed that Paul's whereabouts must be discovered. Paul must see the letter. After that decision, it was only a matter of choosing who would depart Antioch in search of Paul.

Luke, the physician, was chosen. To ensure that Luke would be able to overtake Paul, the church decided to provide him with a horse. It was a decision that demanded sacrifice on everyone's part, for as you know, it is rare for an individual to be in possession of a horse. Nonetheless, a horse was Luke's only hope of searching out *and* finding Paul.

There were two reasons for choosing Luke. One, he was an excellent horseman. Secondly, physicians had been held in high esteem ever since Julius Caesar had given all the physicians in Rome the honor of Roman citizenship. Beyond that, Luke could attend to any infirmities Paul or Silas might have.

After Luke's departure the brothers in Antioch sent a reply to Justus Barsabbas. The letter thanked Justus and the elders in Jerusalem and let them know that Luke, the letter in hand, had been sent out in search of Paul.

I, Titus, was the last person to speak with Luke before he left Syria. "Titus," he said, "pray that God will give me the wisdom to know which path to take. It is important that Paul be found. He *must* be found."

At that moment Paul and Silas were facing a major dilemma.

CHAPTER 3

"Paul of Tarsus, you have absolutely no idea where you are going, do you?" Silas sighed. They were now four days out from Galatia.

"None!" replied Paul. "We are but looking for the will of God, and that is not always easy to come by." Paul surveyed the landscape that lay before them. "Perhaps it is for us to travel north to Bithynia and turn east to Byzantium and then onward to the Orient. On the other hand, Silas, it may be that we shall take the gospel to the very heart of Asia Minor. I do not know. But this I know: We should move forward until the Lord makes it clear to us where we are to go."

For a moment Paul revealed his unspoken thoughts. "Sometimes, when I hear of the madness of the Emperor Claudius, I want to walk right out of this empire and take the gospel to the East. At other times my heart wants to go straight to Rome and declare the gospel to the emperor himself!"

Paul turned to Timothy. "It is good that you are a Jew, young man. It is also good that you are a Greek because the farther we move west, the stronger becomes the Greek culture."

"I am all things to all men," Timothy replied brightly, reminding Paul of an earlier conversation that had taken place between them in Lystra.

The road the three men now traveled was not at all like those Paul and Barnabas had endured in southern Galatia, for it was broad and—unlike in Galatia—the road was safe. (Crime among the Greeks of Asia Minor found its expression not so much in brute force as in cunning of heart.) Best of all, there were inns or way stations along the road about every ten to fifteen Roman miles.

Each night, at whatever inn they came to, the three men sought the Lord and his counsel. But heaven gave no reply; there was only the sense that they should continue to move forward.

"It seems to me we will be finding our way one city at a time," observed Paul late one afternoon. "From now on, in each place we come to, we will tarry a few days and wait for the will of God. If our Lord opens a door or if a word is given, we will remain. Otherwise, we will move on to the next city.

"Of this I am certain: Jesus Christ is to be proclaimed in this heathen world—somewhere north of here. And, once we find that place and he is proclaimed in that city, our gospel will bring forth the ecclesia of Jesus Christ. Until then, I ask both of you to seek out the deepest sense that is within you."

The one city they all began to anticipate was the ancient and legendary city of Troas. As my three friends neared Troas, they took lodging at an inn just outside the city. It was there in that inn that Paul stated his impressions:

"It is not Bithynia. I can tell it, deep in here," he said, pressing his hand to his chest.

"I agree," said Silas. Timothy said nothing, but he was learning to listen *in here.*

"I would that the place could be Ephesus," Paul said longingly. "Yet, every time we have tried to move toward Ephesus there has come this sense that it is not the way we should go—at least, not now.

"When we do not know the Lord's mind, then there is only

one thing left to do," said Paul as he leaned back against the wall of their small room. "We sit down and outwait the Lord. We will enter Troas, and there we will sit, and we will wait."

"How long?" asked Timothy.

"For as long as it takes," replied Paul quietly.

The next day the three men entered the seaport city of Troas, located but a short distance from the ancient ruins of fabled Troy, land of the Trojans, of which blind Homer wrote. The land surrounding Troy is called the land of *Troads* (a name from which the city Troas derives its name).

"Timothy, do you know much about the city of Troy?" asked Paul as they entered Troas.

Timothy was hesitant to say anything. He knew a little about ancient Troy, but he was not about to try to impress Paul, knowing that Paul was well versed in the ancient legends of this place. On the other hand, Timothy did not want to look totally ignorant.

"I have read some of Homer," Timothy finally admitted.

"Then you know the story of the Trojan wars and something of the heroism of those brave people?"

"Well, most of all, I know not to trust large wooden horses," said Timothy with a smile.

"Tonight we sleep in Troas, but tomorrow I shall take you out to the ruins of Troy. After that, we shall return to our room and wait . . . wait until God shows us something more than nothing."

Late that afternoon the three men, having entered Troas, found a room near the center of the city. The next morning, as promised, Timothy was rousted out of bed by a rather enthusiastic Paul.

"It is time to visit Troy!"

The three men were soon climbing among Troy's ruins, for it was only a short walk to what is now only a pile of rubble.

Paul perched himself on one of the overturned stones and began entertaining Silas and Timothy with long quotations from Homer. He then sang an ancient Greek song, to the chagrin of Timothy and Silas. As Paul came to the end of the lyrics, Silas raised a hand in protest, saying dryly, "Your gift lies somewhere other than in music."

This did not deter Paul. Timothy and Silas were then treated to a long discourse on ancient Greece, on Homer, and on the stories of Troy. Paul would speak in common Greek, then suddenly change into classical Greek, quoting a poem or an ancient oration.

"Perhaps it is here, in Troas, that we should stay," wondered Paul out loud. "But that is a man speaking. What is the will of God? It shall be in Troas we reside *only* if the Lord gives much clearer understanding than we now possess."

It was almost night when the three men passed back into Troas and to their small room.

"It is not easy to wait on the Lord," said Paul as he sat down on the floor. Timothy, new to this world of seeking the Lord's mind, nodded in agreement. Paul continued, "We have no abundance of money; therefore, the day must soon come when I must settle somewhere. I must begin earning a living."

Paul then glanced first at Silas and then Timothy and announced, "Tomorrow we fast."

Timothy flinched. Noting Timothy's reaction, Paul added, "All right, tomorrow *I* will fast. Now I invite you brothers to join me in eating the last morsels of Lystrian food."

"Then to sleep," added Silas.

Timothy only stared. He had never missed a meal in his entire life.

A few minutes later the candle was extinguished. The men fell to sleep.

I, Titus, must tell you that our brother Paul was not a man

given to signs or visions. Rather, he had a great dependence upon an inward knowledge and understanding of things going on in his spirit. There, deep inside, is the place where Paul dealt with his Lord. Therefore, you must understand that what I am about to tell you was a rare event in the life of Paul. During the night, while Paul was sleeping, a vision came to him. He saw a face and then heard a voice: "Come over into Macedonia and help us."

Now, Macedonia is a land just north of Greece. The two countries, the north called Macedonia and the south called Achaia, are so closely tied they are considered virtually one nation.

It was still dark when Paul slipped down beside Silas and began to shake him.

"Silas!"

Silas groaned.

Timothy opened his eyes. Paul was smiling. "It is Greece. We are going to Greece."

"Are you sure?" asked Silas, as he struggled to sit up in what was total darkness.

"I am of absolute certainty."

"Macedonia or Achaia?" asked Timothy.

"Northern Greece—Macedonia. We are in a perfect place. The port of Troas is ideal for a trip across the Aegean Sea. The winds blow from the east in good weather. It is no more than a two- or three-day journey."

"Macedonia?" grumbled Silas, after Paul had recited his vision. "We are in Asia Minor, Paul. Macedonia? None of us has even considered going to Greece!"

"It is Greece," replied Paul emphatically.

By the time the sun had come up, Paul was on the docks asking about schedules of ships sailing for Macedonia.

"Macedonia?" said one of the managers of the docks. "If

your destination is Philippi, there are at least one or two departures each week. One is in port now."

In a few minutes Paul had struck a bargain with the ship's captain for passage to Philippi.

Paul returned to the inn to be met at the door by the innkeeper. He asked in a very gruff voice, "Is your name Paul?"

Paul hesitated. He *always* did when a stranger asked his name.

"It is."

"There was someone here looking for you this morning. I could not remember that *Paul* was your name, but the description he gave seemed to fit you. Are you one of three men from Antioch?"

Paul's response was quick. "Yes. Has someone come to us from that city?"

"Are your friends named Silas . . . and the boy, is he named Timothy?"

Timothy had just stepped out into the street. "I am Timothy, but I am not a boy," he said aggressively.

"You look like a boy to me," grunted the innkeeper.

"Who is it that is searching for us?" asked Paul.

"The man looking for you has written something for you. Here! He said his name is Lucius, or something like that."

"Luke!" exclaimed all three men at once.

"Where is he?"

"Looking for a stable, I think."

"A stable?" echoed Timothy.

"I have a feeling that we are about to receive some bad news," observed Silas. "I cannot imagine any other reason why the brothers and sisters in Antioch would send Luke here by *horseback*."

"Unless I miss my guess, we are about to discover that the

bad news has a name: Blastinius Drachrachma," Paul replied in agreement.

Timothy went limp. "I thought we were through with that man."

"I had hoped the same," said Paul.

Paul read the brief note the innkeeper had handed him. "Luke is in the marketplace. He will stay there every day, sitting on the steps of the synagogue, until we arrive."

"The synagogue!?" exclaimed Silas.

"Luke is a Gentile. Why not the temple to Apollos?" laughed Timothy.

The three men rushed to the center of the city, eyeing every face they passed.

The distinctive voice of Luke boomed across the market. "Silas! Paul!"

Timothy was first to reach Luke, embracing him as he would a kinsman, even though the two men had never met.

"So you are Timothy, then? Only a few days ago I was in your home in Lystra. Your mother sends her love and wonders about your well-being. She also asked that you write."

Timothy blushed.

Even as Paul embraced Luke, he went straight to the point. "Why have you come? I cannot believe that it is only with good news."

Luke's face sobered. "You are correct. It is not good news—it is bad news. In fact, it is very bad news."

"What is it?"

"A letter came to you, in Antioch. It is from Jerusalem, written by Justus."

"Justus Barsabbas?" asked Silas.

"Yes, *that* Justus. It is I who, without apology, opened the letter and read it. Simon and I both knew it was urgent. Once the contents were known, the brothers in Antioch dispatched me to search for you. Paul, the letter is important."

"How did you find us so quickly?" asked Timothy.

"I came by horse."

"Still," replied Timothy, "your task was near impossible."

"What does the letter say?" asked Paul.

"Not here," replied Luke. "Where are you staying?"

"Not far, but the room is too small for all of us. Perhaps the innkeeper can provide us a larger room."

A short time later the four men were in a larger, cleaner room.

Luke began: "Trying to find you has been like going through a maze. You are difficult men to find. Could not one of you develop some distinct characteristic, something unique that is easy to describe?"

"Timothy could grow a beard!" teased Silas.

"Or Silas a thick head of hair," retorted Timothy.

"Hush!" said an amused but slightly impatient Paul.

"The letter has to do with Blastinius," said Luke.

"We are not the least surprised," responded Paul sadly.

"Paul, I tell you, I fear that your woes with Blastinius are not over. Do you wish to read the letter before we talk further?"

"No, I would first hear your words," assured Paul.

I, Titus, must tell you that in the next few minutes Paul heard words that would change his entire existence on this earth—right up until the day of his death.

"Blastinius has taken a vow against you. It is a vow to the death!"

The room fell silent, even though Timothy ached to ask what a vow to the death meant.

"As best as any of us can understand, this is what has happened," continued Luke. "You recall when Peter was in Antioch with you, that Blastinius left the city. Everyone thought he had gone home to Jerusalem. Instead, he went to Galatia. There he caused much confusion among the four young churches there. This continued until he was rebuffed by Timothy. Soon after that he was rejected by all of the Galatian churches.

"Only then did Blastinius return home to Jerusalem. When he heard the decision made by the Twelve, blessing Paul's ministry to the uncircumcised Gentiles, Blastinius was livid. He rejected outright the decision made by Peter and James to allow the Gentiles to hear the gospel. He confronted Peter and he rebuked the elders. Blastinius is utterly opposed to your preaching your gospel to the heathen, Paul."

It was clear Luke did not want to speak the next sentence. He hesitantly drew in a deep breath, then added, "Blastinius knows that you are making this second journey. He knows you are once more out—somewhere—preaching the gospel to the Gentiles and that you will probably raise up more Gentile assemblies. This and other things caused Blastinius to take a vow against you."

"The vow to the death," said Paul quietly.

Timothy and Silas studied Paul's face. There was not a single indication as to what Paul was thinking or feeling. It was only that Paul's eyes blazed.

"And the words of that vow?"

"Blastinius has vowed, before the throne of God, that he will follow your every step as long as you live. Wherever you go on this earth, Blastinius will come behind you. He will search out every place you have preached the gospel. He has vowed to then go to that very place and preach his gospel to those same people. If they refuse his gospel, he will do everything he can to destroy that assembly by *any* means possible. If they do respond, he will circumcise them and cause them to follow the law of Moses. In other words, he will destroy every ecclesia you raise up.

"He has also sworn that wherever his feet tread, he will

warn the Jews in that city against you. He will also tell the local government about you in the most unfavorable way possible. Blastinius has even sworn to warn the *heathen* against you. Blastinius will destroy *all* your labors."

(Timothy has said that hearing those words was the worst single moment he ever lived.)

Paul sat quietly. Nothing of his feelings showed. It was as though all Paul's life God had been preparing him for this hour.

Luke continued.

"If Blastinius cannot convert the Gentiles you preach to, I think it is safe to say he will seek not only to destroy the assemblies you raise up, but he will turn to the Jews, as well as the Roman government, for help in doing so.

"Paul of Tarsus, you have won to yourself a formidable enemy, as skilled, gifted, talented, . . . and determined . . . as you are. *And*, I must admit, an enemy far more articulate than you. He is also cunning and deceptive. A man who is a natural leader, willing to suffer the agonies of traveling, as you are, . . . for the sole purpose of destroying you. You have *this* man in your life to hound you until one of you is dead."

Paul's response came slowly and thoughtfully. "A sworn enemy. A man of incredible gifts. A master of the holy Scriptures. A zealot of zealots."

Paul then added, "Is that all? Luke, is this all you have to tell me?"

"There is more," said Luke. "Blastinius was outraged to hear that you were once again going into heathendom to preach your gospel. Blastinius will shadow every movement you ever make. Expect him."

"Luke, as you were passing through Galatia, did you speak to the churches in Galatia about all this?"

"I did with the ecclesiae in Derbe and Lystra. They will tell the other two churches. By now I assume all four churches know of Blastinius's vow."

"What was the feeling of the brothers and sisters in Lystra?"

"When I told them, some cried, others moaned. Others prayed. They know Blastinius. They are of the same mind as the brothers and sisters in Jerusalem and Antioch: Paul has won to himself a gifted, clever, unrelenting enemy. They fear for you and for the work you are now about to do."

"Does his vow include murder?" asked Timothy.

Luke blinked.

"I doubt it. Blastinius still sees himself as a follower of Christ. On the other hand, he also sees himself as a zealot for the law of Moses. Blastinius feels *personally* responsible for safe-guarding the law. To answer your question, I do not know. But I do assume Blastinius will stoop to making himself a friend of the Roman Empire if it serves his purpose. An assassin he is not; nonetheless, he is a *friend* of assassins. Most of all, anywhere Blastinius travels he will go straight to the synagogues. More than anything else he will use the synagogue to stop you."

"I thought I had problems enough," said Paul with a touch of irony.

Silas, seeking to break the somber mood, said to Luke, "Tell me, why is it that they chose you to find us?"

"I suppose it is just because I am one of the few people in the Antioch church who knows how to ride a horse!"

It was at this point in the conversation that Paul mentioned my name. "Luke, I wish you had brought Titus with you."

"Why?" asked Luke, who did not always hold this nephew of his in the greatest of esteem.

"Titus was present in Jerusalem when the Twelve made their decision. It would be good for a Gentile such as Titus to be here, to witness to the decision of the Jerusalem elders and the apostles. And, of course, to bear witness to the authenticity of the letter the apostles sent to the church in Antioch commending us to the preaching of the gospel to the heathen."

Paul then added, "Luke, will you stay with us for a time?"

"I am willing, for a time."

"Are you willing to take a sea voyage? In two days we leave Troas."

"To where?"

"The Lord has spoken to me in a vision. We will board a ship bound for Philippi, northern Greece."

"To Macedonia!" exclaimed Luke in wonder. "Then yes, absolutely. I have dreamed of the sea. And Greece! I would be most pleased to see Greece. I will do whatever I can to aid you."

"Good! I value your counsel, especially now."

It had been a most disturbing day. That night, three men did not sleep very well, but Paul was *not* one of them.

The next morning Paul asked the unexpected of Luke.

CHAPTER 4

Luke, would you consider selling your horse?"

"Well, of course! It is, after all, a gift from the church to help in finding you. But why this question? Have you been robbed?"

"Oh no, not robbed," said Paul matter-of-factly. "But we have very little money."

"But the church in Antioch, did it not . . . did they not . . . ?"

"No, they did not," answered Paul, dismissing the question with a wave of his hand, indicating he did not wish to discuss the matter.

But Luke would not be silent. "What an oversight, of all of us! I don't think the subject of money was even brought up, was it? A terrible oversight! But what about the churches in Galatia . . . ? Did they not give . . . for the spread of the gospel to their fellow Gentiles?"

"Luke, there were many things going on when we passed through Galatia. The matter of money entered the mind of no one."

"How could we *all* be so forgetful?"

"Do you really want an answer to this question?"

"Yes I do," remonstrated Luke.

"Frankly, I am not sure," replied Paul. "But perhaps the brothers and sisters have become accustomed to my working for a living and my preaching the gospel for free. Perhaps they do not recognize that although I *can* earn my *daily* bread, the expense of travel is beyond my reach." Paul smiled. "Perhaps they think the money I need for travel is given to me by an archangel."

"The horse will be sold immediately, archangel or no," declared a frustrated Luke.

"Sell the horse on this condition only. Whatever you are paid for the horse, you must lay aside some of that money to pay for your return journey to Antioch. Remember, Luke, when you return to Antioch you will be traveling *on foot.*"

"I do not mind walking back to Antioch, and I am certain the horse does not mind my doing so."

"Then it is agreed. The horse will be sold, and you will keep back for yourself what is necessary for your journey home. The rest of the money we will use for our travels to Greece."

"I have a feeling that you will have little money left," observed Luke.

"That is of no great importance. I have received word from the Lord to go to northern Greece. *That* is important. I will go to Greece; once there I will ply my trade in the city market. Now, Luke, in selling the horse be very careful. It is my understanding the traders of Troas have a reputation for being notoriously difficult to deal with."

"Never mind that, Paul. I know how much we paid for the horse in Antioch, and I know how much it is worth in Troas."

The voice of Timothy interrupted their conversation: "Beware the Greeks . . . buying horses."

Silas groaned, "Timothy has a humor that neither Jew nor Greek would own."

By afternoon the horse was sold. The next morning the four men set out for the docks of Troas.

Should you visit Troas, you will find the harbor there is large and filled mostly with ships bearing grain. But the largest of the ships, and the ones that will catch your eye, are the *biremes* and *triremes*, Roman ships of war. Fitted on each side of these vessels are banks of oars manned by slaves chained to stocks deep in the bellies of the ships. They row to the command of drum and whip.

As the four men boarded the ship, Paul paused, turned, and looked back at Troas.

"I have felt at home in the few days I have been with you, Troas. You are like the city in which I grew up. I know your ways, your customs, your language. Someday I will come back to you. Oh ancient Troy, may you hear the great news of Jesus Christ."

(Just six years later it was there in Troas that Paul passed through one of the darkest days he ever lived. It was in Troas that Paul waited for me, Titus, fearful that I was dead!)

A few minutes after the four men boarded the ship it slipped out of Troas. By nightfall the ship had docked safely on an island in the Aegean called Samothrace. The next day the ship set sail for the city of Neapolis, which is the port city adjoining Philippi.

At the very moment the ship neared Neapolis, far away in the city of Rome the Emperor Claudius was about to sign a decree that would profoundly affect the lives of hundreds of thousands of Jews. It was a decree Paul came to loathe and one that almost cost him his life.

CHAPTER 5

Mount Ethos! We are nearing Neapolis and Philippi."

The ship, holding close to shore, made its way into the newly constructed harbor of Neapolis, which is tucked under the ridge of the Pangaean mountains.

"Never have we been so close to Rome," said Paul. "To be in Philippi is to be . . ."

"You will fare well in Philippi," interrupted one of the passengers. "Roman citizens always do. Philippi is more fiercely loyal to Rome than any other city on earth. Philippi is a Roman colony like no other. Her citizens think of themselves as living *in* Rome rather than being a colony of Rome."

(The man's words later proved to be wrong. Philippi's patriotism toward the empire would cause Paul and Silas, both Roman citizens, to almost lose their lives in Philippi.)

Late in the evening the ship docked in Neapolis. When a ship arrives in a port at night the passengers usually choose to spend the rest of the night on board the ship rather than risk the dark streets. Just at dawn the four men stepped onto the beautiful, marble-covered Egnatian Way, the greatest of all the roads leading to Rome, and made their way to the center of Neapolis.

"We are about eight miles from Philippi," noted Paul.

"Long ago these hills held an abundance of gold. That gold is what made Greece great. When the gold ebbed, so did the Greek empire. We are in the heart of Greek and Roman history. Philippi is that center."

The steep climb up the hills revealed to the men a rich, fertile plain nestled amidst the Pangaeus mountain range. As they crested the hill they caught their first glimpse of Philippi. Paul stopped.

"Here, on *this* very spot, is where it happened—one of the most important battles of all time. Brutus and Cassius battled Octavian and Mark Antony for ownership of not only Greece but *all* the Roman Empire. Until the day of that battle Rome had been a republic. Since that battle, Rome has been under one man's rule—Caesar's. Just after the battle, the victor, Octavian, turned Philippi into a Rome in miniature. Anyone born in Philippi is born a Roman citizen. Brutus, the vanquished, committed suicide here. Even today, if you make a truly disastrous mistake in Philippi, the thought is to follow Brutus's example and commit suicide.

"Brothers, not one of us has ever seen Rome, but today we will get the best possible idea of what it is to be in Rome. Everything in Philippi *is* Rome. Though we stand in the middle of a Greek world, the language spoken in Philippi is Latin, not Greek. Nor will you see Greek coins in the market. The accepted coin is the coinage of Rome."

"That should cause no problem," replied Silas. "We have *neither!*"

Just a few steps farther the four men saw a large marble marker with these words engraved: *Colonia Augusta Julia Philippensis*.

They had come to the outskirts of Philippi.

"Look at all the Roman soldiers," said Timothy.

"You can easily tell which ones are the veterans," replied Luke. "Look at those hard-bitten features—and scars."

Nor did it take long for the men to discover who were the Romans, for they showed forth the arrogance of Rome itself.

Watching the passersby, Silas remarked, "Not only is the language Latin, everyone dresses in Roman garb. I feel like I am in Rome."

"There—the Philippian Acropolis. It is a thousand feet above us," exclaimed Paul.

(Should you visit the city of Philippi, you will find it is located in the first of three Macedonian districts called *Prima Macedonia*. Philippi's population numbers around thirty thousand. The city is self-governing, and its citizens are bent on keeping it that way, for they know that if there is trouble in Philippi, then Rome will immediately revoke their unique privileges.)

The other three men soon began to notice that Paul was searching the faces of almost everyone they passed. Paul was looking for the man he had seen in that vision.

The men reached the center of the city and entered the *agora* (the marketplace). Each man felt he had suddenly stepped into Rome. The food, the merchandise, the clothing, the language, even the appearance of the people . . . was *Roman*.

"I am *in* Rome," said Timothy quietly.

Paul, looking around intently, had one question he was driven to ask.

CHAPTER 6

W here is the synagogue?" He asked the question of people passing by, over and over again. But the answer Paul got was a blank stare. No one even understood his question.

"My Latin is not *that* bad," grumbled Paul.

Finally the answer came. "There is no synagogue in Philippi." The sentence was followed by a harsh observation: "This is a city of *Romans*, not Jews!"

Paul responded wryly, "It is possible, sir, to be both."

Paul's disappointment was obvious. Without a synagogue Paul had no certain way to introduce the gospel to Philippi.

"There must be some Jews here. But one thing is certain," he said emphatically, "there are fewer than *ten* Hebrews in this city."

Luke's face showed an uncertainty at Paul's comment. So also did Timothy's.

"If there are more than ten Jewish adults in a city, those Jews are required to build a synagogue."

"If there are less than ten?" asked Luke.

"If there are less than ten Jews in a city, on the Sabbath they gather at the nearest river. This place is called a *proseuche*. They continue meeting by the river until the day they are *ten*."

With that fact settled, the men began spreading out across the marketplace, asking if anyone knew where Jews gather on Saturday. It was three days before the Sabbath. For two of those days Paul wandered the streets asking if anyone knew of Jews in the city. The answer was always the same—no.

It was Timothy who found the answer. He was told: "There is a river. It is called the Gangites River. I've seen a group of people gathered there every Saturday. They sing."

Early on the morning of the Sabbath the four men passed out the northeastern gate (called the Gate of Augustus) and walked for about a mile and a half until they came to a narrow path which led to the Gangites River. The men paused beneath an overhanging grove of trees. There they waited.

About an hour later a small group of women crossed over a nearby bridge and made their way to the other side of the river. There they sat down and began to offer prayers and praises to the living God.

After watching for a few minutes, Paul and his companions joined them. Warm greetings were exchanged, but Paul could hardly conceal his surprise that virtually everyone present was a God-fearer, *not* a Jew, and that the entire group was composed of women. It was evident the leader of this little band of worshipers was a woman named Lydia.

This most remarkable woman would come to play a unique role in the lives of all four of these men. She eventually became the central person in the spread of the gospel in northern Greece.

It is not easy to describe Lydia. She is a strong woman, and yet that strength has a certain gentleness to it. I, Titus, can tell you one certainty of this woman—she is in every way remarkable.

Lydia had once been married, making her home in a city of Asia Minor named Thyatira. After she was widowed, she moved to Philippi to ply her craft, the making of purple cloth.

She had risen to the top of her guild and was now the city's leading manufacturer of purple cloth.

(Purple cloth is of great importance throughout the Roman Empire. Only the emperor himself is allowed to drape a full purple cloak about his shoulders. For that reason purple is associated with power and wealth. The most sought-after of all purple cloth comes from Philippi. Even the purple cape which Caesar wears comes from that city. For this reason, Lydia's guild is the most respected of all guilds in Greece.)

That morning, beside the Gangites River, Paul proclaimed Jesus Christ to those women. And as Paul spoke, Lydia's heart was touched. Already a proselyte, she received Jesus Christ as her Lord. The effect of her belief was profound not only in her life; it later affected the lives of many souls living in Philippi. Among the other converts that day were Euodia, Syntyche, and Clement.

(To this very day there is still no synagogue in Philippi. It seems that virtually all Jews who come to Philippi end up becoming believers in Christ.)

The little gathering spent almost the entire day asking questions, listening, crying, and rejoicing. Toward evening the entire group was baptized. Shortly thereafter, the four men bade the gathering good-bye and returned to the inn where they were staying.

Timothy was euphoric. "When Paul came to my city it was so difficult for him to find a way to begin. Lystra proved to be so difficult for the gospel. Not here! We went out to a river, we met a few people, the word of God was presented, the Holy Spirit came, and the hearts of *all* the listeners received!"

"There is little chance that it will continue to be so easy," observed Silas. "Those who follow *The Way* have a tendency to get in trouble for their faith—no matter how they seek to avoid it."

There was a knock on the door. It was the innkeeper. "There is someone here to see you."

Luke went downstairs. There stood Lydia.

"Please ask Paul and the others to come down. I wish to talk with all of you."

The other men were already making their way down the stairs.

"You cannot continue to live in this miserable inn. It is filthy and rat infested. I have a home that is quite adequate for all of you. The air is clean, and I have servants who will meet your needs. You can give all your attention to proclaiming this marvelous and wonderful Lord in whom I have just believed." Lydia's eyes filled with tears, and her voice broke as she spoke, "You have given me a great treasure: you have given me my Lord. I cannot abide the thought of your living in this place. If you have judged me to be faithful to the Lord, come to my house and stay."

Paul would have none of it. "There are rats in all inns," he responded. There were so many reasons *not* to accept Lydia's invitation. But Paul had never met anyone like Lydia. (Neither has anyone else.) Her response to Paul gave all of us insight into this remarkable woman.

"I expected you to refuse," she answered. "I came here knowing you would. But I shall win this matter in the end. Now, you must know that I have invited all my friends and all my acquaintances—and I have many friends and acquaintances—to be present in my home tomorrow just before dawn. I expect you to be there. I expect you to proclaim the Lord Jesus Christ to these, my friends."

Paul stood in silent amazement. Timothy turned away, trying to stifle a laugh. Silas, his dry wit fully intact, observed, "Paul, this woman has just spoken to you. Have you grown deaf during the night?"

Paul managed to stammer a lame thank-you, then added: "We will be there to tell your friends—and your acquaintances—of the riches of our Savior. But we cannot accept the invitation of your hospitality, though given so graciously. I and my friends, you see, are obliged to pay all our own expenses. It is the practice of my life."

Lydia was indignant. "You will never be allowed to do such a thing when you come to live in my home." Lydia turned to walk away, then turned again. "As I have said to you, Paul, I will win this matter in the end."

For a long moment Paul did not move. Finally, after a full minute, he began to shake his head. "Never have I . . . never. Absolutely never," he murmured.

Timothy was beside himself. The other three men stared at him, not fully understanding what had provoked his gales of laughter. He tried several times to say something, only to begin laughing again. At last he composed himself long enough to get out a few words.

"Paul had a vision. A man from Macedonia calling out, 'Come over to Macedonia and help us.' Paul, you have been looking for that man ever since you arrived. Well, this morning you have found him. And his name . . ." Timothy began to laugh again. "His name is Lydia!" Luke and Silas now joined in Timothy's laughter.

Paul did not know whether to be embarrassed or angry. But one thing is certain—the next morning, as they had been instructed, all four men arrived at Lydia's home. Stepping inside, the men were nothing less than astounded. The room, spacious and beautiful, was filled. An atmosphere of congeniality and warmth pervaded the entire home.

Timothy leaned over and whispered to Paul, "This is definitely *not* Lystra."

"Nor Derbe, nor anywhere else I have preached my Lord," rejoined Paul.

Not only were people of wealth present but also merchants, slaves, and the very poor. There was a mixture of every kind of person in the city. Lydia had exercised all her influence to gather these people into her home. Paul observed that Lydia had made sure her friends had not only brought their friends but also their servants and slaves.

As was customary, everyone sat down according to their rank in society. (There were many, many meetings held in Lydia's home in the coming weeks, but that was the first and only meeting when social standing was observed.)

Timothy noticed that as Paul spoke, it was the calmest he had ever seen Paul in such a situation. It was as though Paul were back home in the Greek world of his youth.

Paul told the story of Jesus Christ and then told the story of how he had encountered this Lord on the Damascus Road.

When Paul finished speaking, Lydia immediately announced that there would be more meetings in her home. A few never returned. (In the months to come Lydia even lost some of her best customers.) But it can also be faithfully said that most of those present that morning returned, and most of them became followers of Jesus Christ. A few weeks later terrible persecution fell upon this group. *Not one* of the people who believed on the Lord ceased being part of the ecclesia.

It was in those early morning meetings the ecclesia in Philippi was wonderfully born. During those days of beginnings, most of the believers were women. But not for long. Lydia used her influence to reach the women's husbands.

Word soon spread through the city that there were *meetings* in Lydia's home. But another word also spread through the city—there was a new physician in town. It seems Luke was becoming well known in Philippi. The results were not small.

CHAPTER 7

Luke's fame in Philippi began when he treated some of the infirmities of Lydia's servants. When many were greatly helped, others heard and began to inquire of him. Not long afterward women were bringing their husbands to Luke for the curing of their many ailments. Soon a number of men became brothers in Christ. The number in the gathering began to grow.

What are the gatherings in Philippi like?

The Philippian believers sing beautifully. That is because Silas (unlike Paul) could sing *very* well. Each morning and evening, there in Lydia's living room, Silas taught them a few simple songs. Timothy helped. (Luke is as gifted in singing as is Paul.) Like other Gentiles, they loved to talk; and they had questions unlimited.

From the very outset, in answering questions and telling the story of Pentecost and onward, Paul warned the Philippian believers that he and Silas might be forced to leave the city at any moment; therefore, the church would have to learn—from the very beginning—to minister to one another.

"You must care for one another and function together without *me*," he constantly repeated. And function they did, almost from the first day. Sharing was, and is, a large part of all

Philippian meetings. And love for one another flourished early on. That bond of love has never diminished.

As to learning of the past, because Silas was from Jerusalem, he told of the beginnings of the gospel and of the church. Silas spoke so vividly about the crucifixion and the resurrection of our Lord, it enthralled them all. He testified fervently to having seen the risen Lord. In the days thereafter he continued telling the story: the events leading up to the Day of Pentecost and onward right up to their arrival in Philippi.

Because of the way the Greek mind works, everyone in the room wanted to know more, for Greeks are masters of inquiry.

Paul was so pleased when these new believers interrupted him. And even more when everyone began sharing—that is, sharing their own experiences of the Lord Jesus Christ. Many a night was full of tears, laughter, and joy.

On occasion someone would become quite ill, especially among the poor and the slaves. First Silas, and later Paul, began to lay hands on those who became ill. Paul urged those who were healed to tell absolutely no one. Both men owned a wisdom that had come from the Lord Jesus in saying this to those who were healed.

Then there was the agora. Paul found space in the marketplace to open a small tent-mending business. Twice each day, just before the market shut down at eleven in the morning and just as it was opening again at four in the afternoon, Paul would stand in the market and proclaim Jesus Christ. (As is true of most of the markets in any city, it is quite easy to draw a crowd.)

Each time Paul spoke, a few stayed to ask questions. Not many, but always a few. And, while he sat at his space in the market, there were often those who sat down before him to ask questions or simply listen to Paul talk. Later, a few of these curious ones might be seen slipping into the early morning meetings.

I, Titus, must tell you of one other thing which happened

on that first morning that Paul spoke in Lydia's house. Lydia had done what she said she would do—*win!* Her approach to having the four men move into her house had been both wise and serious. She began by confronting Timothy.

"You have bites all over you, and many of them are infected. It is because of that filthy inn where you are staying." She then turned to Paul. "You have no right to subject this young man to your own convictions. He suffers bites because of *your* personal determinations. Timothy will live in my house."

Paul was about to protest.

"And look at both of you: lice in your hair, bites all over your bodies. You and Silas are both a terrible sight. Is there not something in Jewish law about cleanliness?"

"Paul does not have strong convictions about the ordinances found in the laws of Moses," interrupted a bemused Silas.

Paul threw up his hands. "I concede. Timothy can come and live here."

That was all Lydia needed. "This is excellent for Timothy," she said, "but still not good enough. The four of you need to be together for prayer and fellowship. It is not right that you men split up. Further, Luke needs a clean place, not only to live but also to carry on his work. My home is perfect for that."

"Divide and conquer," muttered Paul, awaking to Lydia's strategy.

"Paul, you are losing," whispered Silas loudly.

"I think you are too," added Timothy.

"Very well. You *do* win. But I insist that we will all sleep in the same quarters," conceded Paul.

It did little to insist when dealing with Lydia.

Her response had a note of finality about it.

"Timothy will sleep with the servants in one of the rooms beneath the house. Paul of Tarsus, you will have your own room. Silas and Luke may stay in the room next to you. I will hear no more of it."

Paul was once more about to protest when he glanced over at his companions. All three shrugged their shoulders. Philosophically, Timothy observed: "Come over into Macedonia and help us, and when you get there stay in clean quarters."

Silas chuckled. Paul feigned anger. Luke had already moved toward the front door, bound for "that filthy inn," to ensure that Paul not see him laughing.

"I think you have met your . . ." started Timothy.

"One more word out of you, young man," said Paul gruffly, "and you will be going home to Lystra." It was Paul's way of confessing defeat.

That marked only one of two times in all of Paul's travels that he had a clean room all his own.

From Luke came healing of body, from two of God's faithful servants came healing of soul and resurrection of spirit. It was a situation that even Simon Peter might have envied.

Paul had never been in a city where God's word had gone forth with such swiftness and ease.

But even such joyful surroundings could not heal a growing agony in Paul's heart. It was that letter from Jerusalem that Luke had brought to him which . . .

CHAPTER 8

Timothy knocked on Paul's door. There was an indistinct response. Quietly, Timothy edged open the door. Paul was sitting in the corner, his face covered with tears. With great difficulty Paul tried to say something to Timothy.

"Paul?"

"I am afraid."

"Afraid?"

"Yes. There has been so much blessing, so quickly."

"And you are afraid of that?"

"No, it is the coming of Blastinius I fear. He *will* come. One day he will come to Greece and even into this very house, and he will be more prepared than he was when he came to Galatia. Timothy, I do not know how to deal with that. And Blastinius's vow. What shall I do?"

"You will warn the brothers and sisters of Blastinius's coming?"

"*That* is my struggle, Timothy."

Timothy waited.

Paul began again. "It has never been my way to warn God's people. I have never frightened God's children with words about dark things that *might* happen. If I warn them well, I shall stop Blastinius; he will have no power here. But in defeating him, I shall be defeated. God's people will begin, after that, to see enemies everywhere.

"Blastinius has made himself my enemy; shall *I* make him mine? He is in my life—forever—until one of us dies. The damage he has done, and will do, will last forever. Shall I spend the rest of my life warning churches about this man? Shall I ingrain fear in the hearts of God's children?"

The tears continued to flow. "If he wins, if he destroys the churches I raise up, shall I become embittered? I *will* if first I fight him and *then* lose.

"Will you hear me become defensive? When I stand to speak, will you see that bitterness seep out? *Defensive*, simply because I have been attacked?

"Defending one's self, attacking one's enemies, is the way of small men, insecure men, men who feel they have something to defend—regardless of the destruction it causes among God's people.

"Shall I warn and defend? And in so doing, steal from these innocent people their innocence? Shall their minds be filled with shadows of coming dangers?

"I grew up in a world filled with rules. So also did most Jews. A world filled with warnings: warnings about the Gentiles; warnings about what would happen if I broke God's law; warnings about a God, who, if I did not do good, would not like me anymore! Warnings upon warnings. In that world of laws and rules, I saw shadows and dark figures everywhere. That world, for me and for all Jews, was filled with the chance of terrible possibilities. I have never allowed this atmosphere to creep into my ministry or into the lives of God's people in the churches I have raised up. I have built on the foundation of Christ."

Paul struggled. "Shall I replace the law, not with Christ, but with warnings and fears? Shall I warn of Blastinius's coming?

"Be my witness, Timothy. Did I ever give warnings? Or cause a spirit of foreboding? Remember my times in Lystra. Did I deliver anything but Christ to the assembly?"

Timothy slipped down beside Paul. "This is the reason for the tears?"

"Would to God that the man Blastinius had never entered my life," was Paul's reply.

"Paul, it was God who placed him there."

Paul bowed his head and began to cry. "I know . . . I know. And this is all I have wisdom to do: to stay here in Philippi as long as possible, and in so doing to grow here in this city a strong ecclesia. I pray to God that I can do that. Then . . . then . . . perhaps . . . when Blastinius comes . . ."

What Paul did not know was that his time in Philippi was almost over. Far away in the city of Rome, events were taking place that would change both Philippi and Paul. What the Emperor Claudius had done with his pen would remove Paul from Philippi. That news of Claudius's deed was already on its way to Philippi.

CHAPTER 9

The first ships from Rome carrying news of the emperor's newest decree reached eastern Greece just a few days after the decree was signed. And news it was! Sailors disembarking from the port of Neapolis began running through the streets shouting the news.

"Claudius signed an edict banishing all Jews from Rome!"

Within an hour, every human being in Philippi seemed to know. And as far as the people in Philippi were concerned, an edict in Rome was an edict in Philippi. Fanaticism for Caesar ran deep in this colony. If Claudius did not want Jews in Rome, that meant Philippians did not want Jews in Philippi.

Had there been a synagogue in Philippi that day, there would have been a riot, and Jews would have been dragged through the streets. Every Jew in the city would have been forcefully removed from the city. But there was hardly a citizen in Philippi who could name even one Jew. In fact, there were only two men in the city who were known to be Jews, and they were from out of town.

When word of the decree reached Paul, he was outraged. (The thought that Philippi might react against him personally did not enter Paul's mind.) Within a few moments Luke, Timothy, and Silas were called into Paul's room.

"That monster! That man who moves outside of any law or any restraint. That wicked one! That man of lawlessness!"

"Strong words, Paul. But how does this decree affect you?" asked Silas.

"This means I cannot go to Rome!" Paul exclaimed. "I wish to see Rome! To preach the gospel there. To see the ecclesia raised up there. How can I do that when all Jews are banished from the city? Need I remind you, I am a Jew!"

"Then you do not plan to leave Philippi?"

"No!" replied a startled Paul. "Why? Leave here? No, and I plan also to go to Rome . . . someday."

Paul paused.

"Can there be any reason to leave Philippi? I am a Roman citizen. So are you, Silas. Luke and Timothy have nothing to fear. You two are Gentiles."

"One-and-a-half Gentiles," corrected Timothy, trying to ease the tension.

"Timothy, you are spending too much time with Silas," Paul retorted. "You are picking up *his* humor. Anyway, here in Philippi, their loyalty to Rome notwithstanding, we shall ignore this decree."

The next morning, all the brothers and sisters in Philippi huddled together in Lydia's house and offered prayers to the Lord for the Hebrews who were being forced out of Rome.

When asked of his view of this decree, Paul's words were slow and pensive. "This is not the first time Jews have been ordered to leave Rome. The other time, the Jews were not long out of Rome before the city rulers hurriedly invited them back." Paul smiled. "It seems there were not enough honest Italians living there to run the city!"

Paul's insight proved true. A few years later the Jews were

allowed back into Rome. But not soon enough for Paul to go there as a free man. As for Philippi, his time remaining there could be measured in hours.

CHAPTER 10

The girl's hideous screams had become part of the city's life.

She had been brought to Philippi from Delphi, the city of oracles. Her owners brought her into the market every day, hiding her in a small, colorful tent where she sat behind closed curtains until someone came forward to pay for her advice.

"Find your answers here," her owners would call out to the passing throng. "If you have a question, this oracle has the answer you need to hear." (Those who paid to seek her advice were sometimes amazed, even startled, at her words. She seemed to know things that simply could not have been known.)

As the slave girl sat in the enclosed tent she often wailed and screamed with such pathos as to chill the blood of the hardest heart. On other occasions her madness left her, and she appeared to be perfectly sane.

In the world of the Greeks, oracles are considered to have powers granted to them directly from the god Apollo. The most elite oracles come from the order of the Pythons and the order of the Eurydeidai. They are called the Oracles of Delphi. The slave girl was of neither of these orders but was nonetheless respected, for she did belong to one of the lesser Daphni orders and was therefore considered a priestess.

On a few occasions this slave girl had predicted future events with perfect accuracy; yet, at other times those who sat before her met nothing but incoherent babble, leaving the hearer to interpret what her snarls and growls might mean. Her three owners had obtained a great deal of wealth from her tragic madness. Their entire income came from this girl.

On rare occasions she left the tent and moved about the marketplace. Sometimes she would stand in the middle of the street, screaming and wailing at the top of her voice. Such screams were followed by grotesque noises and gestures. To the onlookers, this meant that the gods were speaking to her, giving her wisdom so great it caused her to have fits. When these screeches and howls reached an intolerable level, you could be sure that a line would soon form in front of the multicolored tent.

On one of the occasions when the girl was wandering through the agora she accosted Paul. He ignored her. But as days passed, it became her habit to walk behind Paul, taunting him.

On the day after Philippi had heard of the edict of Claudius, Paul's thoughts were completely concentrated on his problems with Blastinius and with the emperor's new edict.

Until Paul entered the market area, the girl had been sitting silently in her tent. Suddenly she thrust her head out from behind the canvas door. Her raven black hair covering her face, she began to sniff the air like some wild animal. She then pushed her way into the crowd, turning first one way, then the other. Her fingers began to claw the air. Then her body contorted. Almost as if in a dance, she walked from one side of the street to the other, seemingly to be looking for something or someone.

Timothy described her this way: "She looked like a blind soul listening to faraway voices."

No one had ever seen her quite this mad. Everyone turned to watch her strange dance and listen to her loathsome growls. Suddenly she began to snarl and snap, then turned and ran—toward Paul. As was often his custom, Paul was about to stand and preach the gospel to the marketplace crowd. The girl took her place right in front of him, whimpering, whining, and crying. She pulled back her hair and then began stomping with her feet. She turned and faced those who had gathered.

"Hear him!" she screeched. "Hear him! Listen to this man."

Paul stared at the girl, having no idea what he should do.

"This man has come from the most high God. Listen to his message."

At that moment her three owners arrived, as confused as anyone. One of them grabbed her and began pulling her back toward her tent. She struggled against him, screaming again and again: "Listen to this man. Listen to Paul. Listen to Silas. They have come from the high God. They have a message for all of you." She then broke from her owners and began running back toward Paul, screaming as she came.

To Paul's credit, he never looked for trouble, nor was it in his mind to do anything spectacular. What he did that day was wholly spontaneous.

Paul whirled about and pointed at the girl. "Go back to your owners." She did not hear him. "Go back to your owners," he said again. For one brief moment the girl stopped her screams. There came a brief instant when she seemed to capture her sanity and in that moment sent a message to Paul through her pleading eyes. It was a cry for help from a young, innocent girl caged inside madness.

Paul's heart suddenly filled with sorrow and understanding. In almost blind rage, Paul thundered, "Come out of this young girl!"

As soon as Paul had uttered those words the girl's body froze. For a moment she stood as motionless as a statue. Then her body began to shake wildly, her arms flailing the air, her head jerked back. The shaking became more intense. Suddenly, there came a bloodcurdling scream, and the girl fell to the ground. Instantly, her owners were at her side.

Paul turned and walked away. It had been enough for one day. Returning to his room, Paul's thoughts turned again to his shattered dream of going to Rome with the gospel.

"Claudius, shall I never see Rome? Blastinius, will you destroy the Lord's work?"

In the meantime, the owners of the slave girl discovered she had lost her power and they had lost their income. The former oracle was now nothing but an ordinary girl, whole and sane. These men had wide investments in Philippi and vast debts, all procured on the basis of future earnings from the girl's strange gifts. Their rage turned toward Paul. "That Jew will pay," one of them swore.

For the rest of the day, the marketplace was filled with talk of what had happened. The next morning the entire market was filled with people waiting to see if the stranger from Tarsus would return to take his place among the tentmakers.

It was not a good day to be a Jew.

The city's citizens were already disappointed that they had no Jewish community to force out of the city, thereby demonstrating their loyalty to Rome. At that moment the only known Jews in the city were Silas and Paul, and they had been preaching some foreign, non-Roman god. Was this not unlawful? The slave owners lost no time in stirring up the people and some of the city leaders by reminding them of this fact.

The market was soon filled with a loud chorus of, "Jew, Jew! Out with the Jew!" Hearing this commotion, others began pouring into the agora. Most had no idea what was going on, but that was not important. That there was excitement was all they needed to know.

Word immediately reached the magistrates that there was a commotion in the marketplace. Most of the magistrates were

Greeks, not Romans; nonetheless, their one great responsibility was to placate Rome. Any laxity on their part could mean great trouble for the city. When they learned the disorder in the agora was caused by a Jew, that was all they needed to know. Details were irrelevant.

"There are Jews among us? Causing trouble? What are Jews doing in our city? Philippi shall have no Jews. *Rome* has no Jews. Bring them here! Now!"

All this time the slave owners had been badgering the crowd. "Do you not realize that you have lost a city treasure? Where will you go now for advice? The gods are angry. They have departed this girl. Why? Because we have allowed a *Jew* in the city. A Jew in the city of Philippi. No wonder Claudius threw them out of Rome. See what mischief they have done in our beloved city! Not only have they deprived us of the gifts of this child of Delphi, they also dare to preach some foreign god. Who knows what wrath will fall upon us!"

As their words escalated, so did the crowd's agreement, now chanting but one word: "Jew! Jew! Jew!"

One of the slave owners walked to the bema and addressed the magistrates: "There are Jews in our city. Is that not unlawful? Foreign Jews no less. They have disturbed our city and advocated customs that are not lawful for subjects of Rome. Why do you allow such anti-emperor conduct?"

"Call the Roman garrison," ordered the magistrates without hesitation.

Once the Latin captain of the garrison appeared, the magistrates put on a demonstration of loyalty, tearing their garments.

"We have just now learned that there are Jews in our city! They will not be here long."

By this time Paul had been located. So had Silas. Both had

been grabbed and dragged through the streets. Neither man knew what was going on. Nor would they be allowed a trial.

"Beat them with rods!" ordered one of the officials as soon as the two men reached the bema.

The crowd cheered with delight.

Turning to the lictors, one of the magistrates cried out, "Beat them, and beat them hard. When you have finished, throw them in jail. Tomorrow, throw them out of our fair city. We shall be finished with Jews before Rome is!" The crowd cheered again.

Months before, the brothers in Antioch had told Paul to never again take a whipping that could be avoided by declaring his Roman citizenship. Paul was doing his best to comply, for he kept shouting, *"Civis Romanus sum,"* but the crowd's cries were too loud for his voice to be heard. No one heard. No one cared.

The lictors forced Paul and Silas to the ground, then stripped them to the waist. The money pouch around Silas's waist was ripped open, and coins scattered across the pavement. Child and adult alike scrambled to retrieve the coins, while the rest of the crowd laughed with glee.

The lictors grabbed some birch rods that were always kept on the bema for just such occasions. Both men were now pushed over a stone column about three feet high. It was at that point the crowd caught sight of Paul's back, with its mass of scars from previous beatings. Everyone cheered. Here was proof of Paul's criminality. The magistrates smiled with satisfaction at their own wisdom in ordering this outlaw to be scourged.

The lictors, too, grinned with perverse delight as they silently vowed to outdo the previous inflictions.

With some in the crowd holding the two men down, and

with a lictor standing beside Paul and another beside Silas, the two felt the first scorching blows of the rods.

I suffered greatly and was shamefully treated in Philippi.

The beating was brutal and continued far longer than usually permitted. Both men's backs were ripped open, blood spattering both crowd and pavement. This was the *third* time Paul's back had undergone the merciless brutality of Roman rods. This one was the worst of the three.

Three times I was beaten with rods.

Finally, the magistrates signaled their satisfaction. The jailer had arrived by then and proceeded to drag the two men off toward the jail.

What happened during the night has become known to virtually all the Gentile believers throughout the entire Roman Empire. Years later when I, Titus, visited Philippi, I asked that I might see the jail where Paul and Silas were imprisoned.

Though many have heard this remarkable story, few know the details.

CHAPTER 11

The jail in Philippi is located *inside* a hill not far from the Atrium. The top of that hill is called the acropolis. At the bottom of the hill is the jail. Long ago, Roman soldiers had ordered slaves to bore in the stone and hew out a room. If you should come to Philippi and visit this jail, you will find the prison is nothing but a man-made cavern.

Standing outside, the only evidence you see of the prison is an iron grated door fastened into the stone, a Roman soldier standing guard. Coming closer, you can look through the door's grid and see the prisoners inside. There are no windows, making the prison not much more than a suffocating hole. Once inside, you find an enormous room divided into three sections. On your right is a large iron cage, on your left another. In these two cages are kept the assorted drunks and petty thieves peculiar to the city. As you walk farther in, you come to an area that serves as a dungeon. The bars of this cell have been sunk deep into the rock. You will notice inside, fastened to the walls and the floor, fetters and chains used to fasten the wrists of prisoners. There are also wooden stocks made for the prisoners' ankles.

Only the most dangerous of prisoners are kept in this cell, yet it was into this room the jailer dragged Paul and Silas. Having locked their feet in stocks and fettered their wrists to the chains, the jailer informed his two prisoners, "Tomorrow, about sunrise, you will be thrust out of this city. You must never return."

The jailer stepped out of the stone fortress and locked the grated iron doors. The two men, their backs burning like fire, turned on their sides. Their dried blood caked their clothes to their bodies.

Prisoners in the outer cells always pushed as close to the prison door as possible in order to get fresh air, but in the dungeon there was nothing except stale air and stifling heat.

Paul and Silas fell into merciful sleep. Late that night Silas awoke with a raging fever. "Lord Jesus," he whispered through swollen lips.

As soon as he said that, he heard a voice say, *Rejoice when men do these things to you.*

Silas broke into a wide grin. Paul smiled back. "Paul," said Silas, his voice choking, "this is the first time I have had the privilege of suffering for my Lord."

"Then let me assure you that it does not get any easier with repetition," coughed Paul.

These few words were followed by a long silence. Then, to Paul's astonishment, Silas began to sing. Paul began to laugh, then joined his brother in song.

> *Hear my prayer, O Lord;*
>> *And let my cry come to you.*
>> *Do not hide your face from me*
>> *In the day of distress.*
>> *Let the groanings of the prisoners*
>> *Come before you.*
>> *According to your great power,*
>> *Preserve those about to die.*

We can surmise, from what happened next, that there was someone—not of this earth—who was listening.

CHAPTER 12

Somewhere in the heavenlies, the Lord heard their groans and their praise. When the psalm had ended, the two men began to sing the shepherd's song. The other prisoners, now awakened, listened in disbelief. By the time the two men had come to the end of the shepherd's song they were singing so lustily one would not have known they were half dead.

It was Silas who first noticed the earth quiver beneath him. At first he paid no attention to it, but then came a hard jerk. The entire prison fell silent. Everyone present was anticipating that *something* would follow. Suddenly there was a violent jar. Again silence followed. Then came another jarring, even greater. The earth seemed to have gone mad. The room of stone began to crack. Fissures swept across the floor, then ran up the sides of the walls. The wooden stocks, though deeply anchored in rock, contorted and broke open like splinters.

The shaking became more violent. The silence was broken by screams arising from the prisoners. The iron bars that caged the prisoners began to twist and snap, then crashed to the floor. The iron door snapped off its hinges and fell forward upon the ground. In terror, the prisoners moved back against the stone walls, fearing the entire cavern might collapse upon them.

Awakened by the earthquake, the jailer grabbed his sword and rushed out into the night. When he saw the door to the prison lying on the ground, he was horrified. *Surely they are all gone*, he thought. His second thought was of the Brutus tradition. He would have to fall on his sword; it was the only honorable thing to do. Torch in hand, he rushed into the room. Because he saw no prisoners huddled close to the doorway, he assumed that, truly, all had escaped.

(I, Titus, know this jailer. Today he is a believer, and I count him both friend and brother. He has told me of what it was like that night. There was no doubt in his mind that every prisoner had fled. "Like Brutus, who had lost the battle against Octavian and Mark Anthony, I was readying myself to follow his example by falling on my sword.")

Paul and Silas could see the silhouette of the jailer framed against the open door, sword in hand. They watched in horror as he clasped the butt of the sword and turned its point toward himself.

"Do not harm yourself!" cried Paul.

"No one has escaped!" continued Silas. "None of us! We are all here."

"Either way, I am as good as dead," murmured the jailer, as he dropped the sword and fell to his knees. Turning his face toward the darkness of the dungeon, he addressed the voices he had heard.

"Sirs," he called out in desperation, "what must I do to be saved?"

The jailer asked one question, but Paul thundered the answer to another, more important, one.

"Believe on the Lord Jesus Christ, and you *will* be saved!"

"I believe! I believe!" cried the jailer.

Paul and Silas, chains still dangling from their wrists, stepped out of the shadows. The jailer lunged at Silas's feet and began to weep, while Paul, in a commanding voice, told the other prisoners, "Stay where you are!" The terrified prisoners complied. A moment later a Roman soldier from the nearby garrison rushed in.

"None have escaped," said the jailer reassuringly. "These two prisoners will come with me. Take up your place beside the prison door. That is, what was once a door!"

Paul and Silas followed the jailer out into the night, down a lane toward his home.

"Something has happened to me! Everything inside me seems to be light and bright—bright as the sun. What is happening to me?"

Entering his home, the jailer called his family together. He told them what had just taken place. Already frantic because of the earthquake, the jailer's wife was, at first, terrified about the fate of her husband. But little by little she came to listen and to understand.

The jailer began cutting the clothes off Paul and Silas. He then washed their wounds and poured oil all over their backs. It was at that time the jailer noticed the leather cord around Paul's neck. The jailer's mouth dropped open. "A *diptych!* You are a Roman citizen?"

"I am."

"The magistrates have beaten a Roman citizen . . . in Philippi?"

"No," said Silas. "That is not exactly correct; you have beaten *two* Roman citizens."

For a moment, the jailer could find no words. "I . . . I . . . I have imprisoned two citizens of the city of Rome. . . !"

Paul and Silas reassured him that they would lay no charge against him. "As you are now, we are followers of Christ. Revenge and recrimination are not ours."

"Stay in my home until first light," stammered the jailer.

"Then I will go to the magistrates and tell them what has happened. This transgression is not a thing to hide." (He need not have bothered—a leading lady of this city was already hard at work locating the magistrates.)

About an hour later the jailer, his wife, and his mother and father, along with his oldest son, all sat together and listened to Paul tell the story of Jesus Christ.

"This Jesus is your salvation."

All believed. Then, in that most unlikely of moments, the entire family, along with two very beaten men, walked out to the Gangites River, and five new brothers and sisters were baptized in Christ.

By the time the party arrived back at the jailer's home there was one very angry woman waiting there. It was Lydia. During the night she had located the home of every magistrate in the city. She had personally gone to their houses and confronted them for their barbaric treatment of Roman citizens.

"You have beaten two Roman citizens!" she repeated again and again. "You beat them without a trial; you beat them without a hearing, and without even a charge. You flouted their rights; you have ripped open their flesh. They cried out again and again, '*Civis Romanus Sum,*' and you paid no attention."

Each protested in the same way, "But we did not hear them."

"How could you?" she retorted. "You made no effort to silence the mob or to hear even one word of defense. You call yourselves *strategoi*, you call yourselves *praetors*—" (Those were the last words the magistrates wanted to be called, for it reminded them that as city leaders they answered to Rome for *all* things.) "You are not governors at all. You are uncivilized savages!

"I shall go straight to the Roman officials—*all* of whom are my friends," she threatened. "By tomorrow the governing of

this city will be back in the hands of Rome. And you, you barbarians, will be in disgrace."

The magistrates began begging Lydia not to report the incident to the Roman officials. After all, every one of them had
seen their own homes damaged by the earthquake. They were
now terrified, not only of Lydia and the Romans, but also of the
gods. They knew they had done *something* wrong!

Lydia, playing to their fears, agreed that the gods were dis-
pleased with them. "After all, you harmed Romans!" she repeated menacingly.

Lydia then added her demands: "You must go to the prison
and set Paul and Silas free, and ask forgiveness." Terrified and
humbled, the men all agreed and followed Lydia to the jailer's
home.

Upon arrival, the magistrates inquired of the jailer, "The
Romans, where are they?"

"In my home."

"Where?"

"In my *home!*"

"Not in the prison?"

"What prison?" responded the jailer. "The place is hardly a
cave. It will never be a jail again."

"Who has escaped?"

"No one!" answered the jailer, half in anger.

"We did beat two innocent men?"

"You did. They are *both* Roman citizens," continued the
jailer contemptuously.

"See!" said Lydia, warming again to her role as adversary.
"You have incurred the wrath of Jupiter. Perhaps you will even
see unleashed the anger of a God greater than Jupiter."

(Word of the beating of two Romans was the only topic of
the marketplace when it began to open.

"The men who were beaten yesterday were Roman citizens. That earthquake . . . the gods are surely angry!"

That day all living in Philippi had heard, and *all* professed their innocence. And all agreed the gods of Rome were punishing the city. Adding to that the fact that the previous day Paul had cast out a demon caused an entire citizenry to view those two men in a totally different light. Much good was to eventually come from these events.)

"Turn them loose," said one of the magistrates.

"I will not. I did not beat them. I did not order them jailed. You do it," said the jailer.

"Go into the house and tell the two men to leave the city," said one of the magistrates to the guard.

By now, Paul and Silas had learned that the city fathers were outside. And that Lydia had also arrived! The guard came into the house and quietly repeated the magistrates' orders.

"The city fathers would dare order *us* to leave! You tell those so-called magistrates to come in here and *ask* us to leave," declared Paul.

The guard hardly knew what to do. Magistrates on the outside, whipped Romans inside. He chose to obey the Roman citizens.

As the guard turned to go, Paul had something else to say. "Those men have beaten us publicly when we were guilty of nothing. Nor will we leave this city until we have received an apology from *all* of them. Nor will they order us out of the city. They will request it of us, and they will do so *kindly*." The guard departed. "Pity the poor magistrates when Lydia hears what the guard says," laughed Paul.

A few moments later the entire *strategoi* were standing in the jailer's house, wringing their hands and apologizing profusely.

"Please, please leave. Forgive us of our wrong. We beg you to leave, *today.*"

Paul stared at each man, then said, "I have been in your city only a short time. I have done no wrong. My companion has done no wrong. We have dear friends in this city; we will visit them before we leave. Until then we will be under *your* protection. You will also extend protection to my Philippian friends after I have left the city!"

"Yes, yes, anything. Only leave."

"I will remember that promise. Be sure of that," threatened Lydia.

Without a word, Paul turned and walked out of the house. Silas took a slightly longer route; he made sure he passed each one of the magistrates and fixed each with a withering stare.

The two men emerged from the jailer's home, and Lydia began to cry as she sought to find some place to touch them that would not cause them pain.

By the time they reached Lydia's house, there were perhaps a dozen brothers and sisters awaiting them. Everyone cheered as the two men walked into the room.

"We have prepared warm salt water for your backs. Shortly I will have new clothes for your bodies," said Lydia, weeping through every word. As the two men were led into an adjoining room, the brothers and sisters began quietly singing.

Luke greeted his friends. "Lie down on the floor. I will begin working on those backs of yours." At Paul's request, Timothy was asked to join them.

"Oh, Paul," said Luke, as he examined Paul's back, "we had so hoped that this would not happen to you again. This back of yours is in shreds. Antioch will not like this news."

Paul's response came as a surprise. "Luke, I have something very, very serious to speak to you about."

C H A P T E R   1 3

I have had less than three months in Philippi, Luke. Now I am forced to leave. Never before have I been in a city so short a time. It is too short a time for an assembly to be well founded. In Galatia I was always with an assembly four or five months. Luke, the holy ones here need more help than has been given."

While Paul continued, Luke poured herbs and oil on Paul's back and then wrapped strips of cloth around him.

Despite his pain, Paul managed to come to his point. "I know you have planned to return to Antioch soon, but I implore you to stay and help these brothers and sisters. They need you, Luke. They need ministry concerning their Lord. Show them how to worship him, how to live with one another. Help the men grow into a brotherhood. And the sisters, the same. Show all of them how to take care of the ecclesia. Give them the Lord. Share with them all those practical things they need to know . . . the kinds of things the assembly in Antioch has learned over the years. Show them more about how to gather, how to function. *Then* leave. The Holy Spirit will do the rest."

Paul sat up and looked straight into Luke's eyes. "How long can you stay?"

"No more than two months. Then I must return."

Paul then turned to Timothy. "Silas and I will be gone within a few hours. You must remain here and colabor with Luke. You have proven your courage in Lystra. You know how to exhort the Lord's people. You know how to encourage God's people. And you have to preach your Lord. As you know, many in the marketplace have listened. Some have believed. After the events of this night, others will, too. Even now there are husbands considering following their wives by being immersed into Christ. They will need direction in their new life. You and Luke must give that help."

"In Israel, you would be considered a Jew. But here in Philippi they don't like Jews. Here you are a Gentile. I remind you of your stated desire, to become all things to all men so that you might win some."

Timothy smiled. "Your words, Paul, not mine."

"Then you will stay?"

"I would be honored."

Turning again to Luke, Paul added, "If you hear any word from the assemblies in Galatia or anything from the saints in Antioch, send that word to me immediately."

"Where?" asked Luke.

"Yes, where . . . ?" replied Paul. "I think I do know! Send word to me in . . . Thessalonica!"

"The capital of northern Greece?"

"But also send a copy of any letter you write to me to Amphipolis and Apollonia. I will be passing through those cities on my way to Thessalonica. The point is, send me any news."

"Your concern is Blastinius?"

Paul wrenched. "What did you put in that oil, Luke?"

"Herbs!"

"It feels like fire! But, yes, Blastinius. Always Blastinius. I am sure Blastinius *will* come here. Here! To Philippi. Either that or his friends," Paul sighed. "I am about to leave a very young, impressionable, innocent assembly. A young church, a *persecuted* church. How shall the citizens of Philippi act toward the brothers and sisters? You both must be ready for that answer, whatever it is.

"Philippi—the most Gentile of all the churches I serve. There is not a single Jew among these believers. These dear ones do not even know what legalism is." Paul laughed. "Most have never even heard of Moses."

"I wonder why," said Timothy teasingly.

Again Paul flinched, then continued. "There is no knowledge of the Hebrew Scriptures here. There is hardly anyone here who could even tell you who David is. I have laid a foundation of Christ. Further, I leave them no Scriptures. They have no writings of any kind. All that these dear people have is what has been given in less than three months. Can this foundation possibly hold? Philippi will be the ultimate test of a gospel only briefly given!"

Paul paused; his voice cracked. "In all this I have not warned them about law, legalism, Pharisees, ritual . . . *circumcision!* Nor of Blastinius. I have never warned them of anything. Not one word. If Blastinius came here tomorrow, he would be welcomed like a king."

"Will you warn them of Blastinius?"

"I have only tonight to speak to the church. Shall I waste my time talking about a man I do not like . . . ?" Paul's words trailed off in a quiet chuckle.

Paul changed the subject. "Tell me, Luke. Have you ever memorized any passages of Scripture?"

"Only a few."

"Timothy?"

"Not many that I could accurately quote."

"I wonder if Lydia . . . I doubt she would know many passages either. There is not a scrap of Hebrew scroll in all Philippi. The three of you get together and write down what you can remember. Make copies, and give them to everyone who can read."

"That will be no more than three, in *Latin*. And no more than four, in *Greek*," observed Timothy.

Paul let out a long breath. "Not much chance of God's people making the mistake of depending on Scripture rather than on Christ! Brothers, your path is clear. Speak to these new believers about the Lord. Show them how to know him.

"Now, Luke, care for Silas; this is the first time he has been beaten with rods."

"Are you implying that a third beating makes it easier?"

"No, but I do know how the next few days will go for both of us. Silas does not."

Lydia stepped into the room.

"Lydia," said Luke, "Timothy and I will be staying in Philippi for a month or two. I believe it would be wise if the ecclesia met here just as often as possible during that time."

"This is good," said Lydia. "We are not ready to be so quickly left alone." Then, turning, Lydia handed Paul a bundle of clothes, and Silas another.

A few minutes later Paul and Silas stepped into the living room, dressed in clothing that could only be described as beautiful.

"Befitting a Roman citizen," commented Luke.

Paul walked over to the jailer. "Observe, my dear brother in Christ, that the actions of this city provided me with new clothes, clothes more costly than ever I have worn before."

"Ah, but bought at so high a price," said the jailer.

By now the room was full. Paul sat down, awkwardly leaning against the wall, then quickly leaned forward. His first words were, "Please do not hug me!" Everyone laughed congenially. Throughout the evening Paul hardly referred to the events of the previous day. His thoughts were on the assembly and its future.

Paul spoke for about two hours. His words were high, spiritual, and often extremely practical. He spoke things of Christ no one in that room had ever heard before.

Timothy leaned forward and whispered to Silas, "Will he mention Blastinius?"

He did not. Before Paul could finish sharing his heart there was a knock at the door. It was the local law enforcers. They had come to escort Paul out of the city. Paul explained to them that he was not planning to leave so quickly. They insisted. But their words were tempered, and their offer appealing.

"A Roman garrison will accompany the two of you out of the city, on horses, to the first inn you come to on the Egnatian Way."

Paul acquiesced. There were a few brief prayers. The meeting came to an end. By the time Paul and Silas had reached the door everyone was crying.

There in the street Luke had a final word to say, a word spoken to Paul but not wasted on the guards. "You two men are in no condition to travel. For the magistrates to demand this is inhuman. You need many days to recoup your strength." He then spoke to the guards directly, "I must go with these men."

"Wait," he added. Luke then reentered the house. A moment later he returned with the small leather bag that denoted his trade.

Paul needed Luke more than he realized, for he had passed through three devastating experiences, all in just a few days. Shortly before the beating he had learned of the vow of Blastinius, as well as the edict of Claudius against the Jews in Rome. The beating itself had come as a terrible surprise to Paul. He had not expected such things on this journey—certainly not in Greece, the seat of civilized behavior. These events had not yet overwhelmed Paul, but they soon would. Yes, Paul needed Luke and all the graces of God.

As the three men moved into the street, the brothers and sisters began moving toward them, softly singing a song of encouragement.

That is the most gentle, most loving people I have ever had the privilege of knowing, thought Paul.

As stated, the guards led the two Roman citizens out through the city gate. It was there that the men found two horses awaited them. The guards helped Paul onto one and Silas onto the other. Luke took his place beside the soldiers.

"This is the first time the Roman Empire has ever provided me with transportation, but it is still not quite equal to the cost they extracted," said Silas. "I am not used to exchanging my blood for a horse ride!"

The first inn they came to was some ten miles from Philippi. When the innkeeper saw the Roman soldiers and heard their demand for a room, he courteously complied—an unusual practice for any innkeeper.

Luke was not satisfied with the room they were given. Perhaps it was because he was a physician, or perhaps it was in remembrance of what Barnabas had once done for Paul. Luke insisted that the room be burned, washed, and cleaned, and that fresh straw be provided. The innkeeper grumbled, but the silent glare of sword-bearing soldiers persuaded him to act quickly.

While the room was burning, Luke asked both Paul and Silas to step out into the morning sunlight. There he moistened their bandages with water and herbs, then gently removed the bandages, replacing the blood-soaked cloth strips with new ones.

"It will be days before these wounds heal," complained

Luke. "I repeat, it is inhuman to have sent you out of the city this way."

"Men do strange things to protect their positions," replied Paul. "Even to the inconvenience of Roman citizens."

The voice of the captain of the garrison could be heard from within. "See to it that these men get rest and quiet. Serve them your best food, and dare not charge them even a denarius. And the physician, treat him as you do the others."

The guards departed.

Once Paul and Silas lay down, they fell asleep and did not awake until late the next afternoon. All the while they were under the watchful eye of my uncle, the beloved physician. What awakened them was the unexpected arrival of Timothy. Luke heard Timothy's voice addressing the innkeeper. Luke rushed downstairs. A few minutes later Paul struggled to the door and urged Timothy to come upstairs.

"I have news." Timothy's face was somber and drained.

"Is it the church in Philippi?" asked Paul anxiously.

"No."

"What is it?"

"We have just received news from Galatia."

"From Lystra?" urged Silas.

"Yes, from Lystra. But there is word, also, from Antioch and Jerusalem as well."

"Is someone dead?"

"No."

Paul heaved a groan. "Then it is Blastinius."

"Yes," responded Timothy sadly, "a letter came from Gaius in Derbe. The letter also includes news from Jerusalem and Antioch, as well as Lystra and Derbe."

Timothy handed the letter to Paul. Paul squinted at the letter and handed it back. "Read it to me."

"I must warn you, Paul, it is not good news."

"Blastinius is never good news," grunted Silas.

"According to the letter, Blastinius left Jerusalem and traveled to the island of Cyprus! He caused a great stir among the churches on Cyprus. Blastinius even attacked the name of Barnabas openly in all the churches. He then made his way to Antioch."

"To Antioch?" exclaimed Paul, trying hard to grasp what he was hearing.

"As you can guess, Blastinius was not particularly welcome in Antioch this time, nor was he in any way successful in his purpose. The church in Antioch is on to him. Therefore, he moved northward, seeking out the ecclesiae in every town and village along the coast of Syria and Cilicia. He has done much damage in some of the small assemblies in these places."

A soft moan escaped from Paul's throat.

"But this is not the main point of the letter, is it?" asked Silas.

"You are correct. After passing through northern Syria, Blastinius turned and made his way again to Galatia and to the churches he had sought to destroy so recently."

"No!" exclaimed Luke in disbelief.

"He found no hearers there, either!" interrupted Paul. "In Galatia the issue is over." Paul had never spoken so emphatically.

"That is exactly what Gaius said in this letter," said a surprised Timothy. "You know the Gauls well!" Then Timothy continued, "But somewhere in all this traveling, Blastinius has learned that you have departed Galatia and have traveled as far into Asia Minor as Troas."

"Oh no," groaned Silas.

"Paul, Blastinius is following you," declared Timothy bluntly.

A heavy silence followed.

"He comes. Even now, he comes," whispered Paul hoarsely. "Blastinius, you will find my trail, will you not? Eventually, you will make your way here to Greece, even to Philippi, will you not? Nor is that beautiful lady in Philippi, whose name is *ecclesia* . . . she is not prepared for you." Paul paused, then looked around the room. "I gave the assembly in Philippi no warnings of the coming of this man, not even of his *existence*. That man will destroy the assembly in Philippi."

Paul's words were muffled and seemed to be spoken to no one in particular.

"You need to know one other thing, Paul," said Timothy, clearing his throat. "Blastinius has not only been visiting the churches, he has gone into every synagogue in every town he has passed through. In every place he has gathered the Jewish leaders together and told them in detail about this controversial man named Paul. Blastinius has twisted your words and reinterpreted everything you have said and everything you have done. He has done so in every city where you have proclaimed Christ.

"Blastinius has made you out to be something extremely sinister," continued Timothy. "What the synagogue leaders know of you is that you are a troublemaker in Judaism and a troublemaker in the empire. You have renounced the law of Moses and have written a seditious letter claiming that God has done away with the laws and ordinances of the Hebrews and that men are free of all laws. These have been Blastinius's words concerning you."

"The letter I wrote to the Galatian churches. He has a copy!" said Paul.

"Oh! Oh!" Silas groaned again and again.

"It is a pincer movement," observed Luke.

Everyone looked up at the physician, surprised by his use of a military term.

"He is going to the churches to bring confusion; he is going to the synagogues to make sure that the door to the Jews becomes closed to you. In both cases he is out to destroy first your reputation and then your effectiveness . . . as well as the Gentile churches. I have a notion that soon he will be warning the city magistrates wherever he travels."

"Even as we speak, he comes. He comes, and comes to destroy," said Paul, very slowly. After another moment of heavy silence he spoke again, this time more slowly still. "Every place I go, everything I say, every thing I do, every step I take—he will soon be there."

Very quietly, Silas added, "Philippi."

"I fear so," responded Luke sadly.

"Gaius, in his letter, suggests that some brothers be dispersed to all the churches where Blastinius might go and warn them that he might be coming."

Paul struggled to his feet, wrenching with pain as he did.

"What shall I do? I do not know. How does one deal with such a situation? I could live upon this earth five hundred years and never again meet such an adversary as Blastinius Drachrachma. You would not expect something like this to occur in a dozen lifetimes."

"Should we take Gaius's advice?" inquired Silas. "Should we warn Philippi and the other assemblies?"

Paul did not realize it, but in that next moment he gave utterance to what would one day be his ultimate decision concerning Blastinius.

"No!" exclaimed Paul. "Never!"

"What?" came Luke's astonished response. "You will not warn?"

"No, I would rather . . . No! It would be a temporary victory, only to eventually wreak cataclysmic destruction in the process of stopping him!"

No one in that room fully understood what Paul had said.

That included Paul, for he had spoken spontaneously, out of the depths of his heart, from a place that is deeper than human understanding.

"If we can say nothing about Blastinius, what shall Luke and I say . . . what shall we do in Philippi when we return there?" asked an almost frantic Timothy.

"Indeed, what?" agreed Luke.

Paul's face was blank. "I . . . I do not know . . . ," he responded.

Luke waited. He was sure Paul had more to say.

"Give me time, Luke, Timothy. In a few days I will write to you. This is a matter that has not yet been settled in my heart. I do not, at this moment, understand the Lord's will. I do not understand why Blastinius is in my life. I do not know how to deal with him according to God's ways."

"But I must repeat my question, Paul. In the meantime, what shall I do?" insisted Timothy.

Paul smiled. "Give them Christ."

"That I shall be pleased to do. I have been well mentored. Is there anything else?" asked Timothy.

"Yes, I have a last question of Luke. You are a doctor. Tell me, what does one do with a back on which its scars have scars?" mused Paul lightly.

Luke turned to Silas, his answer serious.

"Silas, this is the only time you have been beaten. You are younger and stronger than Paul. Your wounds will heal. Paul, your wounds are deep. As you said, the scars have scars. I am concerned about infection; it could easily set in. With your permission, I would spend one or two more days with you."

"*Only* if Timothy returns to Philippi immediately," came Paul's quick response. "One of you must *always* be present in Philippi, at least for the next few months. But yes, Luke, you may stay a few more days."

"And if Blastinius comes to Philippi while all three of you are gone?" asked Timothy.

"When he sees you, and remembers what you did to him in Lystra, he will turn and run."

Timothy's response was a grunt.

That very night Paul came down with a high fever. Infection had set in. If it had been some other physician caring for him, we might have lost Paul. But between Luke's prayers, his medicines, his herbs, and his love and concern for Paul, the fever broke a few days later. Even then Luke insisted that Paul remain yet another day or two at the inn before traveling. Unknown to Paul, Luke sent a message back to Philippi asking the assembly there to send someone to take Timothy's place in carrying Paul's luggage. The very next morning a young brother from the church in Philippi appeared. His name was Marcus.

"Marcus is here to be with you until you reach the next city. He will carry your luggage. I am not going to try to make you stay here any longer, Paul of Tarsus. I know that if you can stand on your feet you will leave this inn."

Normally, one would expect Paul to protest such help, but this time he did not. Rather, Paul thanked Marcus for coming and embraced him. As it turned out, Marcus was able to carry not only what Timothy usually carried but everything that Paul would have been carrying as well.

The day after Marcus arrived, Luke returned to Philippi, while Paul and Silas set out in the direction of Thessalonica. At the outset Paul decided it wise to tell Marcus a story.

"Marcus, I wish to tell you of something that happened to us on the island of Cyprus. It concerns Roman chariots and conscription." Paul told of the day on the isle of Cyprus that Roman soldiers forced Paul and Barnabas to turn back a full day's journey to repair a chariot. After finishing the story Paul requested the obvious. "Marcus, please walk ahead of us and watch for Roman soldiers. Signal us to hide. We have no desire to be free labor for the emperor Claudius."

After Marcus left, Paul turned to Silas with yet more bad news. "Silas, I have not so much as a denarius. How much do you have?"

"Luke gave me twelve denarii. Each of them bears the image of your favorite emperor. But did not the brethren in Philippi . . .?"

"No, it apparently slipped their minds. Things happened there so suddenly that helping us with our travel was not something they had time to consider."

"Getting to the next town looks impossible!"

"True, but so is returning to Philippi."

Later, Silas found that Marcus had five denarii. Finding out the dire straits Paul was in, Marcus immediately wanted to give all five denarii to Paul.

"No, Marcus, five denarii will hardly get you back to Philippi."

"Oh, but I am strong. I eat little. I can get home easily. If you do not take the denarii how will you survive?"

"We will manage," said Silas assuredly. "The Lord has a way of taking care of orphans, widows, and the likes of us."

"How could everyone in Philippi have been so derelict?" an exasperated Marcus wondered aloud. "You are far from Thessalonica, banished from Philippi, with no money. When and if you get to Thessalonica, you will arrive without funds. You will starve."

"If we stay in the inns each night and if we buy food, how many days will that see us?" asked Paul.

"No more than six days."

Paul raised his head, put one hand to his forehead, and began adding. "It has been my experience that it takes at least a month, setting up shop in the marketplace, before I can gather enough business to provide food and shelter. Sometimes, only food."

"You mean there are times that you have had to sleep in the marketplace where you work?" asked Marcus.

"Only on a few occasions. The Lord has been very merciful to *almost* always put a roof over my head."

"But twelve denarii . . . pray tell, how can you survive a month or more on twelve denarii?" stammered Marcus.

"Antioch also forgot," added Silas. "It was only the money in our pocket that we had when we departed Antioch."

Marcus shook his head in disbelief.

Silas mulled the situation over in his mind. "There are two things we can do that will aid us. We can keep an eye out for wild berries and whatever else we see that is growing along the road. As to lodging, the weather is good. We can sleep in the fields at night," he continued as he searched the sky.

"My mother had a saying that I remember as a little boy. When in times of famine or when things were not going well for my family, she would tell us, 'We shall get up for breakfast, we shall walk around for the noon meal, and we shall go to bed for supper.'"

Paul smiled, then added, "Outside of some intervention of God, I see us arriving in Thessalonica with no money, nor food, nor shelter. Even under the most favorable of circumstances tentmaking will not provide us with food or shelter for quite some time—at least a month."

"Then we are thrown on the mercies of God," said Silas with a hint of resignation.

"That we are," agreed Paul, "but in the light of past experience, and especially in the light of the last few days in Philippi, I would say that sometimes the mercies of God do not show up at what we consider the appropriate hour."

*I have lived with weariness and pain and sleepless nights. Often I
have been hungry and thirsty and have gone without food. Often I
have shivered with cold, without enough clothing to keep me warm.*

As dismal as were their circumstances, a greater pain would
soon envelop Paul and send him to the verge of despair.

I, Titus, must now tell you of that hour, which was perhaps
the darkest hour Paul ever lived.

CHAPTER 14

Paul went for hours without saying a word as the three men trudged along the Egnatian Way. A few times he did speak—but almost always to himself!

Then there were the nights. Silas would often awake to hear Paul sobbing violently.

Within Paul a perilous struggle was growing. Often he would stop beside the road, fighting just to get his breath. In the fields where they spent each night, Paul's eyes rarely closed in sleep. He would arise the next morning utterly spent. When Paul did sleep, Silas would still hear him crying out in anguish.

Paul was in no less than a battle for his spiritual life. God was breaking an unbreakable vessel. Ill, hungry, whipped, rejected by men, overlooked by the churches, dogged by an unrelenting enemy, all combined to enshroud Paul in a deep sadness.

The beating in Philippi had not only been unexpected, but Paul discovered he had reached that point where he was unwilling to suffer abuses so extreme, unwilling to continue to receive such unjust treatment. What Paul did not realize was that his Lord was perfecting a vessel—far, far beyond our finite ability to understand.

Was Paul affected by the fact that *all* the churches had overlooked sending him help?

Timothy once said, "Yes, but he never gave room to that thought. With a back inflamed, no money in his pocket, thrown out of a city for the fifth time, a wolf named Blastinius at his heels, hungry and exhausted . . . and about to enter another city where rejection was waiting to greet him: Could he continue to endure? To remain unaffected was more than could be expected of any man . . . or at least to bear it well. Yet, that is exactly what Paul did! He endured!"

That day the three men had enough money to buy food for perhaps five days, if they kept sleeping in the fields.

That journey from Philippi to Thessalonica was an unbearable crucible for Paul. No less than the soul of a worker was hanging in the balance. (There was only one other time in Paul's life when he sank this deep into hopelessness. On that occasion it was I, Titus, who witnessed that hour.)

Always, at the heart of all Paul's agonies was the vow of Blastinius. A hound had entered Paul's life. Though the past had been bad enough, looking into the future Paul could see not a single unhindered day for the rest of his life.

Because of Claudius's decree, Paul's dream of Rome seemed to have gone. This was an unbearable thought for Paul. He knew that one day a handful of Jewish believers in the Trastavere district in Rome would be the church in Rome. Paul wanted the church in Rome to be a Gentile church because Rome was a Gentile city. Paul could hardly tolerate such a thought. "I will not be able to take defeat, rejection, failure, and beatings forever," Paul breathed.

And the Daggermen—they would soon mark Paul for death, a fact of which he was certain!

Most of all, Blastinius! That man had placed Paul in a situation where he could not win. Can any man go on ministering, knowing that no matter what he does, his work *will* be destroyed? Can any man give his whole heart and soul, receive rejections, persecutions, and physical affliction, all the while knowing that everything he does is in vain?

Paul was pressed out of his measure, and he knew it! He also knew God was at work in his life, but *what* it was that God was doing he did not know. Above all else, Paul had no idea what God wanted him to do about Blastinius. *This* was the maddening dilemma Paul wrestled with every day.

"How am I supposed to react to a man set on the destruction of all I do? If it were for a year or a decade of years, perhaps I *would* know what to do. But *every* day of my life—forever?!" Paul was being forced to search out the will of God on a level he had never before ventured into.

Each day the struggle was more unbearable than the day before. Sometimes Silas would hear Paul mutter the name *Blastinius.* Other times Silas thought Paul appeared to be praying. On other occasions, Silas could see blind rage etched on Paul's face. But when there was no expression at all on Paul's face, that worried Silas the most. And when Paul cried, which was often, Silas cried with him.

"Paul's struggle became so intense that at times he sat down beside the road and simply groaned," Silas once said. "Once or twice he sobbed so uncontrollably, so intensely, that I thought he might die. Then there were nights I heard Paul groaning in agony. In all this I never spoke a word to him, never intruded in any way. I knew too well that the battle was his alone. Paul was in the throes of a decision that, one way or the other, would change him—and his ministry—forever.

"Would he decide to warn the churches in Philippi about Blastinius? Paul realized how radically that would change that church and all the churches—and himself. Paul was horrified at the very thought of such a thing. When he saw the hopelessness of his situation, that is when he would slip into deep depression.

"'Either way, I lose,' he sometimes murmured."

What was God's purpose in placing Blastinius in Paul's life? Paul was a man of great power and revelation. I, Titus, shudder to think what Paul—intelligent, proud, insightful, indomitable—might have become had God not sent this thorn into his life. Perhaps without Blastinius to provide him with so great a cross, Paul might have become a man dangerous to God's people and God's purpose. Instead, in the end he became a weakened man wholly thrown on a strength not his own. When the Lord placed Blastinius into Paul's life, he struck at Paul's greatest weakness (and Paul's greatest strength). It is remarkable that the men who are closest to the heart of God seem always to be the ones whom the Lord deals with most severely.

Paul once remarked of this crisis, "The greatest crisis a man will ever face, and the greatest test of what he really is, comes when his ministry is at stake. Men will fight like savages to protect and preserve their ministries and invoke God as they do so. Such men lack any capacity to grasp even the most rudimentary understanding of the Cross . . . of loss . . . and of the divine nature of failure! Strength has no strength. Victory, no victory. Power, no power. Strength, victory, and power lie only in weakness. They are laid hold of only in the willingness to fail.

"Power lies in the willingness to utterly lay down all, surrender all, lose all . . . to have what outwardly appears to be an almost insane willingness to lose. Not to lose once, mind you, but to lose over and yet over again. To see all of your work on earth *destroyed*, not once, but many times—then rise again to see the Lord and his sovereign will in the presence of sure defeat. Only there can God's power rescue you!"

Years afterward, Silas spoke of that journey from Philippi to Thessalonica.

"Paul was angry at Blastinius," recalled Silas. "Paul wanted so much to lash out at that man. This was the natural inclination of Paul—to fight. In his rage Paul imagined writing fiery letters to all the churches, exposing and condemning the man Blastinius. Yet, he knew that was his flesh speaking, not his spirit. At times Paul craved to justify himself, to speak out, to write a letter to Jerusalem, to write to Antioch—to tell them what Blastinius was doing."

I, Titus, do not doubt that in his mind Paul composed a powerful letter to the assemblies in Greece, Galatia, Cilicia, and Syria. But I believe his battle was won before it began. Is there any other man on this earth who would have made the decision that Paul eventually made? Yet, the decision he made was so like Paul, for Paul took the high ground. Paul eventually made a decision that was nothing less than noble—perhaps nothing less than unbelievable. Most men would laugh at such a decision! The rest of us would not comprehend it. Paul chose the route of the impossible. He chose loss and defeat. In so doing, God won! In that awesome decision the Lord had found a way to make a strong man weak, to break a man who was unbreakable.

But that moment had not yet come.

CHAPTER 15

Paul, I am surprised. I thought your back was healed. Yet the fever has struck you again. So, also, the infection. We must stop sleeping in the fields. You need decent rest," insisted Silas.

Paul would hear nothing of it, so at his insistence they forged on.

Each morning the two men rose to search for berries and, if possible, to glean grain from fields. Nonetheless, they were ever exhausted. Paul's intermittent fever was stealing his fortitude. How he managed to continue was a constant amazement to Silas and Marcus. The Egnatian Way brought them at last in sight of the city of Amphipolis. Paul knew there was a synagogue in the city, yet rather than staying until the Sabbath to visit the synagogue, he remained in the city only long enough to dispatch a letter to Luke in Philippi.

That letter reflected what was emerging out of the struggle in Paul's heart.

"I still do not know the Lord's mind," wrote Paul, "but this I have to say to you, Luke. I speak in the strongest manner: If Blastinius arrives in Philippi, *do not* prevent him from speaking to the ecclesia."

Paul had come only thirty-five miles in what had taken over

a week. But during that week, little by little, God had begun winning the heart of Paul. And what was it God was winning him to? To the cross of all crosses: the loss of the Lord's work.

When the letter reached Luke in Philippi, Luke read it in the presence of Timothy. Both men were struck dumb.

Timothy shook his head. "This means if Blastinius comes here to Philippi, he will have free reign among the brothers and sisters."

At the time the letter reached Philippi, Paul was in a region called Prima Macedonia, still some sixty-six miles from Thessalonica.

The battle raging in Paul's soul was destroying him. Now more than ever before, Paul talked aloud as he walked. The crisis had to be resolved soon.

"Can I walk into Thessalonica and face almost certain persecution? Can I cheerfully accept persecution yet one more time? Perhaps a beating? Again? I have been beaten on the island of Cyprus, shipwrecked once, beaten and stoned in Galatia, my name a byword in Israel. Beaten in Philippi!

"Can I now go to Thessalonica and joyfully be thrown out of that city—hated, despised, lied about? Can I endure these abuses and not grow bitter?

"I cannot. At least, I fear I cannot. I have reached my end. I can strive so hard no longer. Either God must extend to me graces of which I know nothing, or I will surely falter in the face of the onslaughts that await me, all the while knowing that you, Blastinius, will come to Thessalonica and destroy everything I have done?"

Could our God extend grace enough?

There was a moment in his most desperate hours when Paul stood in the middle of the Egnatian Way, turned around and looked back at the road from whence he had come, and spoke aloud.

"You are coming, are you not, Blastinius? Yes, Blastinius, you *will* come to Philippi."

Paul then turned again and faced toward Thessalonica. "If I come to you, Oh Thessalonica, capital of Macedonia, if the gospel is received in you by both Jew and heathen, and if the redeemed of the Lord assemble . . . ?"

Paul paused and said nothing. Then he turned and once more faced the road over which he had just come.

". . . Yes, Blastinius, you *will* follow me to Thessalonica. You will come down this very road. You will *always* come, will you not? Philippi will see your shadow, then also will Thessalonica."

It was that night, the night of all nights for Paul, bedded down on the side of the road, that he begged his Lord to take Blastinius out of his life. (There would be two more such times.) That long, memorable night Paul tried to alter the will of God. But it was also that night that the Lord spoke to Paul. It was Paul, not God, who was altered.

"You have looked upon my face. I have transported you into the heavens. You have seen things no other man has seen, things which stretch from eternity to creation, and to the end of all things created. You have my *call* upon your life. You have received my *sending*. To you I have revealed *the mystery*. Yet, you are but an earthen vessel; your strength is too strong, your gift too great, your revelation too vast. It is I, and I alone, who have given Blastinius to you. It is good that only I be strong. And good that you always be weak. Find me, and me alone, to be your strength. Blastinius is in your life . . . forever . . . that you may be weak."

When these words flooded into Paul's spirit, so did a world of understanding—understanding of the ways of a Lord who *cannot* be understood. What Paul reached for that night was to lay hold of a standard beyond what any other man might even dare. Paul had already set a high standard by choosing to work for a living. (Paul often said, "The man who preaches the gospel should not live by proclaiming the gospel. I have chosen a higher way. My gospel is free to all without charge.")

Paul yielded to more than the human mind can grasp: He raised the standard of the worker. It was the standard of loss, not gain. Here was something beyond man's reach: Paul yielded to the loss of his ministry. To strive, to suffer, to pass through the crucibles . . . not once but again and again . . . seeing God's work raised up . . . yet all the time *knowing* it would be destroyed.

On occasion Paul may have briefly stumbled, but not far, not long, and not often. In the years that followed we all watched Paul live out that high drama.

Silas stated it best:

"That night Paul yielded up his life to more beatings, to more shipwrecks. He yielded his life up to rumor, to lies and misunderstandings. He willingly yielded to rejection from his own people, the Jews. Then, perhaps hardest of all, he yielded to even the possibility of rejection from the church in Jerusalem and rejection from the brothers and sisters in the very churches that had been raised up by his own hand. Finally, he yielded even to the loss of churches that were not yet born.

"In yielding to the worst possible thing that could happen, Paul won, and Blastinius lost. Angels rejoiced. The Lord had his way."

Paul had passed through the first of three great crucibles provoked by Blastinius.

In that moment Paul saw an even more distant spiritual reality. He yielded up to God any hope that his life would ever contain any success. On that memorable night, Paul covenanted with his Lord the slaying of one of life's greatest gods. He yielded up success. "I yield to living and dying a *failure*." In yielding to failure he won a victory over all things which the future held.

"As best I can understand what happened that night," said Silas, "Paul yielded to God . . . to suffer upon his arrival in Thessalonica. He prayed for the raising up of the church there, and then . . . yielded that very church up to destruction at the hand of Blastinius Drachrachma!"

There was something Paul said of that night that Silas never forgot: "I will enter Thessalonica to see to it that Blastinius wins and I lose. Still, it is for Blastinius to win that church, and any other church, to legalism. I will not stop him. If he is stopped, it will be by the intervention of God . . . or Blastinius's own mistakes. Ah, but for me to know he is coming will force me to a higher gospel, higher than I could ever declare if there were no Blastinius. I shall yet thank my God for that man's being thrust into my life."

When Silas awoke that next morning, he was both surprised and pleased to see Paul sound asleep. For a long time Silas just sat there staring at a man whose face was aglow.

Silas once spoke of his first impression of Paul. "When I first heard of him (and his contemptuous Gentile gospel), I was offended. When I heard that he had rebuked Peter, I was done with him. That changed, of course, after I met him. But on that particular morning, when I sat there looking at a sleeping Paul, I knew I was looking at the finest man I had ever known, or ever would know.

"I knew beyond all question that Paul's struggle with Blastinius had climaxed and the will of God reigned supreme."

A few minutes after Paul awoke, the two men were back on the road. It was a long time before Paul spoke.

"Silas, there is something I have never told you, or any man. It has to do with Galatia. When I arrived there the second time . . . you were with me . . . I saw fear in the eyes of the

Galatian brothers and sisters. Their innocence was gone. They had an enemy—*my* enemy. Suddenly their world was filled with shadows, ghosts, and would-be enemies. Blastinius had caused that. It was his one victory in Galatia.

"Though I make no apologies for a single word that I wrote to the Galatian churches in the Galatian letter, I doubt I will ever write such a letter again.

"Out of their love for Jesus and out of love for one another, the brothers and sisters in Galatia had come together to meet around the Lord. Blastinius's visit to those four churches and his attack on me while there had taken away their innocence. My letter to them, in turn, had caused them to fear. Suddenly, in their minds, there were potential enemies everywhere.

"I have watched men teach other people to fear," continued Paul. "They teach God's people to fear enemies both real and supposed. Such men spend a good part of their time doing nothing but warning. Warning and warning again. Such methods *never* build. It is a way that only destroys. Men create unity solely on warnings. This is not divine. This is man's way of building. They build a false unity. It is a cheap ministry. Men build not at all when they build on fear and hate. A bond of unity will emerge, but no man can build the ecclesia of God by such means.

"I can produce a strong unity in a church if I warn everyone of the coming of Blastinius. So! Let us teach God's people to fear Blastinius and others like him; let us build on fear and warnings. But if we do, what shall we have? We shall have the work of men, not the work of God.

"God's work is often fragile. Churches—the assemblies—are fragile, or so it appears. For some reason, men do not wish to trust what God has done in the hearts of his redeemed; therefore they build walls of protection around the Lord's people. No, that is not exactly correct. Such men build those walls of warnings and fears in order to protect *their* work. The motivation to preserve one's work is a rotten thing, and it cannot be justified spiritually. Nor will the work of such men stand.

"The church in Philippi has never heard the name Blastinius."

Paul pointed back toward Philippi. "Look down that road, Silas. Once that man arrives in Philippi, can the assembly of God stand? Stand without ever being warned of Blastinius?"

Paul then turned around, facing toward Thessalonica. "I do not know if there is a church destined to be born in Thessalonica. I do not know if we will preach the gospel there, nor do I know if men and women will find their Lord and gather together. But if they do, Silas, I make a vow! After all . . ."

Paul's face broke into a broad smile. "If Blastinius can make a vow, so can I. Today I vow to never mention Blastinius's name to Philippi. Or to Thessalonica! I vow to never warn them, or any future assembly, of his coming. Instead, I will but lift Christ higher."

It was the most stunned moment of Silas's entire life. "If it had been necessary for me to respond to Paul's words," said Silas, "then I would have died. I had no tongue nor thought. I could not grasp what Paul was saying."

Paul looked toward the morning sun and spoke again.

"I invite you, Blastinius, come to Philippi! I invite you, Blastinius, to follow me to Thessalonica. Today I rise out of the prison you almost put me in. I arise from my night of sleep and tell you, Blastinius, I thank God that you exist! I thank God that he put you in my life."

"Hearing Paul speak this way," said Silas, remembering back to that hour, "my legs almost gave out under me."

"From this day, I will tell no one of what you have said and done. Nor will I warn them of what you will say or what you will do. I know that you are coming! And *that* has changed my life, my work, my ministry.

"Yes, Blastinius, I thank God you are in my life. I must build with things you cannot destroy, Blastinius. And I will build with that which *you* cannot build. Every time I open my mouth, I must build only with that material that is the Lord Jesus Christ, and him alone."

Paul turned again to Silas, this time his eyes glistening. "Blastinius cannot destroy God's people nor his ecclesia if they are free, truly free, and if they are saturated with Christ! Silas, I shall reach for new heights and for a more complete understanding of grace. I shall proclaim a higher Christ than I have ever preached. I will show God's people how to know him beyond anything I have ever before revealed. I shall build and I shall build . . . and build again . . . but that man Blastinius will not receive the space of even one word. There will be no fearful warnings. There will be no hate nor fear inseminated into the hearts of God's people. When we leave Greece—and leave we will—we shall leave God's people in utter innocence."

Silas was dumbfounded.

Paul raised his eyes toward the heavens. "I invite you, angels of God, to watch what Blastinius does when he comes. I invite you, the messengers of heaven, to hear my message and to watch my life."

Paul turned and faced the road again. "The angels will be watching you, Blastinius. They will watch what you do and how you do it. They will watch your attacks, they will watch your criticism. They will see you use the final extent of your human strength, and they will also watch *me*. Shall law and fear win? Or Christ and grace!

"Silas, I can hardly wait to reach Thessalonica! We have no money, we have no food, my back is infected, we are both hungry and exhausted. Another beating probably awaits us, or a stoning, or something of that sort. Still, I can hardly wait. Why? Because when I get to Thessalonica, I intend to build—not with wood, not with hay, and not with stubble, not with things of this earth. *Every* man's work must know fire. Blastinius is the fire of my ministry. Thank God, I will be tested. Thank God, my ministry will be tested. My message must be tested. Thank God, fire will fall on my work and God has ordained that Blastinius be the testing fire.

"I have departed from Philippi. When I have left Thessalonica, I pray that you come, Blastinius. Then both you and I will know with what I have built. If wood, then I have no business preaching the gospel. I will be in your debt, Blastinius, for having revealed to men and angels that my work is burnable.

"I will awaken every day of my life knowing that I must build with things fire cannot consume! Come, Blastinius, but know this: I intend to build with naught but Christ. See if you can burn that!"

"I almost broke into a cheer!" Silas later reported.

"Come, oh fire sent by the permission of God, fall upon the work that comes from my hand. Come and destroy everything that can be destroyed. When that fire comes, it is my determination you will find nothing but gold, which is Christ; and silver, which is Christ; and costly stones, which are also Christ!"

Paul then raised his hands to the heavens and began to sing.

Silas, knowing nothing else to do, dropped to his knees and began to pray. In a moment, Paul was beside him. There, on their knees, with their arms around one another, the two men poured out the purest prayers of surrender that man or angels or God has ever heard.

Suddenly, it was Silas who invited Blastinius to come to Philippi and Thessalonica. His words were bold, victorious, and triumphant. The two men shouted, cried, shouted some more—wept—defying Blastinius, men, fallen angels, and whatever creatures there may be, to come and destroy the work that God himself had done.

On they prayed. Both men surrendered their bandaged backs to another beating. Paul surrendered himself to more shipwrecks, to hunger, and to thirst. Both of them thanked God that they had no food to eat, nor money, nor shelter. Then they began to pray against one another: "Lord, break this man, break this vessel. . . ." Their words were wild, their prayers were wonderful, their petitions were of the kind this world will rarely see.

Finally, Paul rose to his feet, lifted his arms to the heavens and shouted, "I thank you, Lord. I will yet rejoice for this thorn."

That day, in the middle of the Egnatian Way, the Lord brought forth a new kind of worker.

(Every time Silas ever told this story, he cried. So also his listeners.)

Paul ended his prayer in a grand finale. "Lord, you sustained Moses. Father, you sustained the Lord Jesus. You can surely sustain us a few miles more and a few days more."

Paul then topped all else with yet a new vow. "Your salvation is free, Lord. Let it be known that I shall take no money in Thessalonica for my preaching. I will always provide my own way in every city I enter. I know your faithfulness. This day feed us, for we are your birds of the field."

Silas was shouting, "Amen!" as loud as his voice allowed while at the same time shaking uncontrollably from hunger.

The last words of Paul's prayer were some of the most difficult of all: "Lord, I acknowledge that even the Emperor Claudius is your servant."

Silas began to laugh. That was a statement he never expected to hear coming from Paul.

Silas took up the prayer: "Somewhere in realms invisible,

you have chosen to close the door of Rome to the gospel. One day we will understand why. Lord, one day, we know, that door will open."

The following morning Paul sat down on the side of the road to have a serious talk with Marcus. "You have served us well, Marcus. I have carried none of the baggage, and Silas very little. You have graciously endured my tears and struggles and watched out for conscripting soldiers. It is time now to return to Philippi."

Marcus protested.

"Marcus, you must! The brothers and sisters in Philippi need to hear from us." Paul then smiled. "Second, we are out of money. You will not remain a large, strong young man if you go on. You will be as thin as we are. We have only three denarii. Silas and I will keep one. You have a long journey, and your two denarii will not suffice. You must continue to sleep in the fields and eat sparingly."

Again, Marcus protested but was soon on his way back to Philippi. Before his departure the three men knelt in the road and prayed. Marcus, though a new convert, prayed the most fervent of prayers for Paul and Silas.

That night Paul and Silas slept within view of Thessalonica after what might have been their last meal. The two men now had one denarius left. Undaunted by these harsh realities, the two men, loaded down with their baggage, made their way toward the gates of Thessalonica, singing and praising the Lord. Just before they reached the city's walls, Paul confided to Silas what he planned to do.

"I will get a letter off to Luke when we arrive. I will ask Luke, and I will ask Timothy, and now I ask you: from this day on, for as long as we live on this earth, that we will never make reference of Blastinius to young churches. If we fail to warn, and if Blastinius comes, and if he wins the day, then he deserves to win. If my gospel cannot withstand legalism, it is no gospel at all. But if this gospel does stand, I desire that Blastinius not be remembered . . . not even for his failure.

"In our minds and in our hearts, from this day forward, there is no Blastinius. There is *nothing* for the churches to fear, ever! All things are as they should be. I shall speak of the inadequacies of the law, the adequacies of grace, and the adequacies of Christ."

"Agreed!" responded Silas. "I believe that Luke and Timothy, by the Holy Spirit, will understand."

My two dear friends walked toward Thessalonica, still arm in arm, singing, shouting, and praising their Lord. Their stomachs were empty, but their spirits were full.

Should you visit Thessalonica, you will discover a hill just before you reach the city. This hill allows you to look down at the blue waters of the gulf. Unnoticed by men but surely noticed by angels, Paul and Silas crested that hill and walked through the great marble arch called the Arch of Augustus. It is covered with the carvings of the heads of five bulls, a monument to Octavian's triumph over Brutus.

Just inside the gate you will find a fountain. Silas, seeing this fountain, plunged his head under the cold water. Paul, at the same moment, was glancing about to see if the Jewish synagogue was anywhere nearby.

"Roman citizenship will not do us much good here," observed Paul.

"Roman citizenship helped in Philippi?" teased Silas, as he poured water on his face.

(Octavian, later called Augustus, made Thessalonica a *free* city after he defeated Brutus. The city elects its own magistrates, called *politarchs*. There are virtually no Roman soldiers here; furthermore, the city is not subject to the rule of the governor of Macedonia.)

"I wonder where that synagogue is," was Paul's response.

"I wonder where the jail is," answered Silas. "And where do they beat their no-goods?"

"Remember, Silas, we are still here to lose, to be defeated by the conduct of a man who will surely hound us. Let us now take our last coin and rent a room for the night." Paul's eyes brightened. "The day after tomorrow the Sabbath begins."

The two men obtained a room in the poorest of inns, at a charge of less than half a denarius, leaving them just enough money for some grain to eat the following day.

Paul had no more than fallen down on the matted hay than he slipped into a deep sleep. Nor did he wake until the latter part of the next day. For a few minutes he was too weak to move.

"How shall I ever find strength to begin mending tents or to speak in the synagogue?"

That afternoon Paul and Silas searched out the city. Thessalonica, a city with two forums and a population of about 25,000, is the capital of what is called Macedonia Secunda, and it is the largest city in northern Greece, as well as the most influential city in Macedonia and the land of Illyricum.

By evening Paul had found what he thought would be a good place to set up his tentmaking. Still he wondered, "It will take at least a month—how shall we ever live?" That night, like hundreds of the city's poorest, Paul and Silas slept in the marketplace, a half denarius their sole fortune. On Friday they went back to stay at the inn for another night so they would have a place to clean their clothes and ready themselves to enter the synagogue on Saturday morning. "We eat or we sleep, but not both," observed Paul.

As the Sabbath dawned, the two men put on those garments which marked them as Jews.

"I only hope that the rulers of the synagogue perceive us as two naturally skinny Jews. And let us hope and pray that there will be nothing to occur which will reveal the condition of our backs."

The synagogue in Thessalonica is small. As usual, Paul went to the front and sat down in the place of prominence, as was always expected of a Pharisee. Just before the meeting began, the ruler of the synagogue came to the front, leaned over, and whispered a question that took Paul by surprise.

"Are you Paul of Tarsus?"

This was not the kind of question Paul liked to hear, especially in surroundings such as this. He had no idea if the question boded well or ill.

"I am," he answered hesitantly.

"There is someone who is looking for you. He is a stranger to this city. I believe he is a heathen. I will tell you more after the meeting."

The ritual began. "This is not a meeting in Lydia's living room," muttered Silas. The time-honored ritual droned on. When it finished, the ruler of the synagogue, who seemed to be a friendly person, warmly invited Paul to speak. Paul stood and very matter-of-factly told the people gathered that he would like to speak to them on the coming of the Messiah.

There was an immediate and warm response for this word. Especially at this moment, as this was a time when Jews had a growing belief that the Messiah would soon appear and throw off the yoke of the conquering Romans.

Silas often recalled Paul's message. "It was the finest ever delivered about the Messiah. It was matchless."

Paul took his captivated audience all the way from the beginning of Creation through all the writings of Moses. The discourse was breathtaking, and, at the very moment when everyone thought he was coming to his main point, Paul paused dramatically, looked about the room (almost as one who had wakened to his surroundings), and said, "My time is up. Perhaps on some future occasion we may discuss this matter further."

The ruler of the synagogue exchanged glances with the elders. There was a nod of approval. The synagogue ruler then stood and announced that Paul, if he was agreeable, would be invited back on the next Sabbath to continue his discourse.

Paul very graciously consented.

Despite his best efforts, Silas could not hide his smile, for this marked the first time Paul was given an opportunity to speak in a synagogue *and* was warmly invited back again. Paul had learned to not put all hope of reaching the Jews into one message. When he sat down Paul had not yet mentioned Jesus Christ. He was, nonetheless, preparing the hearts of the listeners to hear of him.

Days of going without food were once more taking their toll. As Paul began to leave the synagogue he also began shaking, but it was only the perceptive eyes of Silas that made note of this fact. He immediately came to Paul's side and very carefully put his hand under Paul's shoulder, helping him to his feet.

In leaving the synagogue, Paul had completely forgotten that the ruler of the synagogue had a message for him.

"Thank you for your words," said the synagogue leader as he came to Paul's side. "We look forward to your coming back. Now, to the matter of the Gentile who is looking for you. I believe his name is Andreas, from Philippi. He requested that if you should appear here, you should look for him at the inn where he is staying. It is the inn that is facing the north forum, the easiest of all the inns to locate. In the meantime, he told me he would be searching the city for you."

"I thank you for this word," said Paul. "We must go to the forum now."

Just then a man approached Paul from behind. "Excuse me,

I am a fellow Hebrew. I heard you today in the synagogue. My name is Jason. May I ask if your Hebrew name might be Saul?"

"It is," said Paul, with a touch of pride.

"Ah! Then you are a member of the tribe of Benjamin. So also am I. You *will* return to be with us next week?"

"God willing," said Paul.

"Do you have a place to lodge?"

Silas was about to answer when Paul intervened swiftly. "Yes, we have."

"I have lived in Thessalonica all of my life. My children are grown and departed; both now live in Israel. May I invite you to come and share our quarters?"

Paul was a little unsure as to what to say.

"You are very gracious and hospitable, sir. Let us see how the next week goes. If my kinsmen in the synagogue invite me back for a *third* week, and if you are still of a mind to offer this invitation, we will accept."

"Has he come?" asked Jason softly.

Paul stared into Jason's face. "You refer to the Messiah?"

"I do."

Paul hesitated. "I will see you next week in the synagogue."

"I will be there," said Jason. There was a certain strength and even a sense of determination in Jason's voice.

A few moments later Paul and Silas had found the inn that faced into the forum. They were about to enter the inn when a voice rang out.

"Paul! Silas!"

"Andreas!" responded the two men simultaneously. There was a joyful moment of careful embrace, followed by joyful praise.

"Quick! To my room. I have something to give you; it was sent by . . ."

"But what of Philippi? What of the church? What is the news of her?" insisted Paul.

"Yes! News, and other things," said Andreas mysteriously.

In a few moments, the three men had sat down on the floor in the small room occupied by Andreas.

"How are things in Philippi?" urged Paul. "The assembly . . ."

"I will answer in good time, Paul, but first I want you to know that the brothers and sisters in Philippi have asked me to offer a profound apology on behalf of everyone for having let you depart Philippi without thinking of your material needs."

"Never mind," said Paul, "we are used to working for our living. Now what of the holy ones in Philippi?"

Andreas ignored Paul's question.

"True. Nonetheless, brothers, you both are men who proclaim our Lord and raise up his assembly. The brothers and sisters in Philippi have sent you a gift along with an apology." Andreas handed Paul a small leather pouch. Paul thanked him and laid it by his side, still anxious to pursue the subject of the church in Philippi.

Silas had been more observant, for he had been carefully studying the face of Andreas. "Paul, I think it would mean a great deal to our brother Andreas if you would please open the pouch. Now."

Paul hesitated and then looked at Andreas. There was definitely anticipation on Andreas' face.

"Forgive me. If it pleases the holy ones in Philippi, I will be delighted to do so."

Paul began to untie the string, then poured the bag's contents on Andreas' bed. Before him lay a number of silver coins and a few bronze coins, but there in the middle of them was something that men rarely ever saw. There were gold coins.

Both Paul and Silas gasped with surprise. Paul picked up one of the gold coins and let it lie in the palm of his hands. Tears filled his eyes. Andreas glanced at Silas. Hot tears were running down his face as well. Andreas' face grew crimson, for it did not take great wisdom to realize how meaningful was this gift.

Paul began to choke. Finally he turned to Silas. "Silas . . . would you say something to our Lord . . . I cannot." Silas knelt between Paul and Andreas. After a few moments of struggle, Silas offered a prayer of thanksgiving to God for his graciousness and provision.

It was a moment of healing for Paul. At last God had shown a merciful hand to Paul. For Paul it was as a seal, an evidence that he had made the right choice out there on the road to Thessalonica.

Andreas joined in Silas's prayer. It was not long before all three were shedding copious tears. Finally, Silas stood, took Paul's hands and pulled him up to full stature.

His words surprised both men. "Paul, I am a practical man. I believe that when we walked into this inn I smelled cheese and vegetables and, if I am not mistaken, perhaps some mutton."

Andreas stammered, "You have not . . . you, you haven't . . .?"

Paul picked out one of the bronze coins and held it up. "A bit more than a denarius, is it not, Silas?"

"A bit more," agreed a smiling Silas. "Come, let us dine."

"No," interrupted Andreas. "Paul will remain here. I will see that the food is brought to him." Paul was about to protest but then relented.

"Thank you, Andreas. May I make use of your bed in the meantime?" Overcome by the scene he had just witnessed, Andreas responded, "Paul, you can *have* that bed. You can keep it for as long as you live on this earth. This room is yours, for as long as it is needed."

"Thank you for coming," came the words of Silas, spoken ever so softly.

"Wait," said Paul, speaking almost in frustration, "Andreas, I want to hear how things are going with the brothers and sisters in Philippi."

"No, Paul. Lie down. Andreas and I will be back in a moment. He will tell you nothing until you have eaten."

"Just one word," insisted Paul. "Andreas, does the ecclesia of God in Philippi still gather?" Paul's voice cracked, and once more his eyes filled with tears.

Andreas shot one arm into the air, then responded, "Absolutely, Paul, absolutely!"

Paul slipped down onto the bed and fell into a deep sleep. Even the smell of food did not awaken a wholly exhausted Paul. Late in the afternoon Paul did awaken, and he ate like a man who had eaten almost nothing in a week.

At last, Andreas began to report to Paul about Philippi of Macedonia.

Let it always be remembered that it was the church in Philippi that sent us help, not Antioch, nor Syria, nor Galatia. Only Philippi," observed Paul.

"Why have the other churches not helped you, Paul?" asked an unbelieving Andreas.

"It is a mystery to me, as much as it is to you. Perhaps it is because when I am present among them, everyone knows that I am working for a living. Beyond that, it is the nature of men to always think someone has more money than they really do." Paul furrowed his brow. "Nonetheless, I often ask myself this question: Why do churches, planted by church planters, not help church planters plant churches?

"By working, we are able to provide for our living. But *traveling* from one place to another—that is a different matter. And entering a new city, that is always difficult and expensive. Perhaps they think that it is no more expensive to travel across nations than it is to stay at home. After all, most of the brothers and sisters have never been more than ten miles away from their home. Few can read or write. Most are slaves. Or freed slaves. Just about everyone has a limited sight of the world outside. You and I have seen more on this one journey than most people would see in five lifetimes. Perhaps that makes a difference.

"Now, Andreas, please send our deepest thanks back to Philippi. I will write a letter of thanks to accompany your return. It is an astounding gift. Kings have been ransomed for less. Silas and I will be able to live on it for a number of months. Some of it we will use to help us until we have firmly established our tentmaking. Whatever is left we will lay aside for our journey back home to Syria.

"Now, Andreas, no more excuses. What is happening in Philippi?"

"It is almost as though the riot in Philippi never happened," said Andreas eagerly. "The brothers and sisters now have a good reputation in the city. Lydia's living room is almost always filled, both for the meetings that are held there before dawn as well as those that are held after sunset.

"There is an indescribable love among us, Paul. All the barriers and partitions between social caste and race are completely gone. The well-to-do have stopped using any names that indicate their social status. Many of the poorer believers have been hired to work in the homes of those who are better off. Slaves are being treated better than they had ever known they could be treated.

"Jesus Christ has done a miracle in the lives of just about everyone who gathers in Lydia's home. As to Luke, he works night and day tending to those who are sick. Whether people are wealthy or poor, Luke charges nothing. He also ministers to the church."

"Then how does he eat?" asked Silas.

"Lydia takes care of that," said Andreas.

Silas and Paul nodded knowingly.

"Some of the soldiers in the city have gone out of their way to protect Luke, as he has helped many of them." Andreas pulled himself up and, with a slight grin, added, "Silas . . . Paul . . . I fear to report to you that Luke is being treated far more like a Roman citizen in Philippi than you ever were."

"And Timothy?"

"That brother is amazing," responded Andreas admiringly. "Luke teaches us songs, gives us practical help, and ministers. Timothy speaks several times each week. The brothers and sisters love him. He is growing. We are all impressed. When I first met Timothy I thought he was very quiet, and . . ."

Paul interrupted, "I know, I had the same impression the first time I met him. Initially, I hardly noticed him. But the second time I was in Galatia, I met a *man*. A young man, yes, but a man."

"Well, be assured that the care and love that have been extended to you this day are but a picture of the care for one another that is going on in Philippi."

"The agape of God!" breathed Silas. "We preach Christ. Those who hear touch him . . . then they fall in love with one another. I will never cease to be amazed at the love and care everyone extends to others once they fall in love with Christ."

"We did overlook one place to care for someone. We apologize, again, for having forgotten, but, on the other hand, you left so abruptly."

"Be assured that we have never received such a liberal gift," said Silas, "not even remotely."

"Have there been visitors?" inquired Paul, the question in no way sounding as important as it was.

Andreas's answer was enthusiastic. "Of course! There is hardly a meeting but someone either comes to the door to listen, or sometimes steps in. After three or four weeks, those people usually either leave or become part of Christ. Timothy has been quite busy immersing new believers."

"Have there been any visitors from outside the city?" continued Paul.

"Let's see, I am not sure . . . no, I do not think so. Were you expecting someone?"

There was a moment of silence; then Silas intervened.

"Not so much expecting, just *wondering* . . . but I would dare guess that someday your door is going to open, and there will be two or three brothers from Galatia coming to visit. Churches tend to visit one another."

"Andreas, the two of us will almost certainly stay in Thessalonica for a while; the gift has made that possible," said Paul. "And with your good report about the assembly in Philippi, I would like you, when you return there, to tell Luke it is time that he return home to Antioch. Tell everyone in Philippi that I was allowed to speak in the synagogue here in Thessalonica and that I was well received. I think I will be able to continue speaking for at least two or three more Sabbaths, perhaps more. And Timothy, tell him that I would like him to come to Thessalonica in the not-too-distant future."

Silas listened, and understood exactly what Paul was doing. He was leaving the Philippian church wide open and defenseless to the possible coming of Blastinius. But Paul's next sentence revealed just how deep was the commitment he had made there on the road to Thessalonica. "If there are any visitors that come from other countries, be sure they are received warmly; and if they desire to speak, let them do so."

If Andreas had seen Silas's expression, he would have seen a man with *disbelief* written all across his face. But then Silas remembered Paul's words: "Every man's work must be tested. If it cannot stand, it should not stand."

"Also, tell the brothers and sisters that I hope either Silas or I will be able to return from time to time, to encourage, to exhort, and to strengthen."

That evening, while they talked far into the night, Silas saw the soul of Paul being healed. Paul had turned the work of God in Philippi over to the church itself. There would be two more crises Paul would face that involved Blastinius, but the main battle had been won.

"I bear Paul witness," said Silas years later, "that not once did he refer to Blastinius in any of the Macedonian churches."

(Thirteen years after that wonderful day Paul wrote a beautiful letter to the church in Philippi, still remembering and still thanking them for that gift.

Yet, sometimes, even to this day, I, Titus, would find myself repeating Paul's words, "Why do churches, planted by church planters, not help church planters plant churches?")

The next day Andreas began preparations to return to Philippi. Paul placed an arm around him and said something to him which he was really saying to the entire church in Philippi. It was said as a witness to the angels.

"My dear brother, let no man take from you the freedom that you have in Christ Jesus."

Andreas, having no idea what was being said to him, replied firmly: "Paul, nothing will."

"Oh, as you return, keep an eye out for young Marcus. If you see him, feed him. He has only two denarii for his entire trip back to Philippi. And tell the gathering that I am grateful to them for sending him. We would never have made it without his strong arms."

It was time for the two men to turn all their attention toward bringing the gospel to Thessalonica. That meant, first of all, returning to the synagogue the next Sabbath, this time to present Christ.

CHAPTER 17

Silas sighed deeply. "Another boring hour," he said as he approached the synagogue. "Religious ritual, in religious buildings—such will never compete with the body of Christ when they get together in a home. Imagine the assembly trying to have a meeting in a synagogue."

"Silas, while you are complaining," needled Paul, "remember that the synagogue is our entrance to the gospel. On the other hand, I admit I look forward to the day when there is a living room in this city filled with believers sharing about Christ."

The two men took their place in the synagogue. By now, word had passed through the community that someone from far away would speak, in a fresh new way, about the Messiah.

It is proper that you know the names of some of the people who were present that day, because some of them are now believers. Two of them are my dearest friends. I, Titus, have spent a large part of my life with those two men . . . both now workers in the Lord's vineyard.

One young man in the room that day was Aristarchus, a most remarkable Gentile. Another young man who was present there that day was named Secundus. Also, a devout Jew named Jason had eagerly returned, hoping to hear more about the Lord. And there was a youth named Demas.

There were about sixty people in the synagogue that Sabbath morning, and Paul held them all in rapt attention for over an hour. Even after this message, he had hardly told them the details of the Messiah who had come. But, oh, he had built a beautiful foundation for telling them more.

"Those of us who are Hebrews," he continued, "have looked forward to the coming of our Messiah for a long, long time. Toward that end, I have great news for you!"

Paul ended his message and sat down. Once more the synagogue ruler stepped forward. "We have no choice in this matter, do we? We must hear what Paul of Tarsus has to say to us next Sabbath about the coming of the Messiah."

As the meeting ended, Jason once more followed Paul out of the synagogue. So did Aristarchus, along with others. Entering the agora, Paul sat down on the steps of one of the heathen temples and began telling them the story of the coming of Jesus Christ. And there, in that setting, they believed.

At the insistence of Jason, Paul and Silas departed the inn that very day and moved into Jason's home, but with the understanding that Paul would pay for their lodging. Jason was loath to accept, but he accepted, knowing that if the two men would stay in his home, he would learn more about his Christ.

The next Sabbath the small synagogue was crowded. People were even standing along the walls. What the synagogue ruler did that day was unprecedented: He dispensed with the ritual and turned the entire meeting over to Paul.

Some of the people present were Jews who had not been to the synagogue in years. Others were God-fearers who were interested in the Hebrew religion. Yet others were simply curious heathen who had heard rumors of a coming deliverer. Once again Paul spoke for over an hour.

Silas had never seen an occasion like this and had to struggle to keep from standing and shouting praises to his Lord. Tears he did not prevent.

That day some believed, others wondered. The synagogue leaders were baffled, for even among them there were those who believed. But the most momentous thing that happened was that the synagogue doors continued to be open to Paul, marking the first time in all Paul's ministry that he had preached in the synagogue for so long.

What had captivated everyone was not only the story of the Crucifixion and Resurrection but also that this man standing in front of them had persecuted the ecclesia and had later met Jesus Christ face-to-face. It was a witness hard not to believe.

When Paul finished, Jason immediately stood up. "I have received this Messiah. Somehow he now lives somewhere deep inside me, and he has changed my heart."

Secundus followed with a similar word. So also Aristarchus and others.

Twenty-one years earlier the Lord Jesus had risen from the dead; now, hundreds of miles away from Israel, a little group of Gentiles began meeting—mornings and evenings—in the living room of Jason's home in northern Greece. (Some meetings were held there before dawn, others after sundown.)

What followed was three months of joy. Among those who believed there were a number of Jews and Greeks, mostly merchants. The rest were slaves, freed slaves, or the very poor. As was true in all other places where an assembly was raised up, everyone tried to spend as much time with one another as possible. And whenever there was a heathen holiday, the assembly would rent a large room and spend the day together. Unless prevented by ill health or work, no one missed a meeting.

Several women in the ecclesia were wives of leading citizens of the city. A number of their husbands also came to believe. The Thessalonian believers turned out to be the most steadfast believers among all the Gentile assemblies. That proved to be a mercy of God. (Of all the churches that ever came from the hand of Paul, the church in Thessalonica would come to know more community rejection than any other church. The believers in Thessalonica learned to live in constant rejection from an entire city—not for a year or two but for over a decade.)

Early on, Silas taught the brothers and sisters to sing psalms and to make up their own songs. In the process, he also taught them how, in the meetings, to speak to one another out of their own hearts. It was also Silas who told these Macedonian Greeks so many stories about how the church in Jerusalem suffered much persecution. Silas was a master at telling stories about the Hebrew faith, about Jerusalem, about Antioch, about Jesus Christ. Unwittingly, his words were preparing the hearts of these dear believers for what was to come. That one contribution, more than anything else, prepared the Thessalonians for the persecution they were soon to experience.

As Silas told the story of how the brothers and sisters in Jerusalem met together, as well as how those in Antioch met, there soon came a noticeable change in the Thessalonian meeting: Paul and Silas often never got a chance to minister in the meetings, as the brothers and sisters took over the meetings completely, testifying to one another of the living Lord who dwelled within them.

"I have told these Thessalonians everything I can remember of those first six years in Jerusalem," said Silas, smiling, "and still they want to hear more."

One night Silas explained to these new believers what *exhortation, encouragement,* and *admonition* meant. The reaction was immoderate. Hardly a meeting passed but someone stood and either exhorted, encouraged, or admonished. Yet what they did, and how they did it, was unique to all the other assemblies.

"Gentiles they are," observed Paul one morning after a particularly glorious meeting. "Greek. Heathen Gentiles. And I could not be more content!"

During the day Paul and Silas worked in the market-place—and, yes, it took them about a month to establish enough business to pay their expenses. And every day, to Jason's loathing, the two men paid for every meal they ate at Jason's house, as well as for their lodging. As it turned out this was a greater testimony than either Paul or Silas had expected it to be. Just a few months later, Paul had to remind some of the brothers in Thessalonica that *he* never ate food from someone's table without paying for it.

The number of believers grew. The growth came mostly by rumor and by the striking way believers cared for one another.

Like any city in the empire, Thessalonica is a place given to rumors. Such rumors are soon passed to the towns and villages nearby. It was not long before these places were hearing of a man from Israel who was speaking in the marketplace, telling the strange story of some god who died and had risen again. A few of the curious came to Thessalonica to hear for themselves. Some believed, which served to create more rumors.

If you had been in Thessalonica at that time, and if you had passed by that place in the market where Paul worked, you would have seen believers, and heathen, sitting with him asking questions, listening, laughing, encouraging, and being encour-aged. Silas has told me that some of the richest words Paul ever spoke were uttered right there in that marketplace while he cut and sewed canvas.

Usually Silas spoke to the brothers and sisters in the morn-ing gathering and Paul in the evening, as it was Paul who went to the marketplace before dawn to set up his table, call out the manner of his skill, and then wait for business. That was neces-sary on Paul's part because, as you know, most business agree-ments made in the marketplace are struck no later than sunrise.

Paul loved every minute of his time in Thessalonica, both in the marketplace and in the meetings in Jason's home. He was a man possessed with two things: his Lord and the Lord's house. To Paul, the ecclesia was the very purpose of creation.

No one present in the meetings in Jason's house had known Christ for more than a few weeks. Except for five or six, none could read. Yet Paul sat there on the floor and spoke to those believers some of the deepest words man has ever uttered or ever heard. He led them beyond those things that are comprehended by the mind and imparted to them the deep things of Christ that only the spirit in a redeemed man can understand. He spoke to them mostly of an indwelling Lord and an indwelling Spirit. He did so in such a wondrous way that one might think Paul mad to believe those simple people would understand.

And yet, they understood! Those dear brothers and sisters would come to the next meetings and, with their own mouths, share the reality of what Paul had made known to them.

Just a few weeks after the birth of the ecclesia (and to the delight of Paul and Silas), Timothy arrived, bearing firsthand news of the holy ones in Philippi.

"At your request, Luke has returned home to Antioch," he reported. "With my having also departed, the brothers and sisters in Philippi are now on their own. The nearest I can figure, the closest church to them is Antioch, over three hundred miles away! But it is a strong assembly; the brothers get together every week, the sisters also. Beyond that, there must be at least four or five times every week when everyone, or nearly everyone, comes together. Paul, the situation in the gathering in Philippi could not be better."

It was one of the best moments of Paul's life. He had passed through his crucible; his healing was almost complete. And well that it was, for a new crisis was imminent.

"I believe," said Paul, "that Philippi will have a sister church right here in Macedonia. You must come to the meetings. All of them. Tell me what you see. Besides, it is important that you come to know the brothers and sisters in Thessalonica."

Paul sighed. "Especially, spend much time with the young brothers here. We have an abundance of young, unmarried men. They are very impressionable. I have to be very careful in what I say to them. They tend to be a little too exuberant at times."

"They are wild!" interpreted Silas.

While there, Timothy made note of many things, one being that Paul prefaced many of his words to the ecclesia the same way he had in Philippi:

"Silas and I may not be in Thessalonica much longer. Listen carefully as I give you practical help, and listen as I give you spiritual help. Learn how to know the Lord. It is for us to live in the physical world, but it is also ours to walk in the invisible realm."

Paul *knew* his time in Thessalonica would be short, and he made every word count.

To the credit of the Thessalonians, they drank in every word. There was almost a glee among the Thessalonians as they considered the possibility that they would be left alone, without help of any kind. It is almost as though they knew what was in store for them.

The Lord was the one who put such a buoyant spirit in the assembly.

I, Titus, have never known a people, before or since, so willing and so able to withstand so much rejection from the city they lived in. If you should visit the gathering in Thessalonica, you will discover that one of their favorite admonitions is that

of the Lord's: "Rejoice and give thanks when you are persecuted for my sake."

Until this very day the ecclesia still meets in Jason's home.
(I am told that nearly every wall in his house has been knocked
down—there is nothing left of the house as it once was except
the kitchen.) Then, and now, their meetings have always been
noisy, filled with laughter and humor, abundant in sharing and
singing, with some of their gatherings lasting far into the
night.

Never forget how very poor those people were. Many coming into Jason's home for the first time came in awe, having
never been in a place so nice, even though his is but a very hum-
ble home. Many of God's people in Thessalonica have no house
at all, sleeping in the marketplace, in the heathen temples, or on
rooftops and in doorways. Many live in one room, crowded in
with others.

It is in Thessalonica that Paul first began to use the phrase
holy ones when he spoke to the believers. I, Titus, can tell you
how much of a blessing that came to be. So uplifting is that
word that its use (calling one another *holy ones*) has spread to all
the churches throughout all the empire. To this very day when I
am greeted "Good morning, holy one!" I am always taken by
surprise . . . and ever grateful in my heart that Jesus Christ has
made me a *holy one*.

Walk into Jason's house, and you will see it packed with the
extremely poor, slaves, freed slaves, some blind or near blind,
others with their faces covered with primitive tattoos. The garments of many are odorous; some have clothes so tattered that
they are but a series of patches. Many have never owned more
than one garment throughout their entire life. You will see
faces wrinkled, skin as hard as leather, eyes blinded by disease,
and arms and legs deformed from lack of food. The slaves, even
the young, often have emaciated bodies, their faces and backs

cut and scarred from mistreatment by their masters. Most slaves, again, even the young, have no teeth, their teeth long since rotted out because of the worthless food they are fed. But you see something else rarely seen among the slaves and the poor.

There they all sit on the floor of Jason's home, calling on the name of the Lord, hearts filled with love for him, mouths quick to speak of him, lips given to testimony, praise, prayer, and song . . . all to the Lord. Every soul in that room loving and being loved by everyone else in that room. And in the midst, a few of the city's wealthiest citizens . . . seeing themselves no better, nor worse, than anyone else in the room.

And so it is in Thessalonica in every meeting in the homes even to this very day.

As in Philippi, so in Thessalonica, some of the wealthier women took it upon themselves to care for the poorest in the church. Some of these poor have even been invited to live out their days sheltered in the homes of the wealthy. (As you know, slave owners have a habit of freeing a slave when he gets too old to work or when the slave is dying, thereby releasing the slave owner from the responsibility of caring for the slave.)

A few months after the birth of the Thessalonian church, one of the believers went to be with the Lord. She was one of the gathering's poorest souls. At her burial, even the most well-to-do mourned her passing more than ever they would weep at the loss of their own kin.

The sisterhood in the church is very strong, for though I, Titus, have seen the wealthy care for the poor, I have also seen the poorest nurture and nurse to health those women who are of high standing in the city. There simply are no rich or poor among the Thessalonians, nor Jews or Gentiles. There are only *brothers* and *sisters* in Christ.

And, as in Philippi, the wealthy believers in Thessalonica do not refer to themselves by any name that indicates their social standing. Everyone goes by a name that reveals no social status. (Today this practice is found in all the churches in the empire.)

As to their singing, Timothy once told me that in the beginning the Thessalonians were the worst singers he had ever heard. But as time passed, they came to sing like angels. I testify that I have been in meetings in Thessalonica when there was nothing but singing, for anything else would have been less glorious.

As to what they heard when the singing ended—when Paul or Silas spoke, they spoke of Christ.

Then there was the matter of hiring. Believing wives insisted that their husbands (when they went into the marketplace to hire) seek out and hire first those who were believers.

"These men are honest men, and they are the hardest workers in the city. Besides that, they are my brothers, and I love them. Hire them!" was the sentiment every husband was used to hearing from his believing wife.

As Paul anticipated, his time in Thessalonica did come to an abrupt end.

What initiated the persecution?

Jealousy.

Almost half of the people who once came to the synagogue no longer attended there! They were now believers meeting in the informal atmosphere of Jason's home.

Paul, sensing this growing jealousy, warned that trouble might lie ahead. What *ignited* the fire was not the shrinking of the synagogue congregation—it was a letter that came to the synagogue leaders.

Do you need to be told who wrote the letter?

CHAPTER 18

Blastinius had traveled from Jerusalem to Syria. On his way he went from synagogue to synagogue throughout Syria and Cilicia. His one topic: Paul. And added to that, Paul's evil in corrupting the Jewish religion! In order to spread his message farther north, Blastinius sent out letters to synagogues in Galatia and throughout Asia Minor. Nor was this circuit letter a gentle letter! It had been crafted by a master. Synagogue leaders made copies of the letter and sent it on to other synagogues farther north. As a result, this cruel letter made its way to northern Greece . . . and eventually even to Thessalonica!

In the letter, by means of direct charges and by subtle implications, Blastinius had portrayed Paul as a renegade Jew—a rejecter of the law of Moses, an enemy of Israel, as well as a man despised by even the Roman officials . . . a troublemaker and an enemy of Caesar. Blastinius's letter seemed perfectly believable to those who read it.

What had turned Blastinius's previous hatred into blind rage? It was Paul's letter to the Galatians. Blastinius had been given a copy of this letter. Having read it, he became certain Paul was a man who must be destroyed. Words like *freedom* were blasphemous to the mind of Blastinius; and that the law of

Moses had been nailed to the cross of Christ and done away with was, to Blastinius, beyond treason. To him, Paul ranked below an insurrectionist, uncircumcised infidel.

It was this provocation that caused Blastinius to make his vow and set out on a journey into the Gentile world . . . to ruin Paul. It was in Syria that Blastinius decided to send out letters to places he might never reach in person. The letter played to the hour. There was hardly a Jew on earth who did not despise the Roman occupation of Israel. And the Jewish traditions were being honored as never before. Hence Blastinius addressed all these passions, casting Paul as the worst of all offenders.

When the elders of the synagogue in Thessalonica read Blastinius's letter, they were appalled. Until then they had assumed that Paul was simply a local phenomenon who had created problems only in Thessalonica. Now they realized he was a man turning the world upside down.

It was obvious they had to stop this insurrectionist. A plan was hatched. Every day the Jews would go into the marketplace and, speaking to the crowd, warn everyone concerning the strangers living in their city and working in the market.

"He is trying to overthrow Caesar. He declares there is another king besides Claudius. He is trying to overthrow the emperor and the empire." These were the words the people in the marketplace heard.

People in Thessalonica *feared* Rome. Nor did they desire to see any more Roman soldiers marching through their streets. Self-protection dictated that they do something to rid Thessalonica of Paul of Tarsus. Within a few days, the synagogue leaders had managed to raise up a small mob and, eventually, to incite them.

At that particular moment Paul and Silas were visiting a very old, very ill brother. The mob, not finding Paul, stormed

Jason's house crying: "We are a free city. Our allegiance is to Rome! We will not tolerate this revolutionary!"

Angry that this troublemaker was not in the house, they decided to grab Jason instead. Aristarchus, Secundus, and a few others watched in horror as the mob dragged Jason through the streets and then on to the city's magistrates.

One voice in the mob cried out, "Those men who have turned the world upside down have come here!" The magistrates had no idea what was going on, but they heard enough to be fearful, though it took them a while to figure out the men being charged were not present. They did, however, recognize the bloodied Jason.

After an exchange of words, questions, charges, and countercharges one of the magistrates resolved the confusion.

"Jason, you will be bonded. Leave seven silver coins here. The money will not be returned to you if these troublemakers remain in the city. If they leave, and that is now *your* responsibility, your money will be returned. It is your choice."

That night the entire ecclesia assembled in Jason's home. All eyes were on Paul. He stood and proceeded to clarify the events of the day. "There was a riot today in the agora—the elders of the synagogue provoked it. We have since discovered that it is because of a letter that has been written to all the synagogues in Asia Minor and that, by some manner, the letter found its way to Macedonia. Because of Silas and me, Jason was dragged through the streets to the magistrates and poorly treated."

"Give me no sympathy," interrupted Jason. "It was a joy to be shamed for my Lord!"

"They have taken a large amount of money from you, Jason." Paul turned his eyes on the other believers. "If I do not leave immediately, the money will not be returned to Jason. I have been legally banished from Thessalonica; I am now considered a criminal. Silas and I have decided to depart tonight, giving the authorities no room for dispute nor opportunity to change their minds. We will depart at the end of this meeting."

There were cries of protest and disappointment.

"Sadly, except for Timothy, the banishment is permanent," continued Paul. "We cannot legally return to you." Several began to weep. Others simply shook their heads in disbelief at so quick a turn in all their lives.

Aristarchus then told of what had happened at the bema. He managed to make the entire incident seem humorous. His ability to do this both surprised and impressed Paul. Silas once said to me, "It was the first evidence of the strength of God's people in Thessalonica, and it alerted us to the future possibilities that were until then hidden in the young man named Aristarchus."

The rest of the evening was taken up with Paul and Silas giving words of instruction and encouragement. Both men reminded everyone that they had—from the beginning—warned them of this day. That night, fear gave way to eagerness and joy.

"Silas, someday you will return to Jerusalem. Be sure and tell them what happened in Thessalonica." It was Secundus, his voice choked. "And tell them that we are grateful for the testimony of the Jerusalem church. Tell them that today we also feel privileged to suffer for Jesus' sake."

Cheers and shouts of "Amen!" followed his words.

Has there ever been an assembly of God's people anywhere who were so willing to suffer and who, when they did suffer, were so quick to rejoice?

Silas called for prayer. All knelt. All prayed, and all wept. There were hugs by everyone.

"So much like the last evening in Philippi," said a stunned Timothy.

Just before Paul stepped out of Jason's house, he took Jason aside. "Write to Philippi tomorrow, please. In the letter tell them what has happened here, and request their prayers. Explain that the situation here is far more grave than what happened in Philippi. We have seen hate in the eyes of many people in this city. They believe that everyone who assembles in Jason's house is an insurrectionist.

"Then tell Philippi to send a copy of your letter on to the four churches in Galatia and to Antioch also. All the other churches need to know what happened here."

As the three men moved out into the street, the entire assembly walked out with them, then on out through the Vardar Gate (the western gate), and from there to the Egnatian Way. From there they all walked together to the Axius River. Once on the other side of that river, Paul and Silas were safe; the banishment ended there. And so, as they walked along the path beside the river, the brothers and sisters began to sing and shout and praise.

"I have never seen anything like this," murmured Silas. "Never. When I tell the ecclesia in Jerusalem, they will be very proud."

Just as the sun was coming up over the horizon, the company of believers arrived where there was a ferry to cross the Axius River. They stood there waiting and singing until the morning's first ferry arrived. Paul presented a few more words of exhortation and once more everyone knelt and prayed, while the man in charge of the ferry looked on in baffled wonderment.

When Paul, Silas, and Timothy moved toward the ferry, the pilot protested that it was not capable of holding all those people. "Only three will board," assured Paul.

The ferry began to pull away. Everyone became very quiet. It was a reverent moment. But when the ferry began to reach the other side, shouts and praises broke out again. Silas returned the shouts. So also Timothy. As the ferry struck dry land, everyone began to cheer wildly.

"The next city is Berea," said the pilot, pointing toward the mountains. "It is some fifty miles south of here. You must be very important people to have such a crowd to accompany you."

Paul thought of the whipping in Philippi, the banishment in Thessalonica, and then the fact that he was a follower of Christ. *Important? Yes!* thought Paul.

But Silas was the one who spoke for both: "There are those in heaven who might consider us to be very important. Upon the earth, I am not so sure."

With that word, the company of three turned south with one question in their minds: Had Blastinius's letter also reached Berea? If so, they would have to bypass that city; if not, they would seek to proclaim Christ in the Berean synagogue.

"His ways are not my ways," said Paul thoughtfully. "I had wanted to move westward. I wanted to go straight from here to the land of Illyricum. From there, I had hoped to sail across the Adriatic Sea, perhaps to the Italian port city of Brundisium."

"In other words, you were hoping you would be able to travel from the port city of Brundisium to Rome," said Silas.

"A fellow named Claudius has prevented that hope, has he not? The Lord did not allow me to go to Ephesus, nor to Bithynia, but, rather, to Greece. Had I had my way, I would be traveling north to Illyricum right now, with my eyes set on Rome. Instead, we are going to a small city in the mountains where men and women go to escape the hottest days of summer. A resort city!"

Paul looked westward and pensively added: "Claudius, what have you done to me?" Then lifting his eyes skyward he continued, "Lord, what is your plan in all of this?" Paul turned back toward Thessalonica: "Blastinius, I expected you to seek my destruction in the churches. But for you to try to turn the

Roman government against me—a government you hate—this I never imagined. And the synagogues. You have contacted the synagogues *everywhere!* You are *more* than I expected."

"Consider this, Paul," interrupted Silas. "If we had left Antioch and gone straight to Rome, right now we would be packing our bags and fleeing the Imperial City."

"Berea instead of Rome? Quite a difference!" added Timothy.

"Let us hope," said Silas, "that no letter from Blastinius has reached as far as the mountainous city. Somehow I simply cannot imagine a letter having reached *that* far!"

No letter had reached Berea, but one had been sent. It simply had not yet arrived.

The Thessalonian adventure had come to an abrupt halt—the Berean adventure was about to begin.

CHAPTER 19

"Friday afternoon—Sabbath will begin in a few hours. I would have chosen some other day to arrive. Be that as it may, we must find an inn immediately," said Paul as they entered Berea. "Timothy, inquire of the finest inn available. After that, meet us in front of the synagogue; I wish to stand in front of it for a few minutes before we go in. Perhaps I will learn *something!*"

Shortly thereafter the three men were standing on the synagogue steps. No one spoke. Each prayed his own thoughts, hopes, and fears.

After that Timothy guided his two friends to an inn with a clean room and fresh straw, decent by any traveler's standards. It was also the cleanest city any of them had ever traveled to. The back streets were wider than any they had ever seen before or since. The next morning, as Paul had done so many times, he reached into one of his leather bags and pulled out his pharisaical garb.

"Thanks to Lydia, you look quite prosperous!"

"And a little less skinny than when we spoke in the Thessalonian synagogue," replied Paul.

As the men made their way through the streets to the Jewish gathering, Paul was less sure of himself than ever before.

Will they have heard of me? he kept asking himself. Had a letter already arrived there from Blastinius? If so, it might be a tumultuous morning.

"Timothy," said Paul wryly, "I have never mentioned this to you before—you look a lot more like a Greek than you do a Jew."

Timothy laughed. Silas feigned astonishment.

"May I ask, then, that you take your place among the God-fearers, not the Jews. If any word has reached here about me, I do not want anyone to have the impression that I am opposing the law of Moses by letting a Gentile sit among the Jews."

Timothy threw his arms out in a great circle and said, "Ah! *Today* I am unclean!"

"Silas, you are spending too much time with this young man."

Each of the three took a deep breath and passed into the synagogue. Timothy was soon struggling to keep his eyes open. He was sleepy, tired, the room suffocating, and the ritual boring beyond words. At the end of the ritual the two Jewish visitors were asked if they had anything they would like to share.

It was Silas who stood, and his words were eagerly received. Paul sat silent, his name left unannounced. At the close of the meeting there was only a little interest but there was also no hostility. This mild reception gave the men a week to find out if the synagogue leaders had been warned against Paul. As best they could discern, no one had ever heard of Paul of Tarsus.

The three men returned to the synagogue the next week. This time Paul spoke. Knowing that his time in the synagogue in Berea might be short, Paul came straight to the point. "The Messiah, whose name is Jesus, has come. He has been crucified, and he is risen from the dead."

This time the two men received a warm invitation to return

the next week to speak again. The Berean synagogue, it turned out, gave Paul the kindest welcome he could have possibly asked for.

When the three men returned the next week they found a table had been placed in the middle of the room. The scroll of Isaiah had been taken from a wooden chest. Such wooden chests can be found in every synagogue. They contain a few scrolls and are kept in the synagogue behind a blue curtain.

At the invitation of the synagogue leaders, Paul was allowed to take his place beside the scroll and quote passages from it. Paul did not always quote the words exactly; nonetheless, his knowledge of Isaiah was masterful. Even the elders of the synagogue were impressed.

As the meeting came to a close, it seemed that everyone in that room accepted Jesus as their Messiah. Many *did* believe. (Perhaps half the synagogue attendees truly did confess Jesus Christ as Lord before Paul was forced out of the city. This is remarkable when one realizes that Paul was in Berea for no more than a month.)

Every day while in Berea, Paul went into the marketplace and preached. He usually did this in late morning, just before the market closed down for the noon meal. He returned again in the afternoon when people reentered the agora. When he spoke there was an urgency in Paul's words, as he felt certain he would not be long in Berea. Unfortunately, the response in the marketplace was not as positive as in the synagogue.

Nonetheless, by the end of the second week the new brothers and sisters were gathering in the home of Phirhus. Phirhus's home was small, but it was large enough for the believers to cram into.

A most unusual thing was going on at the synagogue.

On the next Sabbath the doors were left open all afternoon. Both Jews and God-fearers came to the synagogue and *together* read the scrolls. Most of the people had never before been that close to a Hebrew scroll. Until that day only the elders were allowed to touch them. (The scrolls are used only for public reading.) Among the elders who could read, one after another took turns searching the scrolls until each found a passage on which Paul had spoken, and then read it aloud.

Even the Jews could not always understand what was being read, as the scrolls were written in an ancient, almost-forgotten Hebrew. It was up to the elder, therefore, to not only read the passage in the archaic language, but to read it again in the Hebrew that is spoken in our day.

When the passage was thoroughly read there was much discussion. According to what I, Titus, have been told, never once during this time was there any criticism of Paul. Further, what Paul had said seemed to be borne out in all the scrolls they read. Though Paul continued to be received by the Bereans, it was inevitable that the warm reception would change.

Trouble had been anticipated, and trouble came. But it did not originate in Berea; it came from Thessalonica. And, yes, it was provoked by the doings of Blastinius.

It seemed the leaders of the synagogue in Thessalonica got word that Paul, having been thrown out of Thessalonica, had traveled on to Berea. Learning this, they determined to end his influence there, just as they had in Thessalonica. A delegation of devout Jews set out for Berea.

Upon arriving in Berea, the Thessalonian Jews turned the Berean Jews against Paul. They then proceeded to the city rulers, informing them about Paul, telling bizarre and outlandish stories. They went so far as to read from the letter written by Blastinius. Nor did they stop there. On the next Sabbath, the men from Thessalonica spoke publicly against Paul in the synagogue.

The next day these men were back before the magistrates,

warning them of the chaos Paul would cause in Berea, graphically telling tales about the harm Paul had caused in Thessalonica. "He incited a mob—he denounced Caesar. He is an enemy of Caesar!"

Alarmed by those words, the magistrates decided to take action. If Thessalonica saw fit to banish this man, so would Berea, for Berea was also a free city wanting no trouble from Rome. Further, they wanted no insurrection or riot in the market.

Oddly enough, not once was the name of Silas mentioned. Paul was the sole target of all charges.

Paul was not unaware of these events. He was, in fact, making plans to do the inevitable. "I must leave Berea," he told Silas and Timothy. "I will do what they least expect. I mean to return to Thessalonica. The brothers and sisters there are in dire straits. I will also seek to find some way that will allow me to return to Philippi."

Silas and Timothy's response, as well as that of the Berean brothers, was adamant. "This you cannot do!"

While they were in the middle of this rather heated discussion, a letter came to Paul from the brothers and sisters in Thessalonica. There was every reason for their having written.

It seems that one day in the marketplace, a young brother said something very critical of the Emperor Claudius. "Claudius is a very evil and wicked man; he rules outside of any law!" the youth had exclaimed. His words were heard by men very favorable to the emperor and very unfavorable to the local believers.

Actually, and what was so galling to Paul, the young brother was simply quoting something Paul had said. Just before Paul left Thessalonica—that is, just before the mob invaded Jason's house—Paul had been speaking to the ecclesia, and in the course of the message Paul had expressed some very strong, unflattering words about Claudius. Someone had asked Paul about when the Lord Jesus would return. As Paul responded, everyone in the room became very excited that "the Lord Jesus may return very soon!" Somewhere in the discussion that followed, Paul expressed some very negative feelings about the emperor.

"Ever since the empire ceased to be a republic, the Caesars have ruled outside of any law, but none have been so lawless as Claudius; none have sinned as this man of sin has."

It was only natural that a young brother, new and fervent in the Lord, would take Paul's words into the marketplace . . . and add a few words of his own. The news of this young man's comment had swept through the entire city. As a result, the ecclesia was being totally rejected by the entire city populace. The only place the believers were welcome was in one another's homes. Otherwise they daily met the taunts of citizens wherever they went.

Reading all of this, Paul was speechless. He finally muttered something to the effect, "I do not think I will ever speak again."

Paul was already anxious enough about Thessalonica. Now he was more determined than ever to return there. But Timothy and Silas were even more adamant that he must not. Finally Paul relented. Instead, it was agreed that Paul would leave Berea quickly and travel into southern Greece (Achaia) and there await news from Silas concerning Berea *and* Thessalonica. Silas and Timothy would remain in Berea, and Timothy would make a visit to Thessalonica as soon as wisdom allowed. A meeting of the Berean ecclesia was called before Paul departed.

"Never, not even in Philippi, have I said farewell to an assembly this new in Christ. Silas and Timothy will stay with you for as long as they can—perhaps a month or two. By then we must decide what to do next. I will return when returning becomes a possibility."

The parting was, as in Thessalonica (less than two months earlier), both sad and hopeful. The brothers and sisters, walking with Paul all night, accompanied him down to the seaport city of Dium.

There in Dium, Paul bought passage on a ship preparing to depart for no less than the city of Athens. There was a fond and tearful good-bye as Paul boarded the ship. "Tell Athens of Christ!" someone called out. "Return in God's time!" came another. At the last moment, a few brothers scrambled on board, having decided to accompany Paul to Athens.

Paul gave Silas and Timothy a warm farewell.

As planned, Silas and Timothy remained in Berea to continue aiding the young church. At the same time the two men would also keep in touch with Thessalonica. All three agreed to keep in communication with one another as much as possible.

"I will stay in Athens until you or Timothy come to me. Or until the Lord directs otherwise. In the meantime, write, and write often. Timothy, you were not banished from Thessalonica as were Silas and I. Go there, soon! If you do get to Thessalonica"—Paul smiled—"try to look as much like a Greek, and as little like a Hebrew, as you can." The conversation ended.

Sails were hoisted. A moment later the ship began to pull out of the Dium harbor. Paul and company shouted words of exhortation to those on shore. The ship sailed close to shore all the way to Piraeus, which is the seaport city of Athens. Paul, a Jew who had been raised in a Greek culture, found himself on his way to the birthplace of the Greek culture and the mother of the Greek-Roman civilization . . . to the city of the goddess Athena. "To Athens!" said Paul to himself. "I never once imagined going there."

Would the city of innumerable gods respond to the gospel of Jesus Christ?

CHAPTER 20

Legendary *Piraeus!* The port from which thousands of ships had been launched into the four winds of the world to conquer for Greece. Paul drank in every detail of the scene unfolding before him.

Should you ever visit Athens, you will find it is four miles inland from Piraeus. The statue of Athena, on Mars Hill, is in full view from Piraeus. Athens' golden age had passed away four hundred years earlier, but the city is a thousand years older than that, and it is still captivating. The city was never truly conquered until the iron heel of Rome crushed her some two hundred years ago. She is, rightly so, called *the city of innumerable gods.* Paul discovered that both Piraeus and Athens lived up to that description. There were statues to gods everywhere in the port city.

"The entire four miles we walked were virtually nothing but lines of statues and altars to every imaginable god. One even had the inscription, *To an Unknown God.* Truly, the one god that Athens does not know is the true and living God." Such was the report one of Paul's companions later gave to the Berean church.

Paul himself has recounted his own impressions. "Just

before we entered Athens we passed the great manufacturing center for pottery, the *Keramikos*, its goods known throughout the world. On each side of the road where we walked there is a high wall, an ancient fortification built over three hundred years ago."

Just beyond the pottery works, Paul paused and pointed upward: "The great acropolis. Five hundred feet above the city, built on the site that is revered for Ares, the god of war."

Paul and the Bereans approached the city by way of what is called the Double Gate, located on the west side of Athens.

"It seems that every road of any importance converges here at this gate," observed Paul as they passed into the city. "The road from Corinth, the road from Piraeus, the road from Actium, and the road from Boeotia all end *here*." Paul then added: "All roads lead to Athens! Has Rome heard of this?"

If ever you should travel to Athens, here is some of what you might expect to see.

Just as you pass through the Double Gate, you come to the temple of Demeter. At that moment you will be impressed with its beauty; but later, as you become familiar with the city, you will find that there are temples of equal grandeur *everywhere*. Is there any place in all the world with temples so beautiful and so numerous?

Just beyond Demeter's temple is the great statue of Poseidon, sitting astride a great horse. In Poseidon's hand is the ancient trident, a three-pronged spear, still used in battle to this day. Beyond that are yet more statues, to Zeus, Apollo, Hermes, and Athena. All find honor near the statue of Poseidon. Beyond there you come to the sanctuary of Dionysus.

As you enter the heart of the city, you cannot but discover that young men have come here from all over the Roman Empire to study philosophy. These students are in evidence everywhere. Then comes the Greek marketplace, located near the famous music hall called the Odeion of Pericles.

Passing through the Greek agora, you come to the city's colonnade, and there more idols. In between these idols are statues of heroes of the ancient past, whose significance has long since been forgotten.

It was in the Greek marketplace that Paul secured a room in one of the inns. Once Paul was settled, the brothers who had accompanied him from Berea bade him good-bye and returned home, carrying with them the information of the exact location of Paul's lodging and his request that any news about the churches in Thessalonica and Berea be sent to him immediately.

Paul suddenly found himself very alone, and with nothing to do until the Sabbath. He therefore wandered the city, taking in its wonder and its history. What he soon learned was that the exodus of Jews from Rome was at its height, and that the refugees seemed to be destined either for Israel or the city of Corinth, a city only a short distance south of Athens. This city, Corinth, now being filled with Jewish Romans, intrigued Paul. *Perhaps all is not lost. Roman Jews, concentrated in one Greek city, and that city is nearby*, he said to himself.

As to Athens, Paul found gods of every imagination, including an altar to *modesty*, another to *impulse*, and even an altar to *rumor*. Among them all, the most impressive was the great bronze statue to Ptolemy. Other temples south of the Greek marketplace (in the Roman agora) included a temple to the Olympian Zeus. And on the southeast side of this agora is yet another dedicated to Pythium. In the Agora Square, which sits between the Greek market and the Roman market, is the stunning temple to Theseion.

Athens is quite simply the most idolatrous place on the face of the earth. It was the best and worst possible place for Paul to stay while waiting for Timothy's arrival. There was much to interest the Greek side of Paul, but there was much to enrage his Jewish side.

"It seemed forever before the Sabbath arrived," Paul once noted. "When at last it did, I could not but wonder, has this Athenian tolerance for all things influenced even the Hebrew house of worship?"

It had.

"I believe," said Paul, "I could have stood in that synagogue and announced that the world would come to an end by noon, and no one would have looked up to see who said it."

Because it was a synagogue custom, Paul was asked to speak that day. Even as he rose to declare his Lord, there was a sense of hopelessness in Paul. I, Titus, know that only one person received the Lord that day: a dear sister in Christ named Damaris.

Damaris has reported that it was a very moving and brilliant message Paul brought, but hardly an eye blinked or a hand moved when Paul announced that the Messiah had come.

"Is there anything that has ever entered into the mind of mortal man, or any event that has ever taken place on this earth, that might have stirred that synagogue?" Paul asked himself. "I would have been elated if they had rejected me. I was met with nothing but total disinterest. I gladly take rejection over blank stares."

Paul walked out of the synagogue that morning knowing that he had fulfilled the desire of the Lord *to go first to the Jew*. But the prospect of going to the Athenian Gentiles boded even worse.

Paul had watched little groups of men in Athens carrying on deep discussions about nothing . . . yet speaking always in pretentious, abstract ways that only sounded profound.

"The day following the Sabbath, after much inner debate, I

decided I would do what Socrates had done. I broke into several of these discussions, asking a series of questions. This allowed me the opportunity to also *answer* questions. Nonetheless, there was no one who showed any interest in anything I said. The men of Athens had long ago talked to death all meaningfulness.

"I deliberately addressed the topic of the *Anastasis* (that is, the Resurrection), but their minds were darkened. Long ago they established intricate philosophies of Anastasis that completely surrounded, enveloped, and negated any understanding of the resurrection of Jesus Christ.

"Upon hearing me address this subject, they either laughed or smiled tolerantly. Therefore I left these learned men and went to the marketplace, slightly more hopeful. As soon as I stood to speak, a crowd gathered around me, but after a few moments some in the crowd began to shout, '*Spermologos! Seedpicker!*' (It is a term the Athenians use to describe people who walk around Athens picking up a little teaching here, a philosophy there, and then, weaving these pieces of philosophy together, attempt to speak profoundly on subjects of which they know very little. *One who goes around picking up words.*)

"My accent did not help," Paul admitted. "The Athenians are used to hearing their language spoken with a beautiful, classical accent . . . but my Cilician tongue, flavored with a bit of a Hebrew accent, made me sound to their ears as one who is uneducated and tongue-tied.

"Nonetheless, several Epicureans and Stoics approached me."

"Are you aware that you are in violation of the law?" they asked. (Paul, of course, had no idea of what they spoke.)

"Before you can teach in Athens, you must come before the city council and allow your teachings to be heard. After they hear you, they decide whether or not you are teaching something dangerous, such as fomenting a rebellion against Rome."

I doubt there is any teaching under heaven this city would not tolerate, thought Paul. Over the passing of centuries, teaching had become more of a farce than it was anything else.

Paul immediately petitioned to appear before the rulers of the city in their place of assembly, which is in the Areopagus. "Approaching the hill of Ares from the south, I made my way up the acropolis. Then I mounted the sixteen broad steps leading to the Areopagus. Waiting for me was the court of Pallas Athena.

"They motioned to me to take my place on something they called the Stone of Shame, where a person presents himself before the court in order to defend himself. I took my place before the sons of Socrates, Plato, Aristotle, Zeno, and Euripedes to declare the gospel of Jesus Christ, the colossal statue of the goddess Athena only a few feet away."

The prosecutor stepped over to something called the Stone of Pride. Paul soon learned that the Greeks' so-called tolerance was but a facade. With a voice showing both contempt and amusement he addressed Paul very formally. "Tell us, foreigner, what is this new teaching that you proclaim in the Agora?"

Paul took a deep breath, reached into the very deepest recesses of his being, and pulled out his classical Greek training which he had received in Tarsus as a youth. He was determined to let them know that their world was not unfamiliar to him.

It was not long before his illustrious audience realized that this foreigner was no "seedpicker." Paul had hardly begun before he quoted from a passage in *The Eumenides* by Aeschylus in which the goddess Athena told the story of the origin of the Acropolis. Paul then quoted Plato, out of the tenth book of *The Republic*, speaking of "the great architect of the universe." Shortly thereafter, he stunned his elite audience by quoting from an obscure Cretan poet named Epimenides. He then added a quotation from the philosopher Aratus, who, three hundred years earlier, had written, among other things, a book called *Phenomenon*. The quotation was, "We are his offspring."

There were nods of approval as Paul continued.

In theory, Paul had been brought there to be examined as to whether or not his teachings were dangerous to the province of Achaia, but, in fact, he had been allowed to speak to this body to assuage their curiosity.

Whatever attention they had given him to that point, it was when he mentioned the Resurrection that most began to laugh. One member of the council waved his hand and, speaking for most, said, "We will hear more from you on some other occasion." It was Athenian politeness, which really meant that they were not interested in hearing more.

Paul departed the Areopagus with but one thought: "I can take this place no longer. I am going to Corinth. I will leave word for Timothy to meet me there."

At that moment, someone laid his hand on Paul's shoulder. Paul turned. It was one of the leaders of the council.

"My name is Dionysius. I am a lawyer."

The two men spent the rest of the day together, talking of things eternal. Just before nightfall, Dionysius placed his life in the hands of Jesus Christ.

Besides Dionysius and Damaris, there were several other people who believed on the Lord Jesus Christ before Paul departed the city.

The people of Athens have talked to one another for so long, with so many words, that speech has lost its power. They did not expect to hear anything new or important; therefore, they did not hear. But, sadly, what they did not hear was the greatest news of all!

(Years later an ecclesia came into being in Athens, but even then it was composed mostly of believers who had moved to Athens from assemblies in other Greek cities.)

Paul was about to leave instructions for Timothy at the inn (telling Timothy to meet him in Corinth) . . . when Timothy arrived!

Timothy, keenly aware of Paul's anxiety over the churches, did not even waste a greeting but rather began telling Paul the news from Thessalonica and Berea. Timothy reported mostly about Berea, for that is where he had gone after Paul sailed to Athens. As to Thessalonica, the oppression of the ecclesia by the city had continued unabated. That, in essence, was all Timothy knew of Thessalonica.

"A brother from Berea, Sopater, has visited Thessalonica. As young as he is in the Lord, he has spoken to the Thessalonians and in so doing has brought great encouragement to them."

"I remember this young man well," replied Paul.

(Timothy did not yet know that this Sopater would become a lifelong friend.)

For the next two days Paul, though very distracted, took Timothy around the city of Athens. While doing so he took the opportunity to vent his frustrations concerning the city of endless tolerance. He also shared with Timothy the news that there had been a great influx of Jews into Corinth. "The city is drowning in Jewish refugees from Rome. For that reason I wish to go there."

It was on the last day they were in Athens that Paul did something in the life of a young man named Timothy that Timothy was not at all expecting.

"Silas cannot reenter Thessalonica, nor can I. Silas *can* go to Berea. I cannot. You, young man, *can* go to Thessalonica. I want you to do just that. Stay with the ecclesia there. Meet with them. Minister to them. Encourage them. Exhort them. Then, after a few weeks, come to Corinth. Bring Silas with you. I wish to hear from each of you concerning our two youngest churches." Paul paused. "Meet me in Corinth, and bring good news."

Timothy was reluctant. "You are asking me to do more than visit. You are asking me to minister . . . to do what Silas does, and what you do! Am I not too young? And inexperienced?"

"You are absolutely correct. Go there planning to fail! Anything above that will be glory. My dear young brother, you will never be prepared or experienced until first you lay inexperience behind you."

So, for the first time in his life, Timothy knew what it was to personally carry the burden of the Lord's work. Timothy was not yet twenty-five.

(There came a day, some three years later, when Paul began training six young men. The number eventually grew to eight. I, Titus, was one of those men. So also was Timothy. Of those men, let it ever be remembered, Timothy was the first among us to be called upon to shoulder the responsibility of caring for one of the young churches.)

Paul then gave Timothy, who was still protesting his new assignment, the name of an inn at Corinth where he and Silas were to meet Paul.

"You have been doing quite a bit of preparation, have you not?" said Timothy. "You even know the name of a Corinthian inn?"

"I also know the schedule of a ship bound from Athens for Thessalonica. It is scheduled to depart *tomorrow.*"

Timothy gave a sigh of resignation. "All right, I go to Thessalonica to fail. Anything beyond failure will be, not glory, but a miracle."

The next day Timothy turned north to Thessalonica, and Paul turned southward toward Corinth.

Even Blastinius would never imagine I had come so far, thought Paul.

And he was correct. But Paul had no idea that in the uniqueness of Corinth would come forth the most unusual church ever to emerge from his hand.

CHAPTER 21

My name is Paul. Like you, I am a tentmaker. I was wondering . . ."

The man Paul was speaking to quickly interrupted, "Are you Paul of Tarsus?"

A thousand thoughts rushed into Paul's mind. He was far away from Israel, and certainly no one in the city of Corinth should know his name. *Had one of Blastinius's letters in some way found its way even here? How else could this man know of me?*

Hesitantly Paul replied, "Yes, I am Paul of Tarsus."

The man pushed aside his weaver's beam, stood, and asked: "Are you still a follower of Jesus the Christ?"

This was more than Paul could comprehend. "I am, but how did you know of me . . . I . . . ?"

By now the man had enthusiastically embraced Paul. "I am Aquila from Pontus, a city north of Asia Minor, near the Black Sea."

"Pontus. Yes, I know of it. We are both a long way from our homes."

"I am a follower of *The Way*, as is my wife. We have heard many stories about the assembly in Jerusalem. A few of them included you—that you became a believer by most amazing means! We have come recently from Rome."

"Rome!" exclaimed Paul.

This time it was Paul who embraced Aquila. Paul's mind was immediately flooded with questions. "Rome . . . Rome?" This time it was Aquila who was taken aback.

"Rome!" Paul repeated. "Yet you are a believer! Are there believers in Rome? I knew of no followers of Christ in Rome."

"No, there are no believers in Rome, not anymore. Not since the decree, but there were a few of us until last month."

"How many were you? And how many of those were Gentiles?"

"There were only six or seven. We were all Jews, except my wife."

"Then *today* there are none?"

"None whatsoever. It was such a tiny witness of the Lord in such a great city, and now . . . nothing."

Simultaneously, both men asked the other: "What brings you to Corinth?" Both laughed and embraced again.

"I'll go first," said Aquila. "The emperor threw us Jews out of Rome. Obviously, I had to go somewhere. My wife and I, like so many others, came to Corinth. We were able to sell our house very quickly and were among the first to arrive here in Corinth. We chose Corinth because we wanted to live in a place not belligerent to Jews *and* yet a city near Rome. My wife was born in the Imperial City. It is her home. She desires to return if ever that is possible.

"We arrived in Corinth at a time when there were still houses to be bought. Being a Roman citizen, and therefore allowed to buy and sell property, my wife bought one of the last houses in the city that was sold at a reasonable price. Today there are few houses for sale, and they cost an emperor's ransom to buy. More Hebrews have come to Corinth than to any other city outside of Israel."

"I heard this in Athens."

"And now, Paul, what brings *you* to Corinth?"

Paul's answer came a little more reluctantly. "I am waiting for two friends of mine. They are to join me here. They will be coming from Berea and Thessalonica. Now tell me, is there a gathering of believers here in Corinth?"

"No, there is not. As far as I know, only my wife and I follow the Savior. Now let me ask you the same question. Is there a gathering of believers in either Berea or Thessalonica?"

Paul sighed. "There is in *both* cities . . . at least, I hope this is still true. There has been much trouble, especially in Thessalonica. You might even call it persecution."

"I am not surprised," replied Aquila, as he began closing down his shop. "But if, by God's mercy, there are still gatherings there, my wife will be delighted. She will certainly go visit them as soon as she hears. My wife *hates* to attend meetings in Jewish synagogues. Come, I want you to meet her. Her name is Priscilla, and she loves the Lord passionately." Then, with a twinkle in his eye, he added, "She is also unique."

"You are closing shop? At the busiest of times?"

"Not a very good Hebrew, am I? But be assured, I have enough business for ten men. It seems every new arrival from Rome needs my services. But right now, finding you is far more important than business."

Paul eyed the area Aquila worked in. It was packed with every sort of material. "I've never seen a tentmaker's shop so crowded with unfinished work!"

"The influx from Rome is unbelievable. Hundreds are forced to live in the streets . . . or . . . in tents. Need I say more?"

"You are overwhelmed with business?"

"Exactly!"

"My trade is tentmaking. I hope you will not mind the competition."

"Competition! I am overjoyed you are a tentmaker. Please, take some of my business away from me."

Paul reached down and began helping Aquila pack up his awning, his weaver's beam, and his tools.

This, then, is how Paul came to the city of Corinth, a place that would be both the joy and the consternation of his life.

As they approached Aquila's home, Paul thought seriously about telling Aquila that it was his way of life that, when he ate in someone's house, he always paid for his food. Somehow, that just did not seem appropriate at the moment.

Just as they reached Aquila's home, Aquila rushed past Paul. His voice boomed as he entered the house: "Priscilla, welcome a guest. He is a brother of whom you have heard a great deal. His name is Paul of Tarsus."

In a moment Priscilla was in the street, her eyes revealing her excitement. "Please come into our home." After a few moments of exchanging greetings and information, Priscilla disappeared into the kitchen, only to return a short time thereafter with a sumptuous meal.

Paul soon learned that Priscilla was one of the most articulate, well-informed people he had ever met. She also had a bright personality. He was amazed at Priscilla's grasp of the situation in Rome, as she seemed to know the answer to any question he asked and immediately provided him with insights he would never have otherwise learned.

"The district of Trastavere is virtually empty. I would say that half of the *insulae* have no occupants. You can say, after one hundred and fifty years, the Trastavere district is no longer a Jewish ghetto. Those who owned their own apartments were forced to sell them for almost nothing. Those who rented departed Rome with nothing. Mercifully, Aquila and I lived in the Aventine district. Selling our house was easy. The price was fair.

"But, oh, even in the sadness, there was so much hope

among Aquila's kinsmen. We often heard them say, `We will return as soon as Claudius is dead.' After all, Claudius did not actually sign a new decree; he only reinstated an old one. Legally, Jews have been prohibited from living in Rome ever since the Emperor Tiberius. But no one paid any attention to that until Claudius decided to reinforce that decree.

"The moment I heard Claudius was going to reinstate the decree, I began looking for a buyer for our home. You see, I have a number of friends in Claudius's inner circle. I knew what he was about to do before almost anyone."

"You knew beforehand?" asked an astonished Paul.

"Yes, I often do. I have *many* friends in high places!"

"Paul," said Aquila, "I must confess that I have married not only a heathen, but a smart one; and she has friends everywhere, including those who dust the throne! Rome is her home . . . truly her home!"

Priscilla interrupted. "Aquila and I first met one another in the marketplace. We fell in love and were married almost before I knew Abraham was his grandfather! And can you believe this? When the six or seven believers gathered in Rome heard that Aquila had married a heathen, they had this *long* debate over whether or not I could come to their meetings."

"What did they decide?"

"They didn't. I did!" declared an emphatic Priscilla. "I came in, sat down, and told them to drag me out if they dared!"

"Meet Priscilla!" said Aquila, with obvious pride.

Paul returned to the subject of Rome. "The synagogues?"

"They are all empty."

For the first time Paul realized the hand of God just might be in the expulsion. "No synagogues?" he mused.

It seemed that neither Priscilla nor Paul could ask or answer questions fast enough. All three quickly discovered that they felt very comfortable with one another. It was a friendship that lasted throughout Paul's lifetime.

As Paul stood to leave, he turned to Priscilla and hesitantly said, "My dear sister in the Lord, please understand what I am about to say. It has to do with a commitment I have made. It is that I would eat no one's food without paying."

Priscilla began to laugh. "So the stories about you are really true."

According to Aquila, Paul actually blushed. "And what have you heard of me?"

"I will tell you what I have heard of you," she responded, delightfully. "I have heard that you crucified Moses." Priscilla began to laugh. It was infectious. Aquila and Paul joined in even as Paul continued to blush.

Priscilla continued, in the same vein of good humor, "Along with Moses, I also heard you crucified 613 Jewish laws. As a Gentile, I have but one thing to say: `Good for you.' Now can you also do anything with synagogue meetings!"

"Where did you hear these things about me?"

"Oh, there were always some of Aquila's kinsmen from Jerusalem coming to visit. From them we heard the story of your salvation and even the time you and Barnabas met with the Twelve . . . and confronted them, or so the story goes! And that you will eat with Gentiles like me, and even declare Christ to us unwashed heathen! But mostly that you actually confronted the Twelve on behalf of us barbarians."

"It is true, partially," said Paul. "The Twelve gave Barnabas and me a letter commending us in the preaching of the gospel to the Gentiles."

"Well, it is about time," huffed Priscilla in her inimitable way.

"Actually, Paul," added Aquila, "when we heard this we

were both thrilled. Priscilla and I have always carried a burden for the Gentiles, that *they* come to know our Lord."

"None of your believing friends in Rome came here to Corinth?"

"No, all returned to Israel," answered Aquila.

Priscilla's demeanor changed. "Paul, there are no believers in this city that we can find. We are the only two, and I am lonely. I wish to be with believers . . . especially if some of them are heathen, like me!" Then she added in a feisty manner, "I *hate* going to those horrible Saturday morning synagogue services!"

"How many synagogues are there in Corinth?"

"One, but it is large, and right now it is completely filled and overflowing with Jews coming from Rome," replied Aquila.

"Not only full but hot and stuffy and *boring!*" remonstrated Priscilla.

Paul ventured a question that surprised even himself: "Do you have any idea if the synagogue leaders have heard of me?"

Aquila brightened. "I have absolutely no idea, but I doubt it. We are a very long way from Jerusalem. On the other hand, I hope that they do hear from you. I understand that it is your way, when you are in a city, to always preach first to the sons of Abraham."

Paul shook his head in dismay. "What is it you *don't* know about me?"

The conversation was coming to an end, or so Paul thought. He once again raised the matter of paying for his meal. Priscilla did not hear him but countered with a question: "And where, exactly, do you plan on spending this night, Paul?"

"In one of the inns."

Even as he spoke he realized there would be no room available in the inn where he had planned to stay.

"Hmmm . . ." began Priscilla, "are you aware, Paul, that I

am probably the best cook in all of Corinth? Further, prices for food are outrageous. Especially mine!"

"She speaks the truth, at least about her cooking," inserted Aquila.

"You cannot possibly afford to buy food. Not for long. And the fields are the only place left to sleep." Priscilla paused. "You will stay here, as our brother in Christ. Food and lodging are free, or they are not at all."

Paul stared at Priscilla for a long moment. His only comment was, "You remind me of someone in Philippi. A woman named Lydia."

Priscilla laughed delightedly. "Then she must be a most wonderful woman!"

"I find it very difficult to say yes to your generous offer, I . . ."

"Perhaps my husband has something in mind that can resolve this problem."

"Yes, Priscilla whispered something to me while in the kitchen," said Aquila. "Would you be willing to join me in the making and mending of tents?"

Paul was taken completely by surprise, but his answer was quick. "I would consider working with you, yes—but only with the understanding that you take out of my earnings the expense of my room and food and . . ."

Priscilla interrupted. "*I* keep the records. I will set the cost. And *you* do not argue with my decisions."

Aquila joined in: "We will work together, and we will share the expenses and income, together."

"Are you sure? Am I not taking advantage of you?" persisted Paul.

"Dear brother, if you should stand in the middle of the marketplace tomorrow and yell 'tentmaker!' you would probably be mobbed. Further, if you do so, and they find out that you are a Jewish tentmaker—well, you know our people! You would be overwhelmed with business." Aquila sighed. "Paul, I *need* your help."

"I must warn you, Aquila, there will be times every day when I will have to lay aside the work and go to an inn that my friends and I designated as the place we are supposed to meet. They will be shocked to see the crowded conditions of the city. I need to be there when they arrive."

"We will see to it that your friends find you," replied Aquila.

"And Paul," said Priscilla, "there *is* no place in the city for them to stay. They will stay *here*. And eat here."

Then Priscilla asked forlornly, "Paul, one last question. In Berea, are there Gentiles, like me, in the Berean assembly?"

"*Most* are Gentiles . . . like you. And in Philippi, *all* are."

"Then I will visit these churches. And may God give us such souls here in Corinth."

"That may depend, to a large degree, on how I am received in the synagogue."

"You will be received well, I am sure of it," replied Aquila.

"The Sabbath is close enough. We will soon know."

CHAPTER 22

Aquila, I have rarely been so warmly received by a synagogue. It was as you told me it would be. Crispus went out of his way to make me feel welcome. Never have I seen a ruler of the synagogue so open to the gospel."

Such were Paul's words as he, Aquila, and Priscilla left the synagogue.

"A great deal of this must be credited to Priscilla. When we first came here Priscilla made friends with so many of the people who come to the synagogue. We have had most of them as guests in our home. Priscilla especially went out of her way to become friends with God-fearers."

Priscilla added: "We heard of what happened with Peter in the house of Cornelius in Joppa. We were thrilled to know that the gospel had opened to the Gentiles. I have dreamed since then of non-Jews knowing Christ. I thank God you have come. Paul, those meetings in Rome with just six people were miserable. Christian or not, those gatherings were as bad as going to the synagogue! It is not right for the ecclesia to be Jewish in a Gentile city."

"Barnabas would agree!" replied Paul.

"I have heard what the church in Antioch is like. I cannot wait to be in a meeting with a room full of former heathens!"

Paul had never met anyone with quite the gift of honesty that Priscilla possessed.

"I wish all Jews were as bored with the synagogue as you," he replied.

"I must tell you, Paul," said Aquila, "we cannot visit Antioch; but Berea is near, and so is Thessalonica. Priscilla and I hope to visit the assemblies there."

"That would be encouraging, for them . . . and for you. I hope you arrive at a time when no one is being beaten, jailed, or banished."

"This has happened to you in Macedonia?"

"Yes," replied Paul. "And similar things happened to Barnabas and to Silas, either in Galatia or northern Greece. You can add Syria and Cyprus. Sometimes at the hands of the Jews, sometimes at the hands of the Gentiles."

"Today in the synagogue, when you spoke, why did you not tell the Jewish brethren that the Messiah had come? Did you hesitate because of your past experience in synagogues?"

"I have learned that if I am to be invited back, I must not make that declaration in the first meeting. Nonetheless, I have never before, except in Berea, been received so warmly. I thank the Lord and you for that."

"I venture that at least half of the people in that room are interested in knowing the Lord. Some will surely respond," said Priscilla. "You will return next Sabbath?"

"Yes."

"And will you remain in Corinth to help us gather together the ecclesia?"

"I have, as yet, no word from the Lord. A week, a month, a year—I do not know. So much depends on circumstances and the mind of God."

Every Sabbath thereafter, Paul walked out of the synagogue muttering something to the effect, "Never, never in all my life . . . ," for Paul spoke in the synagogue at Corinth longer than he had at any other place. And the person most encouraging Paul to do so was none other than the synagogue ruler, Crispus.

A synagogue already crowded on the Sabbath was now overflowing, with some even standing in the entranceway straining to hear.

It was on the third Sabbath after Paul arrived that the unexpected happened. At the close of the meeting the ruler of the synagogue stood and declared, "I must tell you what has happened to me. Something here." Crispus pointed to his heart. "I cannot speak for anyone else in this room, but for me I have found the words of Paul to be true. True, not because of the Scripture nor what Paul has said, but true because of what has happened within me."

That day marked the high point of Paul's life in synagogue ministry.

There came a time, ultimately, when some of the Jewish elders asked Paul not to return to the synagogue. It was a mild rejection, and Paul forever considered it to be an act of high graciousness on the part of Jewish religious leaders.

When Titius Justus, one of Paul's earliest converts, heard that Paul would no longer be speaking in the synagogue, he approached Paul with a most reasonable proposal. "Continue to speak. Use my home to do so. You must not stop. You must not leave Corinth."

"Are you sure?" asked Paul. "You know what you are suggesting?"

"I do. But despite the location of my home, it is still my home."

Having a taste for irony, Paul burst out laughing. "Yes, the ecclesia, meeting next door to the synagogue!"

Word spread among the interested and the believers: "The gatherings of the believers will be at Justus's home."

The very first meeting was an overflow. Paul found it necessary to call meetings every morning and evening, *and* one in the afternoon, in order to give everyone an opportunity to assemble. (Eventually Paul even moved into Justus's home, so that he could be on hand at every meeting and spend time afterward with the new believers.)

In the heat of the day, when the market closed, you could also find Paul in Justus's house, answering questions. Even these meetings soon filled Justus's living room.

Paul did not stop there. Justus's living room could hardly hold the people, even though there were almost constant gatherings.

"We will have a meeting, here in Justus's home, on the Sabbath day," announced Paul. "It will be at the same hour that the synagogue holds its ritual."

(I, Titus, have been told that when the brothers and sisters were singing robustly, the sound could be heard through the walls of Justus's house into the synagogue. "A singing invitation to come where life is!" said Priscilla one day, almost euphorically.)

Yet despite these early advancements, Paul's thoughts remained centered on Thessalonica. Several times in the midst of all these blessings of God, he almost left Corinth to return to Thessalonica. Paul was a man distraught.

But peace came to his heart at last, by way of a dream. Paul heard the Lord speak to him in the night hours, "Stay here, for many of the people who are in this city are mine."

Reconciled, the next day Paul walked into the marketplace, and—for the first time—with unbridled enthusiasm preached the gospel. The market was so crowded it was hard to tell who was listening to him and who was ignoring him. Those who heard and believed immediately joined the gatherings.

From the beginning, these Corinthian gatherings were rowdy and zestful. Should you ever visit there, you will discover the Corinthians are an uninhibited people. Functioning in the gatherings came very easily for them. Perhaps, on occasion, too easily.

The ecclesia is an interesting mix, for Corinth is not one city, nor is it two cities; it is three distinct towns. This is because of the incredible diversity of races and cultures. And that diversity called for wise guidance from Paul. Alas, despite his wisdom, this vast diversity created many problems among the believers.

On several occasions I, Titus, have visited the ecclesia in Corinth. You cannot understand the church that assembles there unless you understand the city itself. Otherwise, you will be baffled by all you see . . . as were Silas and Timothy when they first arrived.

CHAPTER 23

Silas and Timothy were seasoned travelers, but they had never seen anything like what met their eyes as they neared Corinth.

Just before reaching the city gates, the two men saw a stone upon which is chiseled the city's full name: LAUS JULIA KORINTHIENSIS. Just before entering the gates, Timothy looked out at the surrounding fields. As far as his eye could see, there were men, women, and their families living in the fields. For many, the hillside was their only home. Many slept during the day and worked through the night. Others slept during the night and worked through the day. For both, cooking was done in the fields. The food was no more than a handful of grain which was their daily pay. Tents of every color, size, and shape imaginable dotted the landscape.

"Thousands upon thousands of people out there," Timothy said with a shudder.

Inside the walls it was no better. Jews fleeing Rome had choked the city's streets. There was hardly room to push through the crowd. It seemed everyone was selling something, even if it was no more than a single pair of sandals or a few slices of dried fruit.

"How do these people ever find a way to sleep?" asked Silas, as he looked at their haggard faces and listened to the ceaseless noise.

"Where do they sleep?" echoed Timothy. "They have filled the marketplace, the doorways, and have even crowded under the stairs. And look up there. The roof of every building is packed with tents and canopies."

"I have never seen so many fires and so much smoke in a marketplace," answered Silas.

"If a man stood on the roof of one of those buildings and looked out into the field, then down at the marketplace, he would have a hard time understanding why anyone would live here, or how they would survive."

Just then a wagon full of corpses passed by them. Timothy groaned. Silas buried his fist in his mouth to keep from retching. "Now I understand the meaning of the adage, 'Corinth is not for everyone'!"

"I have never seen anything like this," said a stunned Silas.

"I hope I never do again," responded Timothy.

"Has everyone gone mad?"

"Look at all the wine shops."

"Look at all the prostitutes."

"Look at all the people; I can hardly make . . ."

"I can hardly hear you!" yelled Timothy. "What did you say?"

"I said, listen to all that noise; I can hardly hear *you!*"

"Have you ever seen so many foreigners?"

"I think *everyone* is a foreigner. These people are all . . . haggling . . . screeching . . . but about what?"

Pushing their way toward the inn where they were supposed to leave a message for Paul, Silas muttered, "What a place for a tentmaking business!"

"I cannot imagine where Paul is staying. There is certainly

not going to be any room in the inn he designated. Let us only hope we find a message from him waiting for us."

The two men continued pushing their way into the marketplace. With great effort, they at last arrived at the inn.

Suddenly a voice rang out.

"You are Jews?"

Silas looked at the man. He did not seem menacing. "I am." Then, with his dry but incorrigible wit, he added, "I am not at all sure what my friend here is; he has not yet made up his mind."

"Would you be Silas of Jerusalem, and would you be Timothy of Lystra?" Both men nodded.

"I have been sent here every day to wait for your arrival. I have sat at this very spot for several weeks. Come, I will take you to your friend."

Timothy looked around at the marketplace. "Silas, you and I have much to tell Paul. But I have a notion he has even more to tell us."

Now, I, Titus, must tell you some things about Corinth so you will be able to fully understand how it was that the unfolding events came to pass.

What Timothy and Silas saw is a sight unprecedented in the empire. Their confusion and dismay are understandable. The diversity of Corinth is not easy to imagine, much less grasp.

Those who live on the west side of the city are Romans; those on the east side are from the Orient. Those living in the central part of the city are native Greeks. Each section has its own culture, its own customs, its own language. (In the case of the eastern sector of the city, it would be languages.) That fact has caused a great deal of confusion both in the city and in the ecclesia. All those cultures, customs, and viewpoints have converged in Justus's house!

To fully understand what caused the Corinthian church so much sorrow during its early years, you must understand the city.

Corinth is an isthmus. It lies between two seas. At the nearest point those two seas are only five miles apart. Corinth is located within those five miles. On the east side of Corinth, on the Aegean Sea, is the seaport town of Cenchrea. On the west side of Corinth is the port city of Lechaeum, located on the Adriatic Sea. Between these two ports . . . *Corinth*, the capital of southern Greece.

Every day, ships from the west arrive in Lechaeum, coming from Brundisium, Italy. Ships from the Orient arrive every day at Cenchrea. Corinth, in the middle, is a gigantic bazaar. Goods, products, and cultures all intersect in Corinth. Goods are bought and sold twenty-four hours a day. In her walls are every language, race, and custom the mind can imagine. Corinth literally straddles two worlds—the East and the West. To add to this madness, there is a trolley that has been built between Lechaeum and Cenchrea. Slaves drag ships overland on these trolleyways. Ships from the Aegean Sea are pulled over to the Adriatic Sea, and counter, ships from the Adriatic Sea are dragged overland to the Aegean Sea. Corinth is the one city in the world where you see ships passing one another on dry land! Even though this is a primitive means of transport, it is still faster and safer than attempting to sail around the perilous Cape of Malea.

Corinth's reputation as a city of confusion and drunkenness and more is known throughout the world. In this melee of buying and selling, misunderstandings in trade are commonplace. Consequently, many lawsuits arise. And why not, with so many languages and so many different views of laws?

Most people coming to Corinth have come long distances and are there for only three to five days. Carousing is the result. Their conduct only adds to Corinth's unseemly reputation.

When ships discharge their cargo on the docks of the two seaports, most of that cargo ends up in Corinth. Buying and brokering never slows, nor do the cries of slave masters and the crack of their whips as they goad their slaves in pulling the ships across dry land.

Day and night, wherever you look, someone is pulling carts or wagons filled with goods to or from Corinth. Sometimes donkeys are used to pull these carts, sometimes slaves. As in all the Roman Empire, the average lifetime of a slave is no more than twenty-five years. The same is true of men freed from slavery, for their lot is no better and is sometimes worse than that of the slaves. A town so interested in merchandising is harsh. Slave owners have a cruel way with their slaves. Freed slaves are treated the same way by those men.

Cenchrea is probably the noisiest place on earth, with the exception of Rome. (It was here that Silas and Timothy first disembarked. They walked from there to Corinth along a road called the Valachaion Way. And while they walked they seriously discussed the idea of turning around and going back to Berea!)

Upon entering Corinth, your ear catches the babble of dozens of languages, none recognizable.

The four major languages are Greek, Latin, Hebrew, and Egyptian. But many more languages than that are heard. Some are from places none of us have ever heard of. As a result you will find men selling their services as translators between merchants, as neither merchant has any idea what the other is saying.

Bales of cotton, piles of fruit, vegetables, and clothing are stacked everywhere.

That Corinth is a Greek city is unmistakable by its architecture. The agora is huge, but because of the crowded conditions of that particular year, crossing it was an adventure. Behind the marketplace is the poorest part of the city (the poorest which I have ever seen except for Rome).

A vast number of people sleep in the agora, on the stone pavement of the streets, in doorways, and in fields. They have no other home. Day and night you see small fires burning. These are fires the poor make to boil their handful of grain. They try to make the food stretch through more than one day, in hope they might set aside enough food for winter and for days when they find no work. Among these souls clothes are not clothes at all but a series of patches on patches. Not many of these people have ever owned anything more than the clothes on their back, clothes they have worn most of their lives. Almost every day bodies are carried out of the fields and burned. Their deaths usually are a result of exposure, disease, or starvation.

Coming through the city gates, what will strike you the most is that the first thirty or forty stores are wine shops! Most of their customers are those who will be in Corinth only a few days. Yet *everyone* seems to be drunk. Hence, Corinth is viewed as a city where all its citizens *stay* drunk.

It goes without saying that these transient merchants and sailors have made Corinth a city of prostitutes.

(When I, Titus, was growing up in Antioch, Syria, I recall that a young woman who had become a prostitute was referred to as a *Corinthian girl*. Such is the bawdy reputation of Corinth.)

Corinth is also a city of idols. North of the market, beside a basilica, is a temple to Apollo. Other temples include those to Hermes, Herakles, Poseidon, Venus Fortuna, and Athena. Then there is the city's Pantheon, located at the western end of the market, where gods innumerable are reverenced.

On the north side of the city is a temple dedicated to Asklepios, the god of healing. Visitors come to this temple from all over the empire seeking cures for their maladies. There are more idols and altars to gods in Corinth than any other cities in the world, except Rome and Athens. There are so many offerings made to the gods that the temple priests cannot offer up all the meat presented to them. Consequently, the priests sell the surplus meat to the city's butchers, who resell the meat in the marketplace.

When the weather turns bad, people huddle together in a close knot, warming one another around fires set in the marketplace. This goes on day and night, people standing in the wind and the rain, never moving. More people die at a younger age in Corinth than perhaps in any other city except, of course, Rome.

As to the crowded conditions, people pitch their tents on rooftops, just as they do in Rome. Never a year passes but that a roof caves in, killing or injuring many. But what I, Titus, recall most is the garbage and filth that cover every street, creating a sickening stench that never leaves.

Then there is the noise. Should you ever go to Corinth, do not rent a room in any inn that is near the marketplace, for you will *never* sleep. Sheep, goats, and cattle are herded through the city twenty-four hours a day, as they are herded to the east and west ports. Joining this noise are the shouts of thousands of slaves bearing cargo on their backs from one side of the isthmus to the other. Further, the hawking of wares never ceases.

If that is not enough to make Corinth a city of misery, there is the monthlong celebration called the Isthmian Games which is held in Corinth every two years. That is the time when Corinth is the most congested. People come to Corinth from all over the world to watch these games.

Finally, thanks to the ancient Greek tradition of rhetoric, Corinth is a city that loves oratory. Great speakers are considered heroes and receive the adulation of the Greek population.

Before you become judgmental of the problems the ecclesia in Corinth is noted for, first visit that city. You will no longer wonder at their problems. Rather, you will marvel that there is an ecclesia there at all.

Having given you some idea of what Corinth is like, we shall now return to Timothy and Silas and their reunion with Paul.

CHAPTER 25

Citizen of Tarsus!"

Paul jumped to his feet, scattering needle and thread everywhere.

"Timothy!" Paul cried, rushing to embrace his young friend. "And Silas!" The next words out of Paul's mouth were predictable: "Timothy, how is she, how is the ecclesia in Thessalonica?"

"Fine, even excellent. I have much news to tell you."

"Tell on, then! Oh! Excuse me. This is a brother in Christ, Aquila. He has come from Rome," said Paul. He then added as he swept his hand all across the marketplace, "As have half the people in this agora."

Silas shook his head. "I've never seen anything like this. The whole countryside is filled with our kinsmen. The inns are full. Tents are everywhere, and many do not even have tents to protect them."

"Aquila was one of the first to arrive here from Rome, and he, dear brother, has a home."

"A home!" exclaimed Timothy and Silas simultaneously.

"That you will visit shortly. But for now, quickly: Tell me of the gathering in Thessalonica, young man. How is she? And Berea? Silas, how is Berea?"

"The believers in Berea are doing wonderfully. They send you their greetings and their love. "

"Has Blas . . . ?" Paul stopped his sentence, cleared his throat, and began again. "Have there been any visitors of note?"

"None whatsoever," replied Timothy quickly, "nor have we heard of any who might be coming."

"Come," said Aquila, sensing there was probably more to this innocent-sounding exchange than would appear. "Continue your words in my home. My wife will prepare a meal for you all."

"Timothy," said Paul, "you are about to meet another Lydia, only more so."

"There are *two* such women in the empire?" laughed Timothy.

A few minutes later the three men entered the home of Priscilla. Silas was about to continue telling Paul the events of the last few months when Priscilla appeared. Before Paul could say anything, Priscilla spoke.

"Welcome! So you are Silas and Timothy. You will be staying in my home. But, oh! I must warn you, I charge much, much money!" Priscilla threw her arms out expansively. "Perhaps more money than you can ever afford. Perhaps more than a king can afford." With that, as quickly as she had appeared, Priscilla then disappeared.

Paul pressed his fist to his forehead. "You thought that Lydia was . . ." The sentence was never ended.

Timothy and Silas were convulsing with laughter. "Once more Paul has met his peer."

"More than my peer. Much more! Actually, when you get to know her," said Paul, soberly, "you will find her to be one of the dearest people you have ever known. And one of the most informed people I have ever met." A moment later, Priscilla reentered.

"I have some water here. I will bring some food shortly. You must be Timothy, and you . . . Silas. Now, before I give you the water you must pay for it." Priscilla's eyes sparkled as she spoke. She then studied the water jar carefully and added, "Hmmm, five denarii. No, six, maybe more." She set the jar down carefully and went back into the kitchen.

"I have found that what they say about Roman women is true. Since making this discovery, I'm not so sure I want to go to Rome after all. The Roman women seem to be very familiar with Homer's description of the women of Amazon."

"Here is some fruit, but I'm sure you cannot possibly afford it," interrupted Priscilla. "Therefore, only stare at it. The water you can drink, but please leave the denarii beside the jar." Priscilla was obviously relishing her role. Once again she disappeared into the kitchen.

Like everyone else who has ever met Priscilla, the two brothers were completely charmed.

Once more Priscilla appeared, this time with a sumptuous meal. "I have changed my mind. *Paul* will pay for this meal and all else that follows. And your lodging too."

Both men laughed. Timothy immediately reached for the water while Silas exclaimed: "Wonderful, Paul—I expect the best room in the house!"

Sitting down, Priscilla turned to Timothy. "You, young man, will be staying in that room. Silas, you will be down the hall. It is a very good room which Paul is paying for." Her eyes narrowed. "Mention money to me even once and you will be sleeping in the fields. Breakfast is served an hour before dawn. You will be present, and you will eat. The noon meal is . . . my, my, *at noon*. The same time every day. You will be present. The evening meal is served just as the sun goes down. If you cannot be present at a meal you will let me know at least an hour beforehand. If not, Paul pays double." Priscilla paused, and then with her hand held forward like the paw of a cat, added, "Again, if you so much as mention money, you will be sentenced to attending the synagogue every Sabbath for the rest of your life!"

Timothy was enjoying the moment far too much.

"Timothy! One word out of you and I'll sell you in the market," reproached Paul. Timothy and Silas once more broke into raucous laughter, even as Paul's face turned crimson. His only retort was, "If you find that you can succeed in dealing with Lady Priscilla better than I, please try."

"*Lady* Priscilla?" asked Silas.

"Yes, she is in some way related to—I'm not sure, she will not explain it to me—one of the governing families of Rome.

"But do not be mistaken, this woman and her husband love the Lord with all their hearts. Furthermore, both are respected by the Jews in the community and much loved by the brothers and sisters in the gathering. In the beginning, the ecclesia met here in their home."

"There is a gathering here in Corinth?" asked Silas in wonderment. "So quickly?"

"Yes, but that story can wait. Right now I must hear from you. Brothers, there is much I wish to hear."

The three men moved to Paul's room and began a conversation that would last through much of the night.

Paul turned first to Timothy. "What is going on in Thessalonica?"

"Paul, do not misunderstand my first words. There is good news. Nonetheless, the church is undergoing fierce persecution. The city seems to have taken it as their occupation to make it difficult for the brothers and sisters there. But hear me, you have never seen a people who care so little about their problems. As you taught them, they are rejoicing in *everything*. They love to sit in the meetings and tell stories of what bad things happened to them during the day. Even as one shares, others break in and tell their own stories. In it all, everything is accompanied by laughter. Then they pause and rejoice. There is more!"

"For good or for evil?" asked Paul anxiously.

"Well, it is all good, except for a little that is *immature.*"

"Wait. What about Berea?"

"Berea is fine," Silas responded. "And Berea has been a great strength and encouragement to Thessalonica."

"Truly?" exclaimed a surprised Paul, his voice choking as he spoke. "Bereans have visited the Thessalonians?"

"Yes, the entire Berean assembly travels over to Thessalonica frequently. There have been two heathen holidays since you left Berea, and virtually the entire body of believers walked all the way to Thessalonica just to spend a day and night with them."

Paul began to weep.

Timothy flung one hand in the air with obvious excitement. "That is not all! Silas, tell Paul, but I don't think he'll believe it."

"Well, Paul, remember that you asked me to write to the saints in Philippi? We did just that. We told them about the grim situation in Thessalonica, that the church was young and had not received much help but had received much persecution. (As though the church in Philippi were not young!) I don't know how they managed it, but virtually every brother and sister in Philippi made the journey all the way down to Thessalonica. It was during one of those same holidays. For one glorious moment in Thessalonica there were brothers and sisters from Berea and Philippi meeting with the believers in Thessalonica. The Bereans were ecstatic. The Philippians were elated. The Thessalonians were overwhelmed. It was a flood of joy for everyone."

Paul's face lit up with a joy that neither man had seen in a long time. "The assemblies have cared for one another," said Paul, struggling with every word.

"Yes, they have cared for one another gloriously," answered Silas.

Paul continued to cry. For several minutes Timothy and Silas sat smiling as Paul shed tears of joy and relief. It was as though in one moment all his fears had vanished.

"Paul," whispered Timothy after a few minutes. "If you'll stop crying for a minute, I'll tell you some more good news."

Paul began to laugh and cry at the same time. "More!?" He tried to regain his composure but managed it poorly.

"I'll tell you the story even if you don't stop crying. Luke returned home to Antioch, as you know. But before he left Philippi he wrote a letter to Antioch telling them all that he had heard the Thessalonica story. By the time Luke arrived back in Antioch, the gathering there had decided to send some brothers and sisters all the way to Thessalonica. In turn, Antioch also wrote to the four churches in Galatia asking if any there would like to accompany the Antioch believers to Philippi and Thessalonica."

Paul broke down completely. He reached over and hugged Silas, then Timothy, and then raised his hands toward heaven. But he still could not speak. Crying was his only avenue of expression.

Timothy continued, "Brothers and sisters from all four of the churches in Galatia decided to send Gaius and a few others to Greece. The saints from Antioch joined—at a designated place—the believers in Galatia, and together representatives from five churches journeyed to Greece. They went first to Philippi, then Thessalonica. That gathering is taking place *right now.*"

Paul forced himself to ask questions, making sure his ears had heard correctly. "You mean Gaius of Derbe and others from Galatia have met Antioch believers . . . and have gone all the way to Thessalonica, *Greece.*"

"Gaius and company left Galatia, joined the Antioch believers, then sailed to Philippi. They had a wonderful time together, we are told. Then they trekked together to Thessalonica. Gaius will return home and visit all four of the churches in Galatia, giving them a report of his trip. All of Galatia knows about Thessalonica. Soon Galatia will be rejoicing about those unstoppable Thessalonians."

Silas inserted, "I have a letter here from Gaius. He wrote it just as we left to come here. He tells you in his letter what he is going to report when he gets back home and speaks to the four Galatian churches.

"Paul, when you visit Galatia again, you won't need to tell them anything about Thessalonica. By the time Gaius finishes reporting, all the believers in Galatia will probably feel they have been there."

Paul was trying hard to grasp everything he was hearing and to regain his composure.

"Philippi? They visited another assembly, and they have been visited by other assemblies? The Gentile churches in Galatia visiting Greece? And Antioch?

"Is not the Phillipian church going through difficult times?"

"The city seems now to have a very good attitude toward the ecclesia. After all, a lot of people were healed, a demon was cast out. Luke built a strong foundation of goodwill with the city by means of his medicine. And remember, that earthquake changed a large number of opinions about you. Philippian believers are not experiencing persecution of any sort.

"Paul, you told Luke that if anyone came to Philippi to be sure to invite them to speak. You meant Blastinius. One of the last things Luke told the ecclesia was that if anyone came to

Philippi, do not prevent them from speaking in a meeting. Well, I'm sure that the *holy ones* in Philippi had no idea what Luke meant, but with the coming of brothers and sisters from Antioch and Galatia, you can be sure that they think it is absolutely wonderful to have visitors from other places."

Paul moaned. "Blastinius will be received as a king." Recovering quickly, he urged Timothy, "Now, tell me more about Thessalonica."

"Well, there's no question that the city has decided to turn its wrath against the *holy ones.*"

"What is it you mentioned about *immaturity?*"

Timothy twisted his face as one searching for words. "Well, let's just say that one of the young brothers did something a little less than wise. It has to do with something you said in one of the last meetings you spoke in before you departed. Do you remember, someone in the meeting asked you what you thought of Claudius?'"

Paul thought for a moment and then frowned. "Oh no! Not *that* meeting."

"*I* wasn't there," said Timothy, "so I don't know what you said. But this I know: That young brother was in the marketplace a few weeks ago and became embroiled in an argument with some of the people in the agora. He made some very rash statements against Claudius. I think his comments reflected your views, Paul.

"Anyway, the law enforcers arrested him, but because of his youth and his obvious immaturity they let him go. Nonetheless, his words were quoted all over the city, which in turn set off a commotion. As a result some brothers lost their jobs. Now, if one of the brothers is known to be a believer in the marketplace, he probably doesn't get hired. The incident has hurt badly. There have been tears, but the brothers are resilient. With them it always ends in rejoicing."

Paul shook his head. "I only answered a question someone asked. A young brother took it to the marketplace, and now a church and a city are in turmoil. Oh!"

For Paul's sake Timothy changed the subject. "Speaking of questions, I have a letter here from the brothers and sisters in Thessalonica. As Greeks are prone to do, they have asked some questions. Most of the questions have to do with the resurrection."

"The what? The Resurrection?"

"Yes. Not the Lord's Resurrection, or his enthronement. They want to know about their own physical resurrection, what it will be like when the Lord returns and the dead are raised. You remember the old gentleman whom you and Silas were praying for when the rioters came to Jason's house? A few weeks ago he fell asleep in the Lord. So, also, has an elderly woman. These two deaths have brought about a number of questions that have to do with the resurrection."

Paul was thoughtful. "I see. And why not? It is true, I didn't speak much about the resurrection, did I? I don't recall saying anything about what happens to the dead in Christ. Thessalonica has good reason to be asking these questions in the presence of the death of two holy ones."

Paul now eyed Timothy intently. "What else, young man?"

Timothy grinned.

"Despite what has happened, the bride of Christ in Thessalonica is doing well. She has been so encouraged by other believers, I doubt she could be doing much better. The only other thing the believers there need, Paul, are some encouraging words from you."

Now Paul had questions. He was especially desirous to know if that deep love the Thessalonians had for one another was continuing. Again and again he expressed his joy that the brothers and sisters in Philippi and Berea had sacrificed to make a journey to encourage the holy ones in Thessalonica.

"Yes, even faraway Galatia has heard of their faith and perseverance. More, Paul, not only Antioch, but all the gatherings in Syria and Cilicia have heard the Thessalonian story. *They*, in turn, have sent word even to the church in Jerusalem!"

As was his nature, Paul began to weep again.

Later, Timothy told Paul of another event in Thessalonica which, at the time, seemed insignificant.

"There is so much love and care in Thessalonica that if someone is out of a job, the others in the ecclesia make sure he is cared for. But it seems that there are one or two brothers who are having a really difficult time finding work . . . especially in the light of so much hospitality and so much free food. To put it another way, they seem to have a hard time getting to the marketplace at dawn to look for work. Jobs seem to just disappear in their presence."

Paul listened to Timothy's unspoken words. "It is odd, is it not," said Paul, "that when men come to the Lord, some become more diligent, and some less?"

"It is not a major concern," continued Timothy, "but sometimes Aristarchus, Secundus, and the other brothers become a little frustrated with their fellow unmarried brothers—the chronically unemployed!"

The discussion continued throughout the rest of the day. There were reminiscences, stories, laughter, and prayer. At one point, Paul grew very serious. "While I was in Thessalonica I said, again and again, 'Watch my life, do what I have done.' Have some forgotten that *I* worked for a living every day I was there? Have some forgotten that I was in the marketplace every morning before dawn, toiling with my hands? Earning my keep? Paying for every meal I ate?"

And so the conversation continued, covering every detail

any of the three could thing of. The three men did not seem to have noticed night had fallen until there was a knock at the door. It was Priscilla. She had prepared a lavish meal for the three men.

(Our sister Priscilla is a master of hospitality. Women from Rome are quite unlike women from anywhere else in the empire; they are considered equal to men, and, in every way, *they* consider themselves men's equal.) Priscilla joined the meeting, listened, and offered insight . . . insight that was *always* helpful. As it was that night and ever after until this very day, one is always impressed with this woman's intellect, her grasp of problems, her observations, and her responses, not to mention her devastating wit and charm.

That evening Priscilla told Timothy and Silas of her own encounter with Christ and how she and Aquila met and fell in love. When they asked questions about Rome, she seemed to know more about that city than you could expect *anyone* to know. (And no one ever mentioned paying for room or food. Priscilla, like Lydia, had won the day on that subject.)

After the meal ended, it was Silas's turn to report about Berea. "Everything is good. The brothers are discovering how to give direction to the church. They are very attentive to the needs of the wives and the single sisters. The women, in turn, guide the men with their insights and are quick to point out oversight or neglect. The sisterhood is strong. They are wholly involved."

Like Timothy, Silas also referred to Sopater. "Unique. Perhaps called to the Lord's work—time will tell. He loves the Lord and has great zeal to go with it." It was an observation about this young man that was not lost on Paul.

Paul ended the meeting with these words. "It is time to bring this long night to a close. Tomorrow I must write a letter to Thessalonica. I wish you to be with me when I do."

CHAPTER 26

The next day, Paul began by speaking about their hosts.

"I would like for Priscilla and Aquila to visit the churches in northern Greece, for neither has ever seen a Gentile church. Priscilla is especially anxious to gather with some brothers and sisters in something *besides* a synagogue. You will not know her long before you learn that she loathes Sabbaths in a synagogue."

"Obviously not a good Jew," responded Timothy expansively.

"Priscilla and Aquila inquired of me as to how I felt about their visiting the other churches. I have encouraged them to do so. And I also hope that someday Priscilla's dream of seeing the body of Christ assemble in Rome will find its fulfillment.

"Now before I begin to write, I have one last question: Did the brothers and sisters in Thessalonica or Berea help either one of you with your expenses?"

Timothy hesitated, then shook his head. Paul looked at Silas. "No?"

"Nothing," responded Silas. "But we had no needs. We are still drawing from the money that the dear ones in Philippi sent to us. As is always true of young chrches, Berea and Thessalonica simply haven't learned to think in those terms."

"Still, I sometimes wonder . . . ," added Paul.

"Paul, I think the fact that we work for a living prevents their thinking in those terms. It doesn't cross anyone's mind."

"I agree," said Paul. "On the other hand, it was not possible for you to work for a living in Thessalonica and Berea during the time you visited. You traveled there; you ministered there; then you traveled here. I don't suppose the emperor—or an archangel—paid your expenses, did they?

"Always work for a living when you are with a church for an extended time. But ideally, when traveling to and from an assembly—or with any travel—the churches should care. And even more so when you are entering a new city to raise up the church. Then should the other churches be quick to help you."

"Please don't mention this in the letter," protested Timothy. "For all the world, they will think we asked you to do so."

"Then I will cloak the subject in such an obscure way that neither they nor you will know what I have said," chuckled Paul.

"Now, tell me, Timothy, how serious is it about these brothers who are not earning their own bread?"

"Not serious, but it does look like it is growing into a consistent pattern for one or two."

"Then I shall say only a few words about a small problem. I will but remind them of my example. I would to God that the ecclesia would watch my life—and then remember. I am loath to give anyone commands.

"And now, it is time to write. We need an *amanuensis*. Timothy, would you please fill this job? An amanuensis is expensive; you are not."

"This is your reason for not hiring a professional—that you get me free of charge?" teased Timothy.

"Well, we can hire an amanuensis, if you wish. But why? You can read, and you can write—something Silas and I could once do but can do no more! I remind you, there is hardly a man in the empire who, having reached the age of forty, has eyesight good enough that he can still read." Paul cleared his throat. "Silas and I are both well past forty . . . or haven't you noticed? You, on the other hand, can still see even very small words as is needed in writing a letter. But if you wish . . ."

"I am willing," responded Timothy.

"Good! Now, first of all, I want the brothers and sisters to know how encouraged I am by your report and how proud of them I am. I also want them to know how grateful I am that their love for one another has continued through this long trial. Let us begin."

Paul paused for a moment.

Timothy unrolled a parchment, then picked up his pen. The apostle's first words were, "This letter is from Paul, Silas, and Timothy . . ."

Timothy looked up. "Why are you putting my name in here?"

"Because you have played a role in the life of the Thessalonian believers!"

"This is embarrassing," said Timothy.

Ignoring Timothy's protestation, Paul repeated himself, and so began Paul's first letter to the church in Thessalonica. It was only the second letter he had ever addressed to an entire body of believers (the letter to Galatia was the first).

This letter is from Paul, Silas, and Timothy.

It is written to the church in Thessalonica, you who belong to God the Father and the Lord Jesus Christ.

May his grace and peace be yours.

We always thank God for all of you and pray for you constantly. As we talk to our God and Father about you, we think of your faithful work, your loving deeds, and your continual anticipation of the return of our Lord Jesus Christ. We know that God loves you, dear brothers and sisters, and that he chose you to be his own people. For when we brought you the Good News, it was not only with words but also with power, for the Holy Spirit gave you full assurance that what we said was true. And you know that the way we lived among you was further proof of the truth of our message. So you received the message with joy from the Holy Spirit in spite of the severe suffering it brought you. In this way, you imitated both us and the Lord.

Paul raised his hand. "Just a moment.

"It is remarkable to me that brothers and sisters from other parts of Greece—both Macedonia and Achaia—have visited Thessalonica to encourage the ecclesia in Thessalonica, only to come away *receiving* far more encouragement than they gave. And Cilicia. Then Syria. Even Antioch. And now Jerusalem. All have been encouraged by the incredible Thessalonian story . . . an assembly in Christ only a few months old, standing up against persecution not unlike what a *seven-year-old* church in Jerusalem had once endured years ago."

Paul motioned again at Timothy.

As a result, you yourselves became an example to all the Christians in Greece. And now the word of the Lord is ringing out from you to people everywhere, even beyond Greece, for wherever we go we find people telling us about your faith in God. We don't need to tell them about it, for they themselves keep talking about the wonderful welcome you gave us and how you turned away from idols to serve the true and living God. And they speak of how you are looking forward to the coming of God's Son from heaven—Jesus, whom God raised from the dead. He is the one who has rescued us from the terrors of the coming judgment.

Once more Paul signaled to Timothy that he wanted to stop for a moment.

"Paul," inserted Silas, "you may wish to tell them how much you have striven, trying to get back to Thessalonica."

"Yes," replied Paul. "But first I want to remind them . . . to stir up their memory of how *we* came there, what had happened to us before we arrived, how beautifully we were received, how they gave up their many Greek idols. Ah!"

Paul took a moment to reflect, then said, "And! And the manner of life we lived among them!"

You yourselves know, dear brothers and sisters, that our visit to you was not a failure. You know how badly we had been treated at Philippi just before we came to you and how much we suffered there. Yet our God gave us the courage to declare his Good News to you boldly, even though we were surrounded by many who opposed us. So you can see that we were not preaching with any deceit or impure purposes or trickery.

For we speak as messengers who have been approved by God to be entrusted with the Good News. Our purpose is to please God, not people. He is the one who examines the motives of our hearts. Never once did we try to win you with flattery, as you very well know. And God is our witness that we were not just pretending to be your friends so you would give us money! As for praise, we have never asked for it from you or anyone else. As apostles of Christ we certainly had a right to make some demands of you, but we were as gentle among you as a mother feeding and caring for her own children. We loved you so much that we gave you not only God's Good News but our own lives, too.

Don't you remember, dear brothers and sisters, how hard we worked among you? Night and day we toiled to earn a living so that our expenses would not be a burden to anyone there as we preached God's Good News among you. You yourselves are our witnesses—and so is God—that we were pure and honest and faultless toward all of you believers. And you know that we treated each of you as a father treats his own children. We pleaded with you, encouraged you, and urged you to live your lives in a way that God would consider worthy. For he called you into his Kingdom to share his glory.

And we will never stop thanking God that when we preached his message to you, you didn't think of the words we spoke as being just our own. You accepted what we said as the very word of God—which, of course, it was. And this word continues to work in you who believe.

And then, dear brothers and sisters, you suffered persecution from your own countrymen. In this way, you imitated the believers in God's churches in Judea who, because of their belief in Christ Jesus, suffered from their own people, the Jews.

For some of the Jews had killed their own prophets, and some even killed the Lord Jesus. Now they have persecuted us and driven us out. They displease God and oppose everyone by trying to keep us from preaching the Good News to the Gentiles, for fear some might be saved. By doing this, they continue to pile up their sins. But the anger of God has caught up with them at last.

Dear brothers and sisters, after we were separated from you for a little while (though our hearts never left you), we tried very hard to come back because of our intense longing to see you again. We wanted very much to come, and I, Paul, tried again and again, but Satan prevented us. After all, what gives us hope and joy, and what is our proud reward and crown? It is you! Yes, you will bring us much joy as we stand together before our Lord Jesus when he comes back again. For you are our pride and joy.

Paul stopped dictating.

"Silas, I need to let Thessalonica know not only that I desired so passionately to return to visit them and strengthen them, but I also wish them to know what happened after I departed . . . I mean, why I sent Timothy from Athens back to Thessalonica. I want them to know what is in my heart.

"Truthfully, this is a little personal, so pay no attention to what I say next."

> Finally, when we could stand it no longer, we decided that I should stay alone in Athens, and we sent Timothy to visit you. He is our co-worker for God and our brother in proclaiming the Good News of Christ. We sent him to strengthen you, to encourage you in your faith, and to keep you from becoming disturbed by the troubles you were going through. But, of course, you know that such troubles are going to happen to us Christians. Even while we were with you, we warned you that troubles would soon come—and they did, as you well know.
>
> That is why, when I could bear it no longer, I sent Timothy to find out whether your faith was still strong. I was afraid that the Tempter had gotten the best of you and that all our work had been useless.

Paul's eyes filled with tears. "Timothy, never have I been more encouraged in all my life as a follower of Christ than I am in all you told me." And Thessalonica stood! The church had survived . . . against all circumstances. Paul motioned to Timothy to write again.

> Now Timothy has just returned, bringing the good news that your faith and love are as strong as ever. He reports that you remember our visit with joy and that you want to see us just as much as we want to see you. So we have been greatly comforted, dear brothers and sisters, in all of our own crushing

troubles and suffering, because you have remained strong in your faith. It gives us new life, knowing you remain strong in the Lord.

How we thank God for you! Because of you we have great joy in the presence of God. Night and day we pray earnestly for you, asking God to let us see you again to fill up anything that may still be missing in your faith.

"I think I will close," said Paul with a sigh.

May God himself, our Father, and our Lord Jesus make it possible for us to come to you very soon. And may the Lord make your love grow and overflow to each other and to everyone else, just as our love overflows toward you. As a result, Christ will make your hearts strong, blameless, and holy when you stand before God our Father on that day when our Lord Jesus comes with all those who belong to him.

"Let us end here, brothers. At least for today. I may add more, but that is all we will say today.

"Oh! The resurrection! I must answer those questions. But let us come back to that after a night's sleep."

Early the next day, Paul woke Timothy and dictated the final words of his first epistle to the church in Thessalonica.

"I need to say something I must always say to Greeks." Paul reflected on his words, then smiled. "The Jews need these words too, but they would never admit it!"

"I am both," said Timothy a bit sheepishly. "Say on."

Finally, dear brothers and sisters, we urge you in the name of the Lord Jesus to live in a way that pleases God, as we have taught you. You are doing this already, and we encourage you to do so more and more. For you remember what we taught you in the name of the Lord Jesus. God wants you to be holy, so you should keep clear of all sexual sin. Then each of you will control your body and live in holiness and honor—not in lustful passion as the pagans do, in their ignorance of God and his ways.

Never cheat a Christian brother in this matter by taking his wife, for the Lord avenges all such sins, as we have solemnly warned you before. God has called us to be holy, not to live impure lives. Anyone who refuses to live by these rules is not disobeying human rules but is rejecting God, who gives his Holy Spirit to you.

"Ah, there is yet something else. Anyone who ever reads these words must know of the love these dear ones have for one another."

But I don't need to write to you about the Christian love that should be shown among God's people. For God himself has taught you to love one another. Indeed, your love is already strong toward all the Christians in all of Macedonia. Even so, dear brothers and sisters, we beg you to love them more and more. This should be your ambition: to live a quiet life, minding your own business and working with your hands, just as we commanded you before. As a result, people who are not Christians will respect the way you live, and you will not need to depend on others to meet your financial needs.

"Paul, you told me to remind you about the question sent to you by the Thessalonian assembly."

"Oh yes. The questions about the resurrection. Let me see the list. No! Read it to me." Paul listened to Timothy reread the questions. Paul then continued:

And now, brothers and sisters, I want you to know what will happen to the Christians who have died so you will not be full of sorrow like people who have no hope. For since we believe that Jesus died and was raised to life again, we also believe that when Jesus comes, God will bring back with Jesus all the Christians who have died.

I can tell you this directly from the Lord: We who are still living when the Lord returns will not rise to meet him ahead of those who are in their graves. For the Lord himself will come down from heaven with a commanding shout, with the call of the archangel, and with the trumpet call of God. First, all the Christians who have died will rise from their graves. Then, together with them, we who are still alive and remain on the earth will be caught up in the clouds to meet the Lord in the air and remain with him forever. So comfort and encourage each other with these words.

I really don't need to write to you about how and when all this will happen, dear brothers and sisters. For you know quite well that the day of the Lord will come unexpectedly, like a thief in the night. When people are saying, "All is well; everything is peaceful and secure," then disaster will fall upon them as suddenly as a woman's birth pains begin when her child is about to be born. And there will be no escape.

But you aren't in the dark about these things, dear brothers and sisters, and you won't be surprised when the day of the Lord comes like a thief. For you are all children of the light and of the day; we don't belong to darkness and night. So be on your guard, not asleep like the others. Stay alert and be sober. Night is the time for sleep and the time when people get drunk. But let us who live in the light think clearly, protected by the body armor of faith and love, and wearing as our helmet the confidence of our salvation. For God decided to save us through our Lord Jesus Christ, not to pour out his anger on us. He died for us so that we can live with him forever, whether we are dead or alive at the time of his return. So encourage each other and build each other up, just as you are already doing.

"Another word!" exclaimed Paul. "I must speak to the holy ones about caring for your needs. . . . See for yourself if it sounds *obvious!*" Paul laughed, then continued.

Dear brothers and sisters, honor those who are your leaders in the Lord's work. They work hard among you and warn you against all that is wrong. Think highly of them and give them your wholehearted love because of their work.

For a few minutes the three men talked about other things that *might* be included in the letter. Most of what was discussed concerned conflicts we are all familiar with in the experience of living together in the ecclesia. With those thoughts in mind, Paul ended the letter with brief sentences covering so many things in so short a space. Having done that, Paul closed with a benediction.

And remember to live peaceably with each other.

Brothers and sisters, we urge you to warn those who are lazy. Encourage those who are timid. Take tender care of those who are weak. Be patient with everyone.

See that no one pays back evil for evil, but always try to do good to each other and to everyone else.

Always be joyful. Keep on praying. No matter what happens, always be thankful, for this is God's will for you who belong to Christ Jesus.

Do not stifle the Holy Spirit. Do not scoff at prophecies, but test everything that is said. Hold on to what is good. Keep away from every kind of evil.

Now may the God of peace make you holy in every way, and may your whole spirit and soul and body be kept blameless until that day when our Lord Jesus Christ comes again. God, who calls you, is faithful; he will do this.

Dear brothers and sisters, pray for us.

Greet all the brothers and sisters in Christian love.

"Paul, be sure it is understood that your letter is to be heard by everyone. Few can read. Some may never have heard a letter nor know what one is," said Timothy.

Paul raised one finger. "Ah! So true!"

I command you in the name of the Lord to read this letter to
all the brothers and sisters.

"Timothy, just before we send this off, read the letter to
Silas and me once more."

Paul listened carefully as Timothy read, then said, "Hand
me your pen, Timothy!"

Paul leaned forward as if to write and then paused for a moment. Tears filling his eyes, in a low, hoarse voice Paul whispered, "Grace, grace, grace . . . ," then wrote these words:

And may the grace of our Lord Jesus Christ be with all of you.

Paul then gave Timothy the following instructions: "Let
the parchment dry until morning, then roll it tight. Wrap it in
leather and seal it in paraffin."

Paul had finished his second epistle, his first to
Thessalonica.

"And now, Paul," said Silas, "you must tell us all the Lord
has been doing here in Corinth."

CHAPTER 27

The church is meeting in a home next door to the synagogue?" asked Timothy, his eyes dancing with unbelief.

"That's not all, dear young brother. The ruler of the synagogue has been immersed into Christ. I personally took Crispus out to the River Tibres and baptized him, along with Stephanas and his family."

"Who else have you baptized?" asked Silas.

"No one. That has fallen to Crispus and Stephanas. We first began meeting in the home of Priscilla and Aquila, but now we meet in the home of Justus. It is his home that is next door to the synagogue. We gather early every morning and evening. And, of course, every time there is a holiday we spend the day together."

Priscilla and Aquila had just walked in. Priscilla added, "Your brother Paul is quite lazy. He speaks before dawn, goes to the market to work with my husband, labors all day long, has brothers and sisters coming by to talk with him. At eleven o'clock, instead of going to rest like everyone else, he comes back to Justus's home and talks with whoever wishes to have some time with him."

"It's not quite like that," said Paul. "Priscilla makes sure that I eat at noon; nothing changes that."

Priscilla continued. "At four o'clock, he is back in the market until the sun goes down. Some days he leaves his tentmaking and preaches in the marketplace. After the market closes at sundown he is at the gathering in Justus's home."

Then came this curious question from Silas. "Every church in every city is unique. Every one of them has a different personality. What is unique about the ecclesia in Corinth?"

Paul threw his hands up.

"Talk! Questions! More questions. They are loud: they talk loud; they sing louder. Louder than anyone I've ever met. They are the noisiest people I have ever known.

"You know I enjoy being interrupted when I am speaking; I have always encouraged this. But in Corinth, encouragement is not needed. You have walked through the city of Corinth: It is wild. There is a mixture of absolutely everything. A little of that is reflected in the meetings."

"Now tell us, Paul, what you think about these boisterous meetings?" asked Priscilla mischievously.

Paul had been found out by her question. "I *love* it!" he said. "The quality of the meetings needs to be lifted. That will come with time, I trust. But yes, I have to confess, I enjoy these rowdy people.

"Timothy, they not only sing loudly, they sing beautifully. They learn a song faster than one can ever hope to imagine. The songs they have written are also beautiful. The Corinthians are lighthearted. It is somewhat difficult to present the mysteries of Christ in such an atmosphere, but I would not change this innate expression of the church for anything."

I, Titus, have been in the meetings in Corinth. I have also been in other meetings in other cities throughout the empire. What Paul said about each church being different in personality was one of the joys of his life. He boasted in the variety that was in the churches. Unlike the synagogues, whose ritual each morning was so predictable, the churches' ways of meeting are unpredictable.

"Does Paul do here in Corinth what he did in Lystra?" asked Timothy.

"What is that?" asked Aquila.

"He will talk with the brothers and sisters for days about a meeting, telling them ways to encourage and ways to bring Christ to the gathering; then he announces a meeting in which they are to try to do what he suggests."

"Yes," said Priscilla. "And sometimes what we try to do is wonderful, sometimes it is terrible! But we love it. And that Paul leaves us to try on our own means a lot to us.

"Paul trusts God's people," said Priscilla thoughtfully, "and as a result God's people trust him."

"Then let me tell you something else about Paul," said Timothy. "He takes a young man, not yet twenty-five years old, and sends him out on a perilous mission to help a church that is in great danger and in great need and is being persecuted. And he expects that young man to have enough sense to know what he is doing. The young man, in turn, feels that he has been thrown to the wolves."

Paul's brow furrowed. "I have no idea what you are speaking of, Timothy, but I will tell you this. No man grows in the Lord nor in his capacity to serve the Lord unless he is pressed beyond his measure."

Paul then turned to Silas. "There will be a meeting tonight. Everyone is expecting to hear from you. There will be another meeting tomorrow evening, and Timothy will speak."

He then added, "I may not come to the meetings."

"Why?" asked Aquila, though he was fairly sure of the reason.

"If I were as young as Timothy and I were going to speak, and there was an old man there who was my father in the Lord

. . . that would make me very nervous and very self-conscious. With that thought in mind, I may not come to the meeting, or I may come late."

That night, Silas and Timothy were privileged to see what the church in Corinth was like when there was a meeting. That is a story in itself.

CHAPTER 28

They sang louder than anyone I ever heard," Timothy later reported.

"Their prayers were exuberant. One after another stood to share a word. Mostly they spoke about Jesus Christ or about something that had happened to them that day. This sharing was interspersed with songs and prayer. Toward the end of the meeting it was predominantly one person after another speaking. The imprint of Paul's ministry was reflected in their words. That is, they centered not on themselves, their problems, or their needs. They centered on the Lord.

"In all my life—before or since—never have I been in a meeting with so many different cultures present and people with so many different ways of expressing themselves. No language predominates in Corinth. There are at least four predominant languages used in the meetings. This doesn't slow anyone down, neither those who know several languages nor those who know only one."

At the beginning of the meeting, the brothers and sisters all gathered around Silas and Timothy, sang to them, then prayed for them. When everyone sat down the air was filled with questions.

At the end of the meeting everyone learned that the next meeting would be in a rented banquet hall. This way everyone in the ecclesia could hear Silas at one time, and Timothy the next night.

Paul came into that first meeting late. His clothes were wet from perspiration. He was obviously tired from his day's labor. His fatigue seemed to disappear as he listened to Silas answer questions and watched the responses of the holy ones.

When the meeting ended, everyone seemed to just move out into the street, there to continue singing and holding on to one another.

Timothy walked home with Priscilla and Aquila, sharing his impressions on the way.

"Such an endless array of cultures in one room is something I have never seen before."

"It is because of the uniqueness of the city. The location of where people live helps you understand," answered Aquila. "You see, the west side of the city is Roman. Romans come to live here when they can no longer bear Rome. That is true even of slaves. And this is an odd thing about Corinth. When a slave is set free by his or her master in Rome, the ex-slave will almost invariably come to Corinth. The reason is to get out of the madness that is Rome and yet to continue to live in a Roman culture not too far from the capital city."

"On the other hand, on the east side of the city," said Priscilla, "everything is Oriental. Dress, language, culture—all come from the East. Their dress is different, their accents are different, and their outlook and way of doing things are completely different."

"And in the middle?" asked Timothy.

"In the middle are the native Greeks. Their way of doing things is different from that of the people who live on either the east or west side of the city."

Aquila added, "Well, when you all get into one room it is a colorful sight to see. Sometimes there is a clash between cultures. What is considered wrong for one has not even been thought of as right or wrong for another. But there has been nothing serious to come up in our fellowship, not yet. What predominates is a love and a care for one another."

"I have a question to ask you, Timothy," said Priscilla, quite seriously.

"The Lord spoke to Paul in a dream and told him that he had many people here. And yet, just about every week Paul comes into a meeting and says, 'I may not be with you very long—the day will come when I will have to leave—so I ask you to watch my life and pay attention to my words. Soon you will be left all on your own.'"

Timothy responded: "Paul has always been looking for a place where he could stay for a length of time, but the pattern indicates that after he has preached the gospel and raised up a people, he leaves not long after that. They are left on their own. Furthermore, Paul rejoices in the fact that he leaves a church. Paul is not, and never will be, one who stays in one place. And on that first occasion when he leaves a church, he never leaves anyone in charge. He calls for all the brothers to come together and, as best they can, to lead the church together. He says the same to the sisters. Out of the brotherhood and sisterhood have always emerged direction and a strong ecclesia. It has its problems, nor would I say that everyone carries an equal load. Some carry none at all, some carry very little, some carry a great deal. That is simply the way it is. Nonetheless, out of all the pain and misunderstanding, the brothers and sisters emerge as one, loving one another. What finally emerges is wonderful, and I cannot describe it. Each stone is different, but all fit some way together."

"It will be a wonder of wonders if such a thing happens in

Corinth. There are three very strong cultures in that room when we meet," Priscilla said soberly.

Timothy went on: "What it takes is Paul's leaving. That is a very dramatic time. The brothers and sisters in Derbe never knew persecution, yet Paul's departure from them did the same thing for them that it did for Lystra, where there was persecution. But it was Paul—not the church—that was persecuted.

"It is just as true of Philippi. Paul was beaten, but the church lived in peace with the city. I've never seen an assembly so knit together and so full of love for one another. Paul's leaving saw to that."

"Well, there is one thing I can say above all else," said Priscilla with a great deal of delight in her voice. "I do not have to sit in a religious building. I do not have to go to the synagogue anymore. I get to go into a meeting with my brothers and sisters; I get to hug them; I get to pray with them. I get to share and speak, and I have the privilege of listening to them speak. And while Paul is among us, I joy and delight in the way he lifts up Jesus Christ to all of us. These are the happiest days I have ever lived. I have found my home. That home is the ecclesia of Jesus Christ."

Priscilla, Aquila, and Timothy exchanged questions and stories for a long time. One peculiarity of the Corinthian ecclesia that Timothy asked about turned out later to be part of a crisis. "The women, I can tell by their features which ones are Oriental. I can really tell which ones are Roman. So the rest must be Greek. In the streets and in the assembly there is a great deal of difference in the women's clothes, the way they do their hair, and . . ."

"It really is marked, is it not?" agreed Priscilla. I'm amazed there has been no problem about . . ."

"There has been a little," interrupted Aquila. "Some of the

brothers from the East want to know why the women from Rome *never* cover their heads. It worries them."

"You see, Timothy," added Priscilla. "Roman women are men's equals in Rome. They are strong. I'm sure you have *never* noticed!"

Timothy smiled and said, "Never."

Priscilla continued: "As far as I can recall, I have never seen a Roman woman wearing anything on her head. And if she is wealthy, she changes the way she wears her hair every day, or every week.

"The Greeks differ. The unmarried young women wear nothing on their heads. That is their way of saying, 'I'm not married.' The women who wear something on their heads are saying, 'I am married.' Those who come from the East *all* wear something on their heads. Watch when you are in different parts of the city. In the western part of the city, we are all uncovered. In the eastern part of the city, all wear something on their heads. In the middle, a mix! That is Corinth. And all that is the church."

"This is one peculiar church!" replied Timothy.

"Tomorrow we will all meet in a banquet hall. Everyone in the ecclesia will be there. Watch the colorful difference!"

"I look forward to it. But I think I'd better explain all this to Silas before he speaks."

CHAPTER 29

The next night Silas ministered to the Corinthian body. It was a colorful sight to see. Orientals of every sort, Greeks, Italians, and even a few Germanic barbarians and Egyptians were present. Silas spoke of many things and answered many questions, but it was his stories about the persecution and suffering of the church in Jerusalem that enthralled the Corinthians.

The next night Timothy spoke. Here was the young firebrand telling the Corinthians his stories of Galatia and all that the four churches there had passed through. (Timothy, as always, was spectacular. The Greeks especially loved to hear him speak.)

When he finished, Timothy was showered with questions from the brothers and sisters. This time they wanted to know everything about the events in Philippi and the persecution in Thessalonica.

"Let's go visit them" was an oft-heard statement. As is true in all the assemblies, there is always a desire to meet other brothers and sisters in other churches. And to know that there were three sister churches so close in northern Greece made everyone want to meet them.

Hearing about these other ecclesiae, and what had taken

place there, gave a new dimension to the church in Corinth. They learned, for instance, that the brothers and sisters in Jerusalem often went arm in arm through the streets of the city, singing. That very night the Corinthians went out into their street doing the same thing, but the *way* they did it was totally different. They were *loud*.

Silas's stories about Jerusalem and about the Twelve—especially Peter—made everyone long to meet Simon Peter. The incredible influx of Jews into Corinth meant there were more Hebrews in the church in Corinth than in any other church that Paul had ever planted. Whenever the Jews heard of Peter working miracles in Jerusalem their eyes lit up. These Hebrews immediately saw Peter, whom they had never met, as their hero. (One day that fact would cause a great deal of pain in the Corinthian church, helping to push the church to the brink of destruction.)

The Greeks, on the other hand, loved Timothy for his fledgling oratorical skills.

In private, Timothy was quiet, almost shy, but when he spoke, he thundered. He had the heart of a Greek. (It can be added that Paul never ceased to be surprised at how much that young man knew, how wise he could be, and how well he could speak.)

In all this it must be confessed that Paul was not a great speaker. Oh, there were times when he spoke with much power and much glory. At those times he had no equal. Nonetheless, though miracles were performed by Paul's hands in Corinth . . . they were *not quite* up to Peter's reputation. And his speaking ranked behind even Timothy. This, too, would be one of the ingredients which later almost destroyed the Corinthian body. There were problems of no small dimension brewing in Corinth.

CHAPTER 30

Timothy and Silas were not long in the city before they saw, firsthand, how quickly the assembly in Corinth was growing. Justus's house, though large, was inadequate. To remedy this problem Justus consented to having a wall within his house torn out to make room for more people.

Although Paul was having a wonderful time beholding God's favor upon Corinth, still he carried a burden for the holy ones who gathered in Thessalonica, for the assembly there was still under constant persecution from the citizens of that city.

In the days that followed, Paul became increasingly anxious to know how the ecclesia in Thessalonica was doing and how his letter was received. It was inevitable that Paul would ask either Silas or Timothy to return there. To Timothy's surprise, Paul again chose him.

"It has been nine months since the gathering in Thessalonica was born. It has been several weeks now since they received my letter. I ask you to visit them and return to me with a report. One thing I wish to know above all else: What is the effect upon them of the city's constant rejection? And, of course, how was my letter received?"

"I thought you were going to ask Silas," replied Timothy mournfully.

But Silas immediately agreed with Paul. "Timothy, it is proper that you go."

"Me! Are you sure? Will they listen to a twenty-five-year-old?"

"Are you refusing to go?" asked Silas, pretending a droll sobriety.

Timothy shut his eyes, then responded, "Paul, what if I fail?"

"Does that mean you are refusing?" asked Paul mischievously.

Once more, Timothy closed his eyes, this time wrinkling his forehead. Then he let out a long groan.

"Tell me, Silas, was that a yes or a no?" asked Paul.

"I have no idea," responded Silas. "A noise like that doesn't give you much to go on."

"I'll go," said Timothy hesitantly.

"Good!"

"But you may be making a mistake, Paul of Tarsus. I am not taking any responsibility for the mess I am about to make."

Silas smiled. "Timothy, the saints in both Berea and Thessalonica esteem you highly. They will look forward to your coming. They will hear. They *may* even respond to you."

Timothy groaned again, then turned to Paul. "Your statement in that letter that Thessalonica was to esteem those whom the Lord had placed over them. I read that, but that wasn't talking about me; that was talking about Silas . . . and you!"

"Timothy, the brothers and sisters in Thessalonica are lovely people. Neither Silas nor I have ever uttered a negative or corrective word to them; yet, they have responded to my every suggestion, no matter how slight. This is their heart. They will do the same for you."

That evening, still unsure of himself, Timothy packed a few belongings. "At least the bags I carry will be light." The next morning before dawn the brothers and sisters in Corinth gathered around Timothy in Priscilla's home, all laying hands on him, praying for him, and sending him out. That is, Timothy was sent to Thessalonica by the church in Corinth. That church sent him with complete trust and confidence.

(I, Titus, add that *that* is the only way any man should ever go—sent by the church, without reservation.)

Several unmarried brothers walked along with Timothy to the port of Cenchrea, where Timothy boarded a ship bound for Thessalonica. The brothers went on board with him, helped him find a place amid the cargo on deck, then sat down with him for a few moments of singing and prayer before sailing. (Timothy walked the entire five miles without carrying his bags. He made *sure* that was done by the other single brothers. When asked why he did this, Timothy answered, "Everyone deserves the privilege of carrying the baggage!")

Just before Timothy left Corinth, Paul had said some things to Timothy that he did not quite grasp at the time. It would be another year before he was to come to understand Paul's mysterious words.

"While you are in Thessalonica, send someone to Berea. Ask that Sopater come and be with you while you are in Thessalonica."

"Why? And why Sopater?"

"Never mind, just do it. Also, spend as much time with Aristarchus and Secundus as opportunity presents. Send all three of them my greetings."

Timothy was bewildered at Paul's words. Paul, on the other hand, knew full well what he was doing, though no one else on earth knew what had been planted in Paul's mind.

What were Timothy's thoughts when, all alone, his ship pulled out of the Cenchrea harbor?

"I felt like the only person in the world. I was scared, and I felt inadequate.

"The last thing I was thinking about as the ship was leaving was something Paul wrote in his first epistle to Thessalonica. 'Submit to those whom the Lord has placed over you.' Paul meant himself and Silas. In no way had the Lord placed me over the brothers and sisters in Thessalonica, and I *knew* it! I also thought they would be insane if they even thought about listening to me! Furthermore, that word *submit* bothered me greatly. I had no desire for anybody on earth to submit to me whatsoever, in any way, place, or form. All I wanted to do was to go there, observe the situation, say a few things about Jesus Christ, and return to Corinth as fast as possible."

Paul had asked Timothy to spend no more than two or three weeks in Thessalonica and then to return immediately to Corinth. Timothy wanted it to be two or three days.

Timothy never fully came to understand who he was. I think he lived his entire youth and part of his middle age never knowing. That is one of the beautiful things about him.

Timothy was received with all the enthusiasm Paul would have received. They flooded him with love, told him story after story, and hung on his every word. Timothy, in turn, did what he could to exhort and comfort, to suggest, and perhaps even to direct. The brothers and sisters in Thessalonica quickly responded. There were problems to be addressed. Some had the potential, it seemed to Timothy, of developing into crises. Timothy dealt with some; others he left for Paul to deal with.

His time with Secundus, Aristarchus, and Sopater was wonderful. Getting to know them caused Timothy to learn their hearts. Each man, in fear, dared to believe he had been called to the work. Timothy was surprised. *And how did Paul know this?* he wondered.

Sitting in the meetings and visiting in the homes, Timothy heard unbelievable stories. Many of the men were shunned in the marketplace when they went, each day, looking for work.

Some of the shops refused to sell food to the women. No slaves had been beaten, but several had been threatened. "Stop going to those gatherings or learn the whip," several owners had said. Children had been mocked by their former friends, taunted by words like *atheist* and *infidel*.

But the ecclesia had found ways to survive in closeness. Those who were not known to be believers brought food for those who were. The unemployed were invited into houses to live and eat. The well-to-do reached out to the hungry and gave work to those who found hiring in the marketplace closed to them. Not one soul had left the faith. Despite mockings, insults, yells, and curses, the Thessalonians gathered, shared their sorrows and deliverances, and rejoiced. Always, they rejoiced. *I have much to tell*, thought Timothy. *Not only to Paul, but to all the Gentile churches. It is a testimony to share for as long as I live. But there are problems. As in all the churches, always there are problems.*

Aristarchus and Secundus shared their frustrations about one such problem. Timothy listened. Sopater listened in wonder. "Nothing like that could *ever* happen in Berea. You Thessalonians are really a strange lot!" was his reaction. It was a small problem that had grown into a large one. Because there was so much opposition to the Thessalonian believers, many saw this as a sure sign the Lord was coming back at any moment. And because finding work was so difficult, free food and lodging were so plentiful, and Jesus was coming back any minute, many in the gathering found it "impossible to find a job." This was wearing on the church's natural hospitality.

"This, Paul will not like," said Timothy to his three friends.

At the end of three weeks, with much affection and tears, Timothy bade the holy ones good-bye and boarded a ship bound for Corinth. His feelings that day were mixed. He was now very glad he had come. He had done better than he had ever hoped. But he also dreaded telling Paul about some of the Thessalonian problems: one was the brothers who do not work; the other, the taunts a few believers had hurled back at those ridiculing them—the taunts including, still, some very unflattering remarks about the Emperor Claudius!

Upon disembarking at Cenchrea, Timothy made his way straight to the marketplace, where Paul and Aquila were making tents.

"Tell me what you can; say it quickly," said Paul as he saw Timothy approach.

"Paul, I believe we should go somewhere in private and talk," replied Timothy.

Paul's brow furrowed. "Is it bad?"

"I do not know. It may not be bad, but it surely is strange." Paul's worry turned to curiosity.

A few minutes later Paul and Timothy were sitting in Timothy's room in the home of Priscilla. Silas joined them shortly after.

"How are the holy ones?"

"They are fine, and they took joy in your letter. The church is still under persecution but is also holding up wonderfully. They are an incredible people. The city has not relented one bit, but they still rejoice."

"But . . . ?"

"Well, as I said, they appreciated your letter very much."

"But?"

Timothy looked more amused than he did worried. "Well, that letter . . . as I said, it was received very well. On the other hand, there were some unusual reactions to it."

"What kind of reactions?" asked Silas, imagining the worst.

"Blastinius?" said Paul.

"Absolutely not. They still know nothing of him."

"Then what is it?" asked Paul in exasperation.

Again, Timothy looked bemused. He took a deep breath and then spoke directly to Paul. "Paul, what on earth did you say about Claudius just a few nights before you were forced out of the city?"

"What do you mean?"

"I mean, you got onto the subject of Claudius and then talked about the Lord Jesus coming back again and about some of the signs that would indicate the Lord was coming back." It was Timothy's turn to be exasperated. "What *did* you say to them?"

Once more, Paul muttered the words he had spoken on a previous occasion, "I must remember to spend more time talking about the Lord's return and about the resurrection of the dead. It seems to be a subject I rarely remember to mention." And I must *never* talk about Claudius. Or, never speaking again might be wiser!"

"Well," said Timothy, "your letter made the resurrection clear, but I do recommend you give time to the Lord's return while you are in Corinth. The Thessalonians know only enough to be in a mess."

Silas interrupted: "Yes, Paul, just exactly what did you say that night in Thessalonica? Neither Timothy nor I were present when you talked about Claudius."

"Never you mind," said Paul pointedly. "Now, tell me what the problem is."

"Well . . . everyone heard your letter read. They became very excited about the Lord coming back. Almost everyone felt he would be back within the next two or three days. For that reason, a number of the brothers have stopped working.

"In fact, Paul, there are several brothers who get up very early in the morning and climb up on a hill just outside Thessalonica and wait for the Lord. They want to be the first ones caught up in the air." Timothy laughed nervously.

Paul did not know whether to laugh or to cry. Finally, shaking his head he said, "Shall I stop speaking, and shall I stop writing letters?"

"I'm glad you find this humorous," said Silas, "because humorous is exactly what it is. Part of the problem in Thessalonica comes from your letter, and part of it comes from that night you . . . what *did* you say about Claudius?"

"Is the whole church reacting this extremely?" continued Paul, ignoring Silas's good-humored taunt.

Timothy ran his fingers through his hair. "First, let me tell you a little bit more about those young brothers. Some have stopped working. It seems perfectly logical to them, so they don't even bother going into the marketplace to be hired. Further . . . they seem to have the gift of arriving at the home of other families—those who have the best cooks in all the assembly—just at suppertime. I am sure that is just a coincidence," said Timothy facetiously.

"Hmmm," said Silas. "Seems to me that these young men may very well be prophets."

Paul buried his face in his hands. Whether he was laughing, crying, or just upset was impossible to know.

"They listen to me too well!"

"Several of the unemployed have moved into the homes of brothers who do work. At first, their presence was well received, but I can tell you that right now some of the holy ones are getting quite impatient with those who are not working. Not only not working, but doing absolutely nothing."

"I wonder if there was not a lazy streak in them to begin with," mused Silas.

"As to the other brothers, I know of only one other person who has done something similar. He closed his business and is sitting at home waiting for the Lord to return."

"Ooohhhhhh, nooo!" moaned Paul.

"I visited this brother early one morning. I remember exactly what he said when he greeted me at the door: 'Perhaps today, Timothy. Perhaps even before breakfast.'"

Paul looked helpless. "Is there nothing more to tell me?" he asked. "Something a bit more sane?"

"Yes, Paul, the church is filled with faith. Faith in the Lord, faith in the gospel, faith in your ministry to the church, *and* faith that the Lord is coming . . . any minute now!"

"And did the brothers and sisters listen to you while there?" asked Silas.

Timothy looked a little embarrassed. "To my surprise, yes, they did. They held out to me the same respect given to both of you.

"Paul, there is a rumor. I am not sure how this rumor got started. The rumor is that there was another letter by you. According to the story, you wrote a letter saying you believe there is no resurrection."

Paul's eyes blazed.

"No resurrection? A letter!? From me? I am a Pharisee, not a Sadducee. Of course I believe in the resurrection. I *saw* the resurrected Lord!"

"Others have quoted you as saying the Lord has already returned."

"Well," said Paul dryly, "I would hope that if the Lord had returned, at least one of us would have noticed." He sighed. "I have never known of any man around whom swirl so many rumors as surround me."

"Could these be stories Blastinius has launched?" wondered Silas.

"I do not know," responded Timothy. "What I heard in Thessalonica was simply too vague."

Timothy leaned forward. "I will confess to you, Paul of Tarsus, what I am looking forward to: I am looking forward to your making some comment about that mysterious night when you talked to the Thessalonians about Claudius and the Lord's return."

"I join in that curiosity," said Silas.

Paul ignored his two friends.

"Tomorrow—not today—I will write the second time to Thessalonica. But I have a sense I must wait until tomorrow."

He could never have expected tomorrow to be so fateful a day.

CHAPTER 31

A large garrison of Roman soldiers entered Corinth the following morning. It was a typical Roman show of force used throughout the empire to quell any potential discontent with Roman presence.

With the garrison came letters from other parts of Macedonia and Achaia. Two of those letters were for Paul—one from Philippi, the other a freshly written letter from Thessalonica. The letters were in Paul's hands shortly after the garrison arrived.

The two letters were similar in news, but the letter from the Thessalonian church had a sense of gravity about it.

It seems a new batch of letters had come to the Thessalonian Jews, filled with attacks on the person of Paul. With these letters were also copies of letters from Jewish synagogues in Galatia. These letters had come originally from Jerusalem and had been sent not only to the synagogue leaders in Thessalonica but also to the Gentile magistrates.

Paul laid the letter aside. "Blastinius! Oh, it is you, yet again, Blastinius!"

After a few minutes of reflection, Paul called Silas and Timothy to his side. "I have received word from the brothers and sisters in Thessalonica. They are now under a new siege of persecution. Here. You may read for yourselves."

Timothy read the two letters out loud. As he did, his voice began to quiver, his young face grew ashen. Silas kept his eyes closed the entire time, but toward the end hot tears began to course down his face.

Timothy was the first to speak. "I do not know how you find the strength to endure this man, Paul."

Silas's words were not spoken so kindly. "This Blastinius has neither heart nor conscience. Sent from Satan, this one."

A moment later, Paul broke down completely. Those agonizing sobs, which Silas had witnessed some seven months before on that dramatic journey from Philippi to Thessalonica, had returned.

"Timothy, you and I must leave Paul alone. He has a matter to settle with his Lord."

Silas had spoken the perfect words. After they left the room, Paul fell on his face and began to cry out to God. At first he asked—as he had once before—to be delivered of Blastinius. But, as before, Paul heard the words of his Lord, speaking from deep in his spirit.

"Paul, you are a man too wise, too filled with revelation of me. You are a man too proud to carry so much light without that light destroying you. You are too strong. Blastinius is my handmaiden to make you utterly helpless and to leave you without hope of any earthly success. I shall not remove him from your life. Through him, I shall render you weak, hopelessly weak. You shall live and move and find your strength in my grace alone."

As it was on the road to Thessalonica, so it was that morning in Corinth. Paul crumbled before the will of the Lord and again yielded to this spiritual dagger that God had thrust into his side.

This marked the second time Paul had asked that Blastinius be removed from his life. (For Paul, there would be yet one more such encounter with his God concerning Blastinius. On that third occasion, as before, *the Lord* would win!)

Later that day, after much weeping, Paul called Silas and Timothy back into his room. Paul was now ready to write that second epistle to the Thessalonian church.

(As you read this letter, you will find the first few sentences to be words of greeting, followed by Paul's expression of his thankfulness to God for the dear ones in Thessalonica and their faithfulness in the face of persecution. After those opening words came the only two sentences Paul wrote in that letter that revealed anything of his feelings concerning Blastinius and those who had become instruments of destruction in Blastinius's hands. In the first epistle Paul ever wrote to a church—the Galatian letter—a large part of it dealt with the problem Blastinius and his company had created in Galatia. In Paul's third letter—which was his second epistle to the Thessalonian believers—-there were only two or three sentences that indicated Paul's feelings toward those who would destroy him and the church in Thessalonica. God was transforming Paul through suffering.)

"Timothy, do you have a scroll and pen?"

CHAPTER 32

Paul sat silent a long time. At last he spoke.

"What I keep hearing from the other churches is that they are rejoicing in the Thessalonians, and their faith is bolder because of them. The churches are growing stronger than ever before in their witness. Thessalonica needs to hear this."

This letter is from Paul, Silas, and Timothy.

It is written to the church in Thessalonica, you who belong to God our Father and the Lord Jesus Christ.

May God our Father and the Lord Jesus Christ give you grace and peace.

Dear brothers and sisters, we always thank God for you, as is right, for we are thankful that your faith is flourishing and you are all growing in love for each other. We proudly tell God's other churches about your endurance and faithfulness in all the persecutions and hardships you are suffering. But God will use this persecution to show his justice. For he will make you worthy of his Kingdom, for which you are suffering, and in his justice he will punish those who persecute you. And God will provide rest for you who are being persecuted and also for us when the Lord Jesus appears from heaven. He will come with his mighty angels, in flaming fire, bringing judgment on those who don't know God and on those who refuse to obey the Good News of our Lord Jesus. They will be punished with everlasting destruction, forever separated from the Lord and from his glorious power when he comes to receive glory and praise from his holy people. And you will be among those praising him on that day, for you believed what we testified about him.

And so we keep on praying for you, that our God will make you worthy of the life to which he called you. And we pray that God, by his power, will fulfill all your good intentions and faithful deeds. Then everyone will give honor to the name of our Lord Jesus because of you, and you will be honored along with him. This is all made possible because of the undeserved favor of our God and Lord, Jesus Christ.

Paul slipped his hand over his face. "In my first letter I broached the subject of the Lord's return. In this letter I must be careful to clarify their misunderstanding."

And now, brothers and sisters, let us tell you about the coming again of our Lord Jesus Christ and how we will be gathered together to meet him. Please don't be so easily shaken and troubled by those who say that the day of the Lord has already begun. Even if they claim to have had a vision, a revelation, or a letter supposedly from us, don't believe them.

Paul reviewed what he had said about Claudius—and other things—on that night when he talked to the ecclesia about some of the events of their day as being possible signs of the Lord's return. What he said in the letter were things he had said before, when he was with them. Much had to do with Claudius. But, alas, the rest of us will never fully understand what Paul was talking about. Paul wrote the above passage in very obscure language just in case a copy of the letter fell into the hands of Roman authorities.

In this passage, for instance, Paul refers to at least two people, perhaps three . . . yet, because Paul used "he," "him," "his," and "they" so often, it is not easy to understand with assurance what Paul is saying. So often, because he also used words with meanings vague to the rest of us, only the Thessalonians knew exactly what Paul was speaking of in this passage of the letter.

Don't be fooled by what they say.

For that day will not come until there is a great rebellion against God and the man of lawlessness is revealed—the one who brings destruction. He will exalt himself and defy every god there is and tear down every object of adoration and worship. He will position himself in the temple of God, claiming that he himself is God. Don't you remember that I told you this when I was with you? And you know what is holding him back, for he can be revealed only when his time comes.

For this lawlessness is already at work secretly, and it will remain secret until the one who is holding it back steps out of the way. Then the man of lawlessness will be revealed, whom the Lord Jesus will consume with the breath of his mouth and destroy by the splendor of his coming. This evil man will come to do the work of Satan with counterfeit power and signs and miracles. He will use every kind of wicked deception to fool those who are on their way to destruction because they refuse to believe the truth that would save them. So God will send great deception upon them, and they will believe all these lies. Then they will be condemned for not believing the truth and for enjoying the evil they do.

The next few words were to be Paul's closing words to Thessalonica. (However, the next morning Paul added more to the letter.)

As for us, we always thank God for you, dear brothers and sisters loved by the Lord. We are thankful that God chose you to be among the first to experience salvation, a salvation that came through the Spirit who makes you holy and by your belief in the truth. He called you to salvation when we told you the Good News; now you can share in the glory of our Lord Jesus Christ.

With all these things in mind, dear brothers and sisters, stand firm and keep a strong grip on everything we taught you both in person and by letter.

May our Lord Jesus Christ and God our Father, who loved us and in his special favor gave us everlasting comfort and good hope, comfort your hearts and give you strength in every good thing you do and say.

The next morning Paul called Timothy and Silas to his room.

"The ones who are not working? I assume that situation still exists. I have spoken in this letter about the Lord's return. This may cause even more Thessalonian believers to stop working and climb up that hill." There was a twinkle in Paul's eyes as he spoke.

"Come, Timothy, let us add a bit to this letter."

Finally, dear brothers and sisters, I ask you to pray for us. Pray first that the Lord's message will spread rapidly and be honored wherever it goes, just as when it came to you. Pray, too, that we will be saved from wicked and evil people, for not everyone believes in the Lord. But the Lord is faithful; he will make you strong and guard you from the evil one. And we are confident in the Lord that you are practicing the things we commanded you, and that you always will. May the Lord bring you into an ever deeper understanding of the love of God and the endurance that comes from Christ.

And now, dear brothers and sisters, we give you this command with the authority of our Lord Jesus Christ: Stay away from any Christian who lives in idleness and doesn't follow the tradition of hard work we gave you. For you know that you ought to follow our example. We were never lazy when we were with you. We never accepted food from anyone without paying for it. We worked hard day and night so that we would not be a burden to any of you. It wasn't that we didn't have the right to ask you to feed us, but we wanted to give you an example to follow. Even while we were with you, we gave you this rule: "Whoever does not work should not eat."

Yet we hear that some of you are living idle lives, refusing to work and wasting time meddling in other people's business. In the name of the Lord Jesus Christ, we appeal to such people—no, we command them: Settle down and get to work. Earn your own living. And I say to the rest of you, dear brothers and sisters, never get tired of doing good.

Take note of those who refuse to obey what we say in this letter. Stay away from them so they will be ashamed. Don't think of them as enemies, but speak to them as you would to a Christian who needs to be warned.

May the Lord of peace himself always give you his peace no matter what happens. The Lord be with you all.

When he finished, Paul made a request.

"Let me see the letter again.

"So! Someone may be writing letters and forging my name? Let us see if we might be able to resolve that problem."

Timothy handed Paul the pen. Paul squinted his eyes and then wrote words so large even *Paul* could read them.

Now here is my greeting, which I write with my own hand—PAUL. I do this at the end of all my letters to prove that they really are from me.

May the grace of our Lord Jesus Christ be with you all.

Paul handed the pen back to Timothy, who then carefully wrapped it in a cloth. Later he sealed the letter in paraffin and slipped it into a leather case.

The very next day the letter was on its way to Thessalonica.

(I, Titus, would have you know that Paul did not write another epistle to a church for *six* years. That epistle Paul would write, ironically, to the brothers and sisters in *Corinth*, the very city he was in when he wrote the two letters to Thessalonica.)

Paul had passed through two crises concerning Blastinius (there would be a third), but his next crisis would be a riot.

CHAPTER 33

In Corinth? Paul in Corinth? I could never imagine he had traveled so far." It was hard enough to believe Paul had traveled as far as Philippi and Thessalonica. But Corinth? "He doesn't know it, but he will have a visitor one day."

It was what Blastinius needed—Paul's whereabouts! He would do all in his considerable power to stop any success of Paul's in Greece. In a few days Blastinius was clear what he would do.

Remember that no one in Corinth knew of Blastinius. Therefore, when he struck, no one was aware that he was behind the ensuing uproar. The city was wide open to his influence.

The first thing Blastinius did was to write a letter to the synagogue in Corinth. The letter was very detailed, telling the leaders there everything he knew about Paul in the worst possible light, as was Blastinius's way. In the letter, he recounted how Paul had persecuted Hebrews in Jerusalem and how he had been beaten in a synagogue in Cyprus. Paul's conduct had brought him a whipping in Pisidia, and Paul was thrown out of Iconium. The citizens in Lystra had justifiably stoned Paul. All was reported in a way that made Paul look like an outcast, a man hated by everyone because of his terrible ways. He came across looking like a man not far from mad.

Blastinius went on to tell of Paul's being whipped and jailed in Philippi and banished from Thessalonica. (All this *had* happened, but never in the way Blastinius told it.) The well-crafted letter implied that Paul hated the Jews, that he despised Moses and all the 613 laws of Moses, and that he was out to overthrow Caesar. Anyone reading that letter would have been terrified of Paul.

Blastinius urged the Jewish elders in Corinth to do everything possible to have Paul expelled from Corinth. Nor did Blastinius end there. He then explained to the Jewish leaders exactly how they could rid their city of Paul. He recommended that they go to the city authorities and reveal to them what kind of man Paul was.

"Tell them Paul is seeking to overthrow both Israel and the Roman Empire."

While Blastinius was at his work, the Emperor Claudius had just appointed Gallio (the brother of the very famous Roman philosopher Annaeus Seneca, who was at the time the tutor of a young lad named Nero) as governor of southern Greece.

When Gallio arrived in Corinth to take over governorship of southern Greece, he came with a reputation of being a very pleasant person and a man of great character. Gallio was much respected and loved in Rome, to the point that two books had been dedicated to him, *De Ira* and *De Vita Beata*.

The Jews in the synagogue, now made aware of the threat Paul posed to them, saw the arrival of Gallio as the most propitious time to use Blastinius's letter to launch their attack on Paul. They chose a man named Sosthenes to be their spokesman before the city magistrates.

Their petition to appear before Gallio was soon granted. In their appearance before him, the Jewish leaders of the synagogue presented themselves as men who were outraged and terrified citizens. They meticulously presented their case to Gallio: "A terrible person now resides in Corinth." Unknown to these men, Paul had become a friend to some of the city leaders. This fair state had come about both by the healing of the sick and by the good reputation of the ecclesia, which some of the city's leaders themselves had visited. Despite these unbelieving Jews' best efforts, and despite the success this approach had produced in other cities, it failed in Corinth.

Gallio listened for a while, then interrupted. "Listen to me, Hebrews. If what you are telling me had something to do with an injury, or if it were a true crime, I would find it reasonable to listen to what you are saying. But what you are speaking of has to do with your own beliefs, about your law and your religion. I wish to hear no more from you. Go settle this matter yourself. I refuse to be involved; I will *not* pass judgment in this matter."

Because Gallio was new in the city, the magistrates and city fathers were listening very carefully as to how Gallio would handle this case. They were struck by his boldness and his insight; therefore they were delighted not only with his decision but with the man himself.

When Gallio concluded his remarks, the magistrates ordered the Hebrews out of the court.

Outside a crowd had gathered, watching the proceedings so as to get an impression of their new ruler. As soon as the Jews stepped outside, some of the onlookers grabbed them and began beating them. Sosthenes took the worst of it. The magistrates in the courtroom had a clear view of what was happening but nonetheless turned and walked out of the courtroom.

This was the first time in Paul's life that the governments of this world did not abuse him when he had been accused. And for the first time, the synagogue had lost.

Nonetheless, from that day Paul knew that his time in Corinth was short. He began his preparation for leaving the ecclesia on its own.

One evening Paul called for a meeting of all the church. Timothy and many others noted the urgency in Paul's words.

"When I leave, and leave I must, Silas and Timothy will be going with me. You will be on your own. The ecclesia here will be wholly in the hands of you, the brothers and sisters gathering in Corinth."

Until that time Paul had spoken to no one about what he planned to do upon leaving Corinth, but rather he had kept his own counsel. But it was at this time Paul began to take action toward carrying out something he had been planning for years (something he had never told anyone).

I, Titus, tell you this: What Paul planned was the most exciting thing ever to happen in my own life . . . *and* in Timothy's!

An air of mystery began to arise. "What is it that Paul is planning to do?"

CHAPTER 34

"It is time. I must depart Corinth," Paul told the assembly. "I will travel from here to Jerusalem, stopping at several places along the way. From Jerusalem I will turn north to home, to Antioch. Beyond that, my plans are not quite completed to the point I can share them with you."

Among those who heard Paul make this comment were Priscilla, Aquila, Timothy, and Silas, as well as Crispus, Stephanas, and a brokenhearted Gaius.

"I will also begin letting my hair grow. When it has grown out sufficiently, *that* is when I will depart Corinth. This very day I have taken an ancient Jewish vow. I plan to arrive in Jerusalem for the celebration of Pentecost and, once there, I will have my head shaved. It is part of the ritual of this vow to do these things."

If those in the room were having a hard time understanding what Paul was saying, it was nothing compared with what he said next.

Silas was thinking that he would, after three years, be going home to Jerusalem. Timothy was assuming that he would be going back to Lystra. Priscilla and Aquila, in turn, were wondering how the church in Corinth would fare once Paul departed. All were stunned at his words.

"Once I arrive in Antioch, I will rest there for a while. *Then* I will leave for my third journey. This time, I *know* exactly where I am going."

"Where?" asked Timothy, before he could even realize he had spoken.

"I cannot go to Rome, that is for certain. I plan, therefore, to go to one of the most influential cities in the world."

Paul took a deep breath.

"Israel has heard the gospel, and churches have been planted all over that land. Syria has heard the gospel, and the church has been planted there. Galatia has heard the gospel, and the church has been planted there. Northern and southern Greece have a witness to Christ and to his assembly.

"Jerusalem, Antioch, and Corinth are among the largest cities in the empire, leaving only Alexandria, Rome, and Ephesus as great cities without a witness of Christ and the church. In Jerusalem I will talk with Peter about the possibility of his going to one of those cities, *Alexandria*. I have been hearing reports concerning Simon Peter. His life is in danger. The Daggermen in Israel grow bolder and more dangerous every year. Several other secret societies have also grown up. There is a great deal of suspicion and unrest in Israel. Peter will one day be on the assassins' list.

"In that respect, Peter and I face a similar problem. My notoriety is growing. You have seen what a letter written against me can do, even here in Corinth. There are those in Israel trying hard to turn the attention of the Daggermen toward me. If Simon Peter should go to Alexandria, that will leave only one great city other than Rome—*Ephesus*. That city—Ephesus—is where my third journey will take me."

Paul hesitated. It was almost as if he did not want to say any more. Timothy saw expectation and excitement in Paul's eyes, but he also saw a trace of uncertainty. Such is the way it is when a man knows that what he is about to do is the one thing in the world that he wants to do the most. Paul knew what a vast and crucial undertaking his next words would launch. We did not.

"Ephesus! You are going to Ephesus?" asked Silas, wanting to understand exactly what Paul was saying.

"Yes, but my heart and thoughts will continue to be with Rome. You have heard the Roman proverb? When one of the emperors dies, the senate immediately announces that this particular Roman emperor *is a god.*" Paul's eyes brightened. "I am hoping that one of these days very soon, Claudius will become a god!" Everyone smiled, for all were familiar with the proverb.

"Now, concerning Ephesus . . ." Paul breathed. "Going to Ephesus may be the last thing I ever do. There are three things I wish to accomplish. Two you already know: One is to preach the gospel to the Jews and the Gentiles. The second is, wherever possible, to see the church of Jesus Christ raised up in the cities I travel to.

"Priscilla and Aquila . . ." Paul again hesitated. He took a deep breath: "I am going to ask a great favor of you. Will you consider moving out of Corinth and making your home in Ephesus? Arriving before I do, making preparation for my coming?

"I would ask of you, when once you have arrived in Ephesus, join yourself to the synagogue and make as many friends as you possibly can. Become acquainted with as many of our Jewish kinsmen and as many God-fearers as is possible.

"And, of course, there is the other matter: Aquila, you and I are tentmakers. I would ask you to set up shop in Ephesus as soon as possible. When I arrive I can then join you." Paul paused again. His next words would be the first to reveal his plan. "I will need to support not only myself but several others."

Priscilla spoke. "You want us to sell our home here; you

want us to go to Ephesus, buy a home there, and wait for your arrival?"

Aquila reach over and took his wife by the hand. She leaned forward and embraced Aquila.

"Yes," replied Paul, and then added: "Would you two please bring this before the Lord?"

"We will give you our answer tomorrow," said Aquila. "I have learned that it is wise to keep important answers separate from the question by at least one night's sleep."

Timothy could not be still. "Paul, there is something else going on here; what is it?"

"Only this will I say to you: It is important that Aquila go to Ephesus before me and establish a tentmaking business. When I arrive, I must support myself, and not myself only."

"What are you saying, Paul of Tarsus?" asked Timothy in an almost demanding voice.

"I will discuss this with you, young Timothy, after we arrive in Jerusalem or, more likely, when we arrive in Antioch."

Timothy jumped to his feet. "*Me?* I'm going to Jerusalem?"

Priscilla clapped her hands in delight. "This is wonderful."

Silas stood and embraced Timothy. "A very fine idea, Paul. It is good that this young man see the city of God. Perhaps while in Jerusalem he can finally decide whether he is a Jew or a Gentile."

"Me? Going to Jerusalem! I am going to Jerusalem!"

"You are thinking you might *not* want to go?" said Priscilla.

Timothy turned to Priscilla. "I would love to go. There is one thing for certain: When I am in Jerusalem, I *will be* Jewish."

Then Timothy paused. "That means I will not be returning to Lystra? Paul of Tarsus," said Timothy, his eyes narrowing, "did you mean that after Jerusalem, I would *also* be going . . . to . . . to *Antioch!?*"

Paul leaned back with a certain satisfaction on his face and said, "Yes, and after that, well, after that, something . . . interesting."

"You will say no more?" asked Priscilla.

"No more."

"Then let us retire."

Timothy, grumbling, agreed.

The next day Priscilla and Aquila gave Paul their answer. "We are not only willing but delighted. We will go to Ephesus and prepare, in every way we can, to make your arrival in Ephesus an advantageous one."

What Priscilla and Aquila had done in Corinth—making Paul's arrival fruitful—they would do in Ephesus with all deliberation.

"I hope to be in Ephesus for a long time," said Paul slowly.

"How long?" asked Timothy.

Paul looked at Timothy rather strangely. "I will give you a riddle. I hope to be in Ephesus for the same length of time that the Lord Jesus spent on this earth training twelve men."

Timothy did not have the slightest idea what Paul was talking about. Beyond that moment Paul spoke no more of his closely held plans. By waiting, Paul was testing his decision . . . by the greatest test of all—time. A week later, Paul asked the entire Corinthian assembly to gather together again. A hall was rented. That meeting began two hours before dawn.

Expectations were high, as everyone in the room knew something exciting was about to happen among them.

Paul stood. "Almost from the day I began to gather with you I have again and again told you I would leave you. Everything you know about Christ, everything you know about how to experience your Lord, everything about the ecclesia . . . everything that has fallen from my lips has all been towards the day I depart."

Paul hesitated. "And so I will be departing from you soon.

So, also, will Silas and Timothy. The three of us will be going to Jerusalem. After that Timothy and I will go to Antioch."

One young brother, sitting in the back of the room, stood up and asked with humor, "Timothy, may I go with you?"

Timothy's response was quick. "Absolutely. All you have to do is pay my expenses and yours, and you carry all the luggage."

After that light moment, Paul continued. "Priscilla and Aquila will also be leaving you." There was a gasp in the room, after which everyone grew very quiet.

"Where?" was the question in everyone's mind.

"Be patient with me. It would be wise not to say where they will go. Not until the very last moment. This world is full of rumors . . . about me. Wisdom dictates that I not tell you until just before we leave."

Everyone understood.

Nonetheless, there were more questions. Then came singing. Then tears. Finally everyone knelt and voiced their hopes and fears to the Lord. (According to Timothy, it was a rich, yet unsettling, moment in the life of the ecclesia in Corinth.)

Everyone showed love for their brothers and sister, who would soon be leaving their midst. What *no one* in the room knew was that Paul had begun writing very confidential letters to others of the churches he had raised up. His plan was taking form.

Because homes in Corinth were so coveted, due to the crowded conditions in the city, Priscilla sold their home within a day—and for a great deal more than they had paid for it.

Priscilla, a Roman citizen, unlike women in other nations, is allowed to buy and sell property. Roman citizenship also guarantees that a Roman citizen cannot be arrested except for serious crimes. Each, then, has a right to appeal directly to Caesar. The only execution for a Roman citizen is by the sword, which means a Roman citizen *cannot* be crucified. Last of all, a

Roman citizen cannot be beaten with rods . . . unless he happens to be Barnabas or Paul or Silas!

On the day before departing, Paul, keeping his word to the church, explained that Priscilla and Aquila were bound for Ephesus. Paul, Silas, and Timothy would travel to Jerusalem, but first they would accompany Aquila and Priscilla to Ephesus for a brief look at the city. From there they would make their way up to Jerusalem to observe one of Israel's greatest festivals.

Paul did not know this journey would hold his second experience of being shipwrecked.

CHAPTER 35

It was almost three hours before dawn. Every believer in Corinth was standing outside the house of Priscilla. With several carrying torches, it was a sight to behold.

Paul stepped into the street. Young brothers immediately took his luggage. Timothy and Silas were the next to emerge. Someone started a quiet song. Aquila and Priscilla then emerged. There were tears in Priscilla's eyes. "I had to take one last look—so much happened in this house."

A few moments later, the five, accompanied by the ecclesia, slipped out of the city and moved toward Cenchrea.

Just before reaching Cenchrea, everyone sat down in a field and there broke bread together. In the midst of breakfast they then took the Lord's supper. After that came the tearful good-byes. Everyone would miss Paul, Silas, and Timothy; but there was even more sorrow at the departure of Priscilla and Aquila.

Paul gave his last word. "After I have settled in Ephesus, I will do everything I can to come and visit you once or twice every year. You have received encouragement, admonition, and exhortation. Now, you must continue doing this for one another. Above all, care for one another. Each of you open your mouths and let the Lord Jesus Christ come out of you.

"Never forget that the ecclesia belongs only to Christ, and Christ belongs to the ecclesia. I have equipped you to build up one another. Now it is for you to build up one another. You will do that as you praise and sing, exhort and share. You will do that in the meetings *and* outside the meetings.

"Most of all, during the last eighteen months you have come to know an indwelling Lord. Live by him."

After these words, most of the believers returned to Corinth to take up their work for the day, but a few went on to the port city of Cenchrea.

(I, Titus, consider Cenchrea to be the filthiest, noisiest town in all the world. Ships continually dock there night and day. Trading and bickering goes on endlessly, everywhere. The only other city so miserable is Rome. But even in Rome the cattle are allowed to be herded through the streets only at night. In Cenchrea, because of the limited space of the port, cattle are herded through the streets day *and* night. During the Isthmian Games, the chaos in Cenchrea is unimaginable. People come from all over the world to attend those games, making their landing in Cenchrea. If ever you should come to Cenchrea, do not spend the night there. Go on to the city of Corinth, as it is impossible to sleep in Cenchrea.)

As Paul had planned, they arrived in Cenchrea on the Sabbath. As he usually did, Paul went into the synagogue. (Priscilla refused to do so!) After the meeting, Paul had his head shaved in the synagogue, his cut hair placed in a small pouch. He would take that sack with him to Jerusalem. There he would throw his hair on the altar in the temple.

That afternoon the company of five boarded a ship bound for Ephesus. It was then that Paul made a most remarkable statement. "I have this request of the ecclesia in Corinth: that sometime within the coming year the brothers and sisters in Corinth begin coming here to Cenchrea, to preach the gospel.

Continue to do so until the assembly of our Lord is established here."

"We have never done anything like that," said one of the Corinthians.

"True, but this is what you must do. I have established the gospel in southern Greece. It is up to you, now, to take that gospel to all the areas of your country. Begin with Cenchrea. There are several brothers and sisters who walk from Cenchrea every week to gather with the brothers and sisters in Corinth. Our sister Phoebe was the first to do so. The number has grown to about five or six people. So you see, it is timely that you brothers come to Cenchrea and establish the Lord's house."

One of the brothers made a very wise observation. "Paul, this is the best thing that you can possibly ask of us, for we cannot do it. We will therefore be stretched." Paul nodded a warm approval.

The ship they boarded that day was one of the largest that sails the Mediterranean. Paul was delighted.

"We'll not need to worry about the Etesian winds in this ship," he thought.

A few minutes after they boarded, the dock slaves came with their poles and began pushing the ship out into the maroon waters of the Aegean Sea. The ship began to turn its prow in the direction of the Cyclades Islands.

Paul moved to the stern. The temple of Aphrodite, looming above Corinth, was clearly in view. And across the Cenchrea harbor were the sanctuaries of the god Asklepios and of Isis. Beyond the temple of Aphrodite they could even see the bronze statue of Poseidon. Tears began to course down Paul's face. "Leaving is not easy."

Timothy turned to face the north, straining to see if he could catch a glimpse of the statue of Athena, far away in Athens.

Out of their sight, other ships, on the other side of the isthmus, were sailing out of the western port of Lechaeum . . . to Rome!

"Ships to the east, ships to the west. Ships sailing south. Others going to the Orient. We must *never* abandon this place called Corinth."

"How long before this ship reaches Ephesus?" asked Timothy.

"It will take only two or three days with good winds; otherwise, five to seven," answered Aquila.

The winds were good, and the weather excellent. Within three days they got their first glimpse of the Gulf of Ephesus. They moved to the bow of the ship as it cut its way into the thick, silted water of the Ephesian port. "This port must be dredged every year because of this silt," observed Priscilla. "One day the silt will win, and Ephesus will have no harbor."

The port of Ephesus was jammed with ships.

The city itself sits on a crescent. To the left are hills, to the right, Mt. Coressus. In the midst of this beautiful harbor rests one of the most beautiful cities in all the world. Ephesus cannot be compared with any other city simply because it is incomparable.

The harbor scene is breathtaking. Every building seems to be made of calcareous stone, except, of course, the government buildings, which are all covered with polished marble.

"There! See the theater," said Paul. "It seats twenty-four thousand people. Slave laborers hewed it out of the side of Mt. Pyron." (Paul had no idea that one day there would be twenty-four thousand people rioting in that amphitheater because of *him!*)

Then all eyes turned toward a high hill north of Mt. Pyron. There glistened the gigantic temple of Artemis, perhaps the most beautiful building in all the world.

"This is the first time I have seen such a wonder," murmured Timothy.

"You would never think that, after it was built, it was once destroyed, would you?" said Silas.

"No wonder they call it the most beautiful city in the world," said Priscilla quietly.

"It is certainly a lot prettier than Lystra," whispered Timothy, thunderstruck by the beauty of the panoramic view.

"Ephesus is over a thousand years old," interrupted one of the sailors. "About six hundred years ago a king named Choesus captured Ephesus and built the temple to Artemis. Her Latin name is Diana. Do you see that river pouring into the harbor? It is called the Cayster River. About four hundred and thirty years ago the Dilean League captured the city."

"What is the Dilean League?" inquired Aquila.

"An alliance of cities. Not long after that, Alexander the Great annexed the entire area. That area is today called Asia Minor."

"What happened after that?"

"About 180 years ago an old man named Attalus lost the city when it was besieged by Rome. It was the best thing that ever happened to us," boasted the sailor. "Asia Minor is now one of the richest parts of the empire, and Ephesus the richest city within it. There is more trading being done here than in any other place in the East. And if you want to make money, this is the place to do so.

"Throughout Asia Minor, no matter what road you are on, you will see road markers *every* mile. Each marker will let you know exactly how many miles you are from Ephesus. The city of Diana is the hub of all Asia Minor."

"I come from Antioch," said Paul. "Our city has about two hundred and fifty thousand people in it. And Ephesus?"

The sailor thought for a moment. "I do not know, but I have heard it is about the same."

The ship found its dock space. A moment later my friends disembarked and soon found rooms in a nearby inn. To everyone's surprise, Priscilla dismissed herself. "I will be back within two hours."

Paul looked at Aquila. "Should not someone go with her?"

"I remind you, Paul; she is a Roman woman."

Paul shrugged.

"Where is she going?" asked Timothy.

"She has been writing to someone she knows here in Ephesus. She has been negotiating for a home, but I did not know she planned to buy it *today!*"

"Today?" said a surprised Silas.

No more than an hour had passed when Priscilla returned. "I have purchased a home." The four men sat in stunned silence.

"Are you not interested?" she asked teasingly. "It is in the area of the city nearest the amphitheater. Come, I will show you."

The four followed obediently. They passed through what is perhaps the largest market any of them had ever seen.

"There are two marketplaces in Ephesus," said Priscilla. She then turned onto one of the side streets. In a moment they had come to the second marketplace, which was called *the state agora* and is located on the southeast side of the city. "That is the Prytaneum—the town hall," said Priscilla, speaking as though she had lived there for years.

"How much can this woman learn in just one hour?" whispered Timothy.

"More than a man can in a week," replied Aquila proudly.

Just off a small square, Priscilla pointed. "There! Paul,

when you return to Ephesus, *this* will be your home. And the living room can hold perhaps fifty people comfortably."

Paul shook his head, raised one hand, and replied: "Well, Priscilla, all I can say is *Praise our Lord!*"

"When will you be able to take this place? When can we move in?" asked Aquila.

"Tomorrow," she said matter-of-factly.

"Only one night in an inn. Tomorrow a home. I can't believe this," said Silas.

For the next two days, the four men helped Priscilla move into her new home. (It was a delightful domestic time for everyone. There was never a question as to who was in charge.)

The reason Paul deliberately tarried in Ephesus was to visit the synagogue on the Sabbath. When the Sabbath arrived, Paul reminded Silas and Timothy that they would simply be visitors passing through. He did not want anything to happen that would prevent Priscilla and Aquila from being well received in the city.

"When I come back I wish to come in peace." Paul took a deep breath. "Timothy, would you please sit in the back of the synagogue?"

"Why?" asked Aquila. Silas and Paul laughed.

Priscilla, staring at the steps of the synagogue, groaned, "Oh! Must I go in this place? To that hot balcony I go! But I shall take some fruit with me and some sewing."

Aquila looked up at the bleak building. "I have to agree with my wife. I hate going into one of these dull places. I miss those wonderful Corinthian gatherings already."

The synagogue was indeed a dreary place but not more so than others. The long ritual began. The room was hot and the air stale. Timothy, sitting in the back with the God-fearers, did notice that there was an atmosphere quite different from most places where Paul had ventured. Ephesus is a long way from Jerusalem. And for some wonderful reason, no one there had ever heard of Paul of Tarsus.

As usual, Paul was called upon to speak when the tedious ritual ended. Paul's pharisaical garb had guaranteed him an audience. Paul began as he always did, speaking of the coming of the Messiah. And he knew exactly when to stop. When the meeting was over, it seemed that everyone gathered around Paul, including the ruler of the synagogue and all the elders.

Some, moved by Paul's words, reached out to touch him. A few had questions, but the questions were not negative. Most simply wanted to stand there to see if there was anything else Paul might say to someone.

"Remain, and be with us next Sabbath, please," said the ruler of the synagogue, as the elders nodded in agreement.

Paul was very gracious. He thanked them humbly and explained that he had made a vow (which was quite obvious in view of the fact his head was shaved) and that he hoped to be in Jerusalem for the Passover. Everyone readily understood that a vow so serious was not to be broken. Paul added that he hoped one day to return to Ephesus and, if he did, he would accept their invitation.

The very next morning the three men said good-bye to Priscilla and Aquila and boarded a small and very crowded ship bound for Caesarea, Israel. The ship was packed with Hebrew pilgrims on their way to Jerusalem.

"The ship will make several stops," explained the captain. "We shall pass Miletus, but we shall dock at Cos; then we shall dock again briefly at the island of Rhodes. From there we shall make straight for Sidon. From there to Tyre, and from Tyre to Ptolemaïs, and finally to Israel's port, Caesarea." He then added: "There is a strong wind blowing from the west. If it continues we shall make good time. It is my hope to be in each port no more than a day at the most."

Timothy turned to Paul. "A strong west wind—is that the Etesian wind?"

"No, the Etesian wind blows from out of the east."

The ship slipped out of Ephesus harbor, while Priscilla and Aquila waved good-bye from the shore. The journey proved to be swift. The three spent one night in Cos, and two or three days later, Silas got his very first view of Rhodes. Could he ever have thought he would one day move to that island? Could he have imagined he would die there on Rhodes, a witness to Christ?

From Rhodes, the ship pushed out into the open seas, passing south of the city of Paphos on the island of Cyprus.

The journey was perfect until the ship began to approach Tyre. At that time a storm blew up just a few miles out from the harbor. All passengers were moved into the belly of the ship. Soon the storm caused the sailors to completely lose control of the ship.

"Unless the gods intervene, she'll be driven onto the rocks," the captain announced.

The cargo was well fastened, and no passengers were in danger of being crushed. Nonetheless, Paul felt sure there were only a few more minutes before they would be in a sinking ship. He looked down at his tools. He knew that neither he nor anyone else would make shore trying to carry them. To make sure no one tried, he hid them.

"Timothy, just the scrolls, nothing else. No food, no clothing, nothing. Only the scrolls."

"We're going to sink?" queried Timothy.

At that moment the ship crashed upon the rocks. Everyone scurried on deck even as the ship began to submerge.

"Can you swim?" Paul was looking at Silas.

"It's a poor time to be asking, but yes, I can."

"We are less than half a mile from shore," replied Paul. "Can you make it?"

"Can you?" asked Silas.

"Yes. I learned how during one very long night in the Middle Sea."

"Timothy?"

"Swim? There's little water in Lystra! But yes, I *think* I can."

Pilgrims bound for Jerusalem and sailors alike slipped into the waters. For those who could not swim there was timber enough in the water to hold on to while sailors and others helped them press toward the shore. It seems that everyone else who could not swim learned to do so very quickly.

Fortnuately, the shore was close and the water, shallow. Silas was the first to reach the shore. Once there, he waded back into the water to bring others to safety.

Timothy managed to get the scrolls to shore, but he himself was spitting salt water. Paul had nothing with him except the small sack that contained his shaved hair. (He was a man determined to carry out his vow.)

Though no one lost their life, it was, nonetheless, a harrowing experience. For Paul, it brought back memories of that terrible night when the ship that he, Barnabas, and John Mark were on sank into the sea off the shore of Pamphylia.

Twice I was shipwrecked.

By evening, the entire party had reached the city of Tyre. There was no place to stay in the inns. The city was already filled with Jews on their way to the Passover in Jerusalem. But there were believers in Tyre. By the time night came the three men had been invited into the houses of God's people. The next day they bought food, clothing, and other possessions.

On the very next day the three men crowded onto another ship bound for Caesarea. Despite the terrible experience of the days before, there was one person who was still very excited. Timothy was about to see the holy city of God, even Jerusalem.

CHAPTER 36

The winds have been kind to you Jews," said one of the sailors as he looked out at the crowd of Hebrews who had boarded the ship. "We will dock shortly."

"It is called Caesarea-by-the-Sea, to distinguish it from so many other cities in the empire called Caesarea," Silas informed Timothy. "Just as there are so many Antiochs. For instance, Antioch-on-the-Orontus is the way they distinguish Syrian Antioch from *fifteen* other cities by that name. You will find Caesarea to be a busy port. Most of the ships docked here will be Greek. Caesarea is a main stopover for ships between Tyre and Egypt."

"How far inland from Caesarea to Jerusalem?"

"About fifty miles. It will be a three- or four-day journey. You *will* find the road very congested. The inns are already full. There will be no place for us to sleep except on the side of the road with thousands of our kinsmen. But tonight it will be different. We will stay with brothers and sisters who are part of the Caesarea assembly. It is a Jewish assembly, but there are some Gentiles in it, including the now-legendary *Cornelius*."

"Is there any chance that I can meet Cornelius?" Timothy responded eagerly.

"Perhaps," said Paul.

"I would love to hear him tell the story of how Peter preached and how Gentiles received the Holy Spirit."

The ship edged its way between the breakwaters and docked in the Roman-built harbor.

"I never get used to the fact that Caesarea is a Jewish city after all. Caesarea, not Jerusalem, is the *Roman* capital of Israel. Ancient and holy Jerusalem, governed by Caesarea. I wonder what King David would think of that."

Silas turned to Timothy. "It is a strange thing for us Hebrews to walk by a heathen temple in Caesarea dedicated to Caesar Augustus, built by no less than King Herod."

"I had no idea the city was so large," said Timothy, as he took in the crowded street. "I always assumed Jerusalem was the largest city in Israel."

That night the three brothers found lodging, not in an inn, but with some of the believers in Caesarea. The next day, at his request, Timothy did meet Cornelius and did hear his compelling story. But most of the day was spent with Timothy listening to Paul, Cornelius, and others speaking about the seriousness of the unrest in Israel. Timothy was in awe. This was a new world for him. Paul, though never saying it, was pleased to see Timothy in the Jewish world, learning its ways, thoughts, and culture.

"I am a Roman, and yet I cannot help saying to you that my sympathies are with Israel," said Cornelius. "Tensions are high—higher than any man living today can remember. Rome's actions of late have been insane! Further, we are told there are rumors that more Roman soldiers will be coming to Israel."

Silas shook his head sadly. "That would be the worst possible move Rome could make."

"I am not sure Rome has any other choice," observed Paul somberly.

"But if there are more soldiers, Israel will one day revolt," returned Cornelius emphatically. "Furthermore, the Emperor Claudius was not wise when he forced the Jews out of Rome. That only fueled the fire of hate in Israel. Beyond that, those who are fleeing Rome are *very* bitter."

"I can assure you, Cornelius, that most of the Jews who fled went to Corinth!" added Silas.

Sometime that evening Cornelius turned to Paul with a question. "Brother, do you have any idea how indebted we heathen Gentiles are to you personally? The attitude of the circumcised toward us has changed remarkably since you and Barnabas met with the Twelve in Jerusalem. We are more tolerated. Sometimes we *almost* feel accepted in the Jewish assemblies. Further, no one within the assembly, absolutely no one, has asked us to be circumcised."

"At no small price," observed Silas. Paul smiled.

"But there are those who are not so friendly to Gentile believers, is that not true?" returned Timothy.

"Yes, this is true. Two thousand years of tradition is not easily broken," was Cornelius's gracious response.

"Do you know, Paul, that the letter you wrote to the four Gentile churches in Galatia has been copied, many times, and passed out just about everywhere? I cannot name a single believer who can read but that he has read that letter. Some find it humorous, others are aghast, a few are infuriated. There is one particular Jew here in Israel, I'm not sure exactly where he lives, but I think it is Jerusalem . . . his name is Blastinius, and he . . ."

"We know Blastinius Drachrachma," sighed Paul.

"Well, he has probably caused more trouble than anyone else in all Israel about Gentile believers . . . and about *you*. He now has a large following. They are zealous for the law. I have also heard that he has been writing letters to synagogues in other places to warn them against you."

"Even to as far as northern Greece," whispered Timothy.

"I see that you are here under a vow, Paul. This is good, and it is good that you go to Jerusalem to observe the Passover. After having read your Galatian letter myself, I can see why there are those who believe you have no kind words for Moses."

Paul didn't seem to hear. "I'm very anxious to meet with Peter," he replied vacantly.

"Spend one more night with us. We will gather the assembly here in Caesarea, and you can report on your journey to Greece."

"Excellent!" said Paul. "The more time I spend with the assemblies in Israel the better. The more I am *seen* in the assemblies in Israel the better."

"How long will you be in Jerusalem?"

"Only to observe the Passover, then I must return home to Antioch. There are some very important letters awaiting me in Antioch."

Timothy's eyebrows rose.

Paul continued, "Blastinius follows my every move. I not only want to read the letters awaiting me; I also want Blastinius to know my destination. Perhaps he will think that I have finally gone home to Antioch, there to end my ministry."

"Perhaps he will if he is in Israel. He may be out trying to find *you*," laughed Silas.

The next night Paul met with over a hundred believers in Caesarea and spoke to them for over two hours. There were questions, dozens of them, but they were questions asked in a kind spirit. And after the questions, Silas and Timothy were both asked to tell their stories, adding to Paul's report about Greece.

The next morning the three departed Caesarea for Jerusalem. Could Paul have dreamed that five years into the future he would be a prisoner in the Caesarean jail?

As the three men made their way toward Jerusalem, Paul spent a great deal of the time answering Timothy's questions and giving him a broad history of Israel. When night came the men slept on the side of the road. Despite the sleeping conditions, they ate well. The church in Caesarea had seen to that and had even sent someone, to Timothy's great satisfaction, to carry the bags of food. If anything was lacking in the food they had been given, it was made up for by vendors all along the way selling every kind of food known to man.

In the evenings Paul continued his discourse with Timothy about the city of Jerusalem, about the meaning and symbol of the rituals Timothy would see. Even Silas was impressed. Years later Silas observed, "I learned more on that fifty-mile walk about this Jerusalem and the new Jerusalem than ever I imagined."

On the second evening of their journey a storm blew up. The three men pulled out the new leather coats they had purchased in Tyre and made ready to spend a wet night on the side of the road. Just then they were invited into a crowded tent.

There could be no sleeping for anyone that night, so Paul entertained everyone with stories about his conversion, about John Mark's adventure in Cyprus, including the night the three of them almost froze in a cold blizzard. By the time he had finished the tale, morning had dawned! A little tired, but filled with expectation, the three took up their journey again.

"While in Jerusalem you must, by all means, meet Mark . . . if he is in Jerusalem. His family lives in Jerusalem, even though I understand Mark may be on Cyprus with Barnabas. It is important that you get to know John Mark because he is an eyewitness to the Lord's resurrection. You also need to hear him tell you that story. Further, six years have passed since Cyprus. John Mark has matured a great deal since he was with me during that Mediterranean shipwreck. One day he will be a fit vessel for the Lord's work."

On the third day, about noon, the men caught sight of Jerusalem. By that time the road was so congested that hundreds were forced to walk in the fields beside the road. Progress was slow.

The moment the throngs caught sight of the city of God, they burst into song. Timothy was beside himself. They were singing the ancient Psalms of Ascent. Over and over they sang them, until the multitude reached the city's gate.

"I have never felt so much like a Jew in all my life," said Timothy.

"Be informed, young man," said Silas, "you still *look* like a Greek."

As the pilgrims passed through the gates, the psalms ended and were replaced by hallelujahs and hosannas. Timothy, overcome, was shouting and weeping at the same time. Timothy, at last, had entered the holy city of God.

It is here, as Paul and Timothy entered the city of David, that I, Titus, end the story of Paul's second journey. His first was a trek into Galatia. (Silas has told us that story.) This second journey of Paul's took place in Greece. From Greece, as you just read, Paul made a brief stopover in Ephesus; and from there he and Timothy sailed to Caesarea and Jerusalem. It is best that Timothy take up the story from here, because in many ways Paul's *third* journey begins at this point.

Let Timothy tell you of his first visit to Jerusalem and, from there, his trip with Paul up to Antioch.

When Paul and Timothy arrived in Antioch, Timothy was asked to speak to the entire church in Antioch. (He stunned us all, delivering the most powerful single message I, Titus, ever heard. We were told he had overwhelmed the church in Jerusalem just a few days earlier, when he spoke to the assembly there. Even some of the *Twelve* called it one of the finest messages on the Lord that *they* had ever heard. We never let him live down that compliment.)

It was that night in Antioch that Timothy and I became friends. Until this day, as I lay down my pen, Timothy remains the dearest and closest friend I have ever known.

Now, it is proper. . . . Let Timothy tell you of the journey of Paul to Asia Minor.

Tell the story well, my dear Timothy, because those were the greatest three years you and I ever lived!

—Titus

EPILOGUE

My dear friend Titus wrote this story you have just read when he was an old man. He penned these words long years after Paul and Barnabas had died. Even Silas was dead at the time Titus began this record of Paul's journey to Greece. I am sad to report to you that soon after completing his task of writing, Titus was arrested while ministering to God's people on the island of Crete. Shortly after his arrest, Titus was executed for his faith.

As promised, I, Timothy, shall continue the story where Titus left off, recounting for you Paul's *third* journey—that is, the story of Paul's travel into the land of Asia Minor and his three-year stay in the city of Ephesus. It was there, in Ephesus, that Paul not only raised up a strong assembly but also trained eight men to take his place.

Titus left off telling the story just as Paul, Silas, and I were entering Jerusalem. It is at this point that I, Timothy, shall begin.

—Timothy

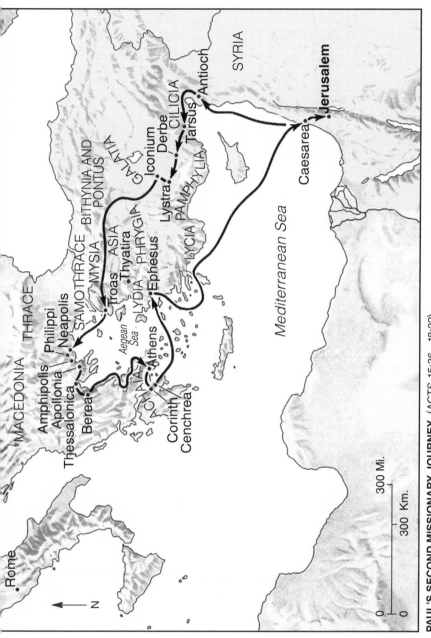

PAUL'S SECOND MISSIONARY JOURNEY (ACTS 15:36—18:22)

If you would like to receive a free copy of *Revolution*, a book that covers the first seventeen years of the Christian story, you may receive one by writing to the author at:

Gene Edwards' Ministry
P.O. Box 285
Newnan, GA 30275
1-800-827-9825

BOOKS BY **GENE EDWARDS**

First-Century Diaries
The Silas Diary
The Titus Diary
The Timothy Diary

An Introduction to the Deeper Christian Life
The Highest Life
The Secret to the Christian Life
The Inward Journey

The Chronicles of the Door
The Beginning
The Escape
The Birth
The Triumph
The Return

Healing for the Inner Man
Crucified by Christians
A Tale of Three Kings
The Prisoner in the Third Cell

In a Class by Itself
The Divine Romance

Radical Books
Revolution
Overlooked Christianity
Rethinking Elders
Beyond Radical
Climb the Highest Mountain